Dark Palace

The Whispers: Book One

Tasha Sheipline

Tasha Sheipline (signature)

Tasha Sheipline

This book is dedicated to a great many people who helped my journey as a writer.

To all those who willingly listened about each new idea as it popped up in my head, thank you for lending an ear. To all those who read through the countless versions, giving me sound advice, thank you for giving your time.
Thank you to my husband and children, for giving me the courage to pursue this dream. Finally, thank you to my two beloved Corgi's, for your constant interruptions. I needed that break anyway.

Chapter One

Boston 1957

The grayish morning held a quiet stillness, with dark clouds to the west promising a miserable, rainy start. Boston rain. Slow and steady. Soaking to the bone. As Adelia Grey smoothed back her shoulder-length chestnut hair with the soft bristled brush, she wondered why she should even bother to take such care. Her thick locks would struggle to lie smooth in the dense moisture hanging in the air. Still, she tried her best to achieve those soft polished waves, though that minor hint of curl remained obstinate, plaguing her with its willfulness. Perhaps, more than anything, she wanted to find something in her life that she herself could control.

"It's hopeless," she muttered as she slammed the brush down on the dressing table. Is it too much to ask to look like one of those fine debonair ladies that grace the cover of Harper's Bazaar? One that could turn the head of every man in a two-block radius? Yes, she supposed that was asking just a bit too much, and she chuckled at the ludicrousness of the thought.

She groaned inside as she stared at herself in the mirror. Her crisp white shirt and plain gray A-line skirt looked so predictable, so pristine. Anyone would think she was barely out of grade school, let alone a college student. She supposed she ought to be grateful for such a rebellious mane, the only thing in her life that offered any shred of excitement these days. After twenty years on this earth, she was starting to find herself rather boring company.

As she studied herself in the mirror, she noticed something off behind her. She moved over to a small wooden stand in the corner and slid the tiny porcelain replica of Windsor Castle back into its usual resting spot. It had only been moved out of place an inch or so, no doubt by her mother as she prepared the room for her return. An immediate sense of comfort settled over her, and she snickered at herself as she realized her own contradiction. No more than sixty seconds ago, she thought herself too boring, yet some insignificant change had flustered her, and driven her into action.

After graduating from high school, she spent the last year enrolled as a freshman at Boston University. With her English-born father being a long-time professor there, the idea of her attending anywhere else had never been entertained. Though her home wasn't far, her parents had insisted that she live on the college campus for the "experience." In truth, she didn't really partake in the college experience as much as they had hoped. Her non-existent social life meant she spent her days attending class, huddled in a lonely corner of the library, or hiding away in the dorm.

As much as she hated to admit it, she wasn't open to much that was unfamiliar. It had been this way for as long as she could remember, with her spending most of her life avoiding all things uncomfortable. This took an incredible amount of work on her part, always pretending to be someone she wasn't, and it proved exhausting at times.

One could say she was now a master at manipulating situations to conceal her general dislike of public interactions. She had developed an impressive list of reasons, or excuses, to avoid such occasions. Never one to want to disappoint her parents, she had become quite good at painting a picture of the normal college girl living life to the fullest. She was content to keep that charade up as long as it felt necessary.

Behind all this, though, was the noise—the relentless, background chatter of everything and nothing all at once. It had always been there, or so it seemed, adding another layer to what made her stand apart from her peers. From everyone.

Taking in the appearance of her old bedroom, she couldn't ignore the familiarity and distance that seemed to wage war against each other. She could almost feel that unspoken tension at her core. While she wanted to be the daughter her parents had envisioned her to be, it just didn't seem possible. She had dreams of becoming an independent woman, who could accomplish great things in this world. If only it wasn't for this overwhelming fear of everything that held her back. It had become second nature to her—its origins unknown—its presence always lingering in the shadows, waiting for the opportune moment to derail anything she set her sights on. That ever-present sense of angst had weaved itself into her soul, and the stronger it became, the more she withdrew into herself.

Her room, in the modest townhouse, was still papered in the pink shade she had known throughout her childhood. The pale-pink coverlet on her bed, that had once been her favorite, was now showing its age in the light tatters of its corners. All around her were displayed the warm and inviting memories of her youth, and she could almost hear the innocence of the space, invoking feelings of safety and home. Yet, in her year at the university, she had changed. Now, these old belongings, still treasured in her heart, felt out of place in a maturing young woman's world. She had a burning desire to grow up—to feel like an adult—but while this room no longer seemed to fit the woman she was today, the thought of it changing scared her. In the past year, she had spent so much time trying to figure out just who she was and what she was bound to become, yet she still found herself feeling lost.

When she had enrolled in college, her father, John, encouraged her to study history. It was his own passion, having taught historical studies for the better part of his career. Her mother thought a degree in education would be a better fit. Elaine Grey often assured her that it was an ideal profession for a young lady. Well, up until she'd married. Then all aspects of a career were expected to be sidelined so she could focus on what was important: raising a family of her own. As independent as her mother was, she still subscribed to a conventional view of roles within the home. Adelia had never told her outright that role was not what she desired for herself. Despite being devoid of an actual life plan, she felt sure her mother's was not her own. Always the dutiful daughter, she just smiled and nodded in agreement, confident there was plenty of time to sort out the details of marriage and motherhood later.

She had grown up in a world surrounded by knowledge. Within academic circles, her father was one of the most-respected professors of medieval studies on the east coast. He'd concentrated most of his work in the period of "the Cousins' War," better known today as the "Wars of the Roses." To say he was passionate about the time period would be a gross understatement. It was a part of his English heritage that had never left him. He had a love for understanding all the complexities of what it took to seize the throne, and relished all the triumphs, failures. and betrayal, like her mother would a good film noir. Whether it be by blood of lineage or blood on a battlefield, her father knew every single detail.

If he had ever wanted a son, fate determined to work against him. Adelia was an only child but, without doubt, his pride and joy. From as far back as she could recall, they'd spent a great deal of time together, and she remembered in crisp detail Sunday afternoons when he would bring her along to the university library. While everyone else was out enjoying the last day of the weekend, John Grey translated old letters to his daughter. The memory was so sharp, she could almost hear his voice echo off the walls, and smell the old leather and ink, as though it were yesterday. Some days, they ventured out to a museum, where he would complain that the placards should be more in-depth. Perhaps her favorite memories were of Friday-evening dinners with her father's fellow academics, who would debate a topic with such intensity, they resembled squabbling politicians more than college professors. This would go on and on until her mother broke in to remind him that they did, in fact, have neighbors.

It came as no surprise that, by the age of nine, Adelia could wow her father's friends with not only her extensive knowledge of the Battle of Agincourt but of all events preceding and following. This wealth of knowledge might have been considered brilliant to some, were it not for the fact that her expertise only really related to history. There had been so much emphasis in her life on history, that every other subject in school took a back seat. She would not have considered herself to be astute in mathematics by any stretch of the imagination, despising whoever thought merging letters and numbers into equations was a good idea. Her grammatical skills were also somewhat lacking. Truth be told, she was almost as adept at writing in Olde English text than in modern language.

After years of molding their daughter to be an intellectual prodigy, they had no doubt what she would choose to study in college. However, she did a fine job of shocking them both when she took a different direction and settled on a psychology major instead.

John Grey, a supportive father to his only child, had given his best fraudulent smile. "Psychology, huh? I suppose there is more of a need for that these days with the world coming back to rights after the war. You could always give it a go. Nothing saying you couldn't change your major later."

Adelia always knew when her father was being insincere on a topic. His posh London accent took on a heavy intonation when he lied. While the man was without doubt devastated, he never gave any outward indication, but she knew him too well not to know. History was his passion but, as much as she loved it, too, it was his identity, not hers.

The truth is, she wasn't trying to buck against her parents' wishes. She had a genuine interest in the human mind and its chaotic inner workings, and loved to examine the complex emotions of people. Other people's emotions—not so much her own. She had developed this interest in her early teens, where being an only child at times proved to be something of a lonely existence. To find a hobby or activity that sparked her interest, she'd dabbled in different things. One time, she went through a Shakespeare phase, reading and rereading his works, delving into the emotional turmoil of Leontes and Hermione in The Winter's Tale, sifting through the dark mind of Richard III, and getting lost in the Forest of Arden with fair Rosalind. Human nature and all of its complexities seemed an infinite space of wonder. Deep down, however, her quest to unravel the mysteries of the mind always led back to the unanswered questions of her inner struggle. She felt like a deep swirling sea, racked with anxiety and insecurity, endeavoring to understand what fate could await someone so confused about herself.

As a child, she enjoyed learning about history, finding it to be one of the ways she could best connect with her father. While she loved studying events of the past, she always took a deeper interest in the people themselves. How people thought, how they lived, and why they acted in such a way always mesmerized her. So, when the chance to study the human mind in more depth came along, it was an easy choice. Whether or not her studies would lead to a lucrative career, she didn't know. One thing was for sure: unlike the vast majority of her schoolmates at the university, she was not determined to waste her parents' money. She studied hard and earned high marks in every class. All she wanted was to be passionate about something, and become adept through her own efforts, but no matter how hard she searched, answers to the deeper questions never came. If studying history left her without certain answers, delving into the human mind was even more perplexing. There were always more questions but never enough answers.

As she sat on the bed, she replayed the past, aware of the room's emotional memory: days of happiness and security, of loneliness and uncertainty. For a moment in the silence, the room came alive around her. She drummed her fingers on the tattered coverlet, and it was as if the faded color was reborn to its original state, tempting her to dive deeper. But she didn't take the lure, snapping her focus back to the moment, like turning off a light switch—something she'd done for years to ease out the often-overbearing noise of the world. I'm a grown woman now. It's time to let go of the past and leave it where it should be—behind me.

The rich scent of her mother's hotcakes hit her as she descended the stairs. Oh, how many of those she had eaten in her lifetime, with their heavy coating of New England maple syrup—its sugary sweetness evoking a rumble from her tummy. With college life, she'd grown accustomed to dry toast on the run, but not today. No, today, it is my duty to choke down at least one or two. I'm sure Mom woke early to make them.

Their house on Baxter Street seemed to be suspended in time, as though nothing had changed. She could expect her summer to be predictable. Her mother would make the same meals she assumed her daughter still liked, while her father would want to visit all the local places they'd gone to in her childhood outings. Neither would see the changes in her, content to think things remained the same—that her absence had just been a pause, and her return meant life could slip back to normal.

Summer was a welcome break from grueling classes and endless term papers, but now her struggle would shift to keeping up the pretense that she was the same old Adelia who used to bound down those same stairs on her way to piano practice. Her parents could not be faulted, though. It was fair to acknowledge that everything they did was an attempt to please their only child. They were happy to have her home, and the least she could do was show appreciation for their efforts.

Despite being glad to be back, each step down the staircase filled her with a dread she struggled to understand. After all, she had spent a happy childhood within these walls—a fact she could not deny. Yet something had always been missing. Something so intangible she could never quite articulate. She had been born into an accomplished family. Her father was an Oxford graduate, who had moved to the States to further his pursuits as a professor. He was highly intelligent in every sense—a learned man who never quit questioning the unanswered. Her mother had also begun a career in education, only to unselfishly give it up to create a home full of love for her family.

Despite her career taking a sideline, she'd continued to be a major contributor for educational publications.

The more Adelia considered her remarkable family, the more unremarkable she felt. As a child, people always asked her what she wanted to be when she grew up, and it was easy to give some basic answer, always knowing she had plenty of time to change her mind. Now, as an adult, she was becoming more familiar with the weight of being out of time. It was a feeling that built in her over the past year as she struggled to find strengths that would make her unique. To date, no profound breakthrough had occurred, which may be why she'd opted to stray far from what her parents envisioned for her in college. She was simply looking for something, anything, she could call her own.

She stood in the kitchen doorway. Her father was seated at the small table, black coffee in hand. After years in the States, he had traded his English tea for a strong brewed coffee. Each morning, without fail, he dined on a single piece of sprouted-wheat bread, and one hard-boiled egg sprinkled with two shakes of black pepper. He'd eaten the same thing for as long as she could remember of her twenty years.

A kind and generous man, John Grey was still rigid in his routines. Each day, he wore a brown, wool suit, with the only variation being his shirt and tie—a cream-colored shirt and green tie on Wednesdays, with a white shirt and blue tie on Thursdays, and so on. Adelia figured her resistance to new things was rooted in the fact that nothing ever changed here on Baxter Street.

Her mother busied herself setting out the butter dish and filling a serving plate with the pile of thick seared hotcakes. She sat it on the painted enamel-top table with a sharp "*clack*." Adelia all but giggled at the sight of the heavy pile of calories she would share with her mother. It was a given that the majority would go to waste; her mother had always been one to cook enough food to feed a whole neighborhood block rather than a small family.

"Darling girl, there you are at last," her father quipped, as though she hadn't been there for a couple of minutes.

"My apologies, Mom," she said, taking the napkin from the table and stretching it across her lap, "I was slow to start this morning." She smiled at her father. "I hope you didn't wait long, Dad?"

His cheeks creased as he grinned. "No, love, we knew you needed your rest after your long journey home yesterday."

"Yes, the bus ride was at least fifteen minutes." She couldn't hold back the smile as her mother pushed the plate of hotcakes toward her. When she took a small one from the top, she caught her mother's raised brow, so lifted a second and set it beside the other. Her mother smiled in satisfaction but Adelia held back the urge to let out a heavy sigh. As loving as her parents were, they had a way of using a silent control over her. It was something she had grown used to over the years, though it felt heavier now that she'd been away from it during the college year.

"So, what are your plans for the summer?" her father asked, giving the folded newspaper in his hand a casual look.

The question took her off guard. Up to this point, she'd assumed she would spend a relaxed summer at home, visiting with friends and helping around the house when her father didn't have her out on a mission. Nothing of any real significance, which suited her fine.

"I haven't any firm plans," she admitted. "I haven't really considered anything in particular. I might find a summer job to earn a little money for the coming school year."

Her father's gaze remained on his newspaper. "Have you considered a visit to your grandmother?"

"Grandma?" she asked, somewhat surprised at the question.

He looked at her for a moment. "Yes."

"In England?"

He lowered the paper. "Yes."

It had been years since she'd last seen her grandma. Her mother's parents both passed on a few years back, and the only grandparent she had left was her Grandma Grey. Considering she resided in England, it had been rare to have the chance to visit her, though her father made the trip alone every few years. Despite the distance, she and her grandma had shared a loving relationship, keeping in touch by post and through the occasional phone call. Marjorie Grey lived in Grace and Favour Apartments for many years, staying on after the death of her husband Colonel Charles Grey. It had been granted to him by King George V for his service to the British Army during World War I. The apartment was located inside Hampton Court, at Richmond on the Thames.

Once again, Adelia was reminded of the remarkable people in her family. Even though she hadn't had the opportunity to spend much time with her grandma over the years, it was still humbling to know that she was a grandchild to such a well-respected family.

She realized her mouth was hanging open so she snapped it shut and sat up. "Oh."

"It is just that, Grandmother may not be around forever. This summer break might be the perfect time for you to pay her a visit. To really get to know her."

"Right." She glanced at her mother. "I certainly hadn't considered leaving you and Mom to travel so far." She turned a hotcake on her plate, a flurry of visuals swirling behind her eyes. "I cannot say I am opposed to the idea. It's just...I would feel like I'm abandoning the two of—"

"I would accompany you over, of course," her father jumped in. "I could stay a week or so, then return home. You would return home closer to the start of school. We would still have some time together."

"The whole summer?" she asked, pushing down the growing knot in her throat. "Would it be a burden for Grandma to accommodate me for so long?"

"You can take on a summer job while you are there. I have an old mate from Oxford who is willing to give you a position at the Palace, as a tour guide of sorts."

She laughed. "Dad, exactly how long have you been planning this?" She wagged a forefinger at him. "You certainly have things well in order, don't you?"

"The idea had not even occurred to me until a week or so ago. I just made some calls to see what could be arranged. Naturally, it is up to you." He snapped his paper straight and returned his focus to it. "There is no obligation for you to go."

She sat for a long moment in silence. Despite her jovial reaction, she found herself not really wanting to go. She could barely visit the college bookstore without falling into a state of near panic. How am I going to go to England for an entire summer?

While her parents had some idea of how much she disliked public places and crowded events, they had always just considered her shy. She was sure they had no idea just how much her condition had progressed—far worse than either could imagine or understand.

Her breath quickened as a swarm of questions invaded her thoughts. Details, one by one, sprang like daffodils in the spring, and she fought hard to push them into the background as she stared at her father, who beamed with delight at his marvelous suggestion. Knowing him, he had planned everything with precision. To object would crush him. She considered the opportunity this presented. It may never come again. She always knew the day would arrive when she had to face her inner struggles head on. Perhaps a trip such as this is exactly what I need to garner such courage. It was far easier to think about courage than it was to muster it up. Yet, if she wanted to embrace change, and there was no doubt she did, the work would have to begin somewhere. England, it seemed, would be that beginning.

"Well, I can't imagine turning down the opportunity to stay in the very palace of Henry VIII." Though she conveyed this with an appreciative smile, she loathed herself in that moment, perhaps more than ever. What a liar she had become. Most of all to those who loved her; the people she should have been able to confide in were the ones to whom she was most dishonest.

"It was Cardinal Wolsey's before," her father corrected. "Then William and Mary's afterwards."

"And Edward VI, and Bloody Mary's, and Elizabeth I..." she added, thankful to be distracted from her inner turmoil.

Her mother gasped. "Oh, for goodness' sake, Adelia, do not call her Bloody Mary. It sounds so—"

"Unpolished?" She snickered to her father.

"I was just going to say tacky," her mother said, "but I guess that's a better choice of word."

"Mom, don't you want to go along too?"

Her mother dug a fork into another hotcake and popped it on her plate. "I have a new project I will be taking on for the publication company. As much as I would love to join the two of you, I would like to get a head start on my work. Besides, I think it would be nice for you and your father to have some time together."

"I dare say Mum is keen on clearing out the house, Adelia. You and I are far too much of a distraction for her."

"Mainly you, John. Mainly you." Though she chuckled, there was a distinct edge of truth in her tone.

"A tour guide at Hampton Court Palace," Adelia said, savoring the sound of it. "I suppose I will have to dress in period garb."

"It will be just like that time you were in the high school production of Love's Labour's Lost." Her father smiled, his pride clear in his expression.

"I was a tree," she snapped. "A very silent one at that."

"Minor detail," he said. "You were still in costume. It was a Shakespeare production, was it not?"

"I suppose. It might be fun to play the part of a courtier at Hampton Court." She nodded to herself. "So long as I'm not cast as the Groom of the Stool."

In truth, the whole prospect of England did sound exciting. In fact, it was probably her dream job. She was not oblivious to her personal limitations, though. For her, dreams and reality were always bitter foes. When the time came, she would have a barrage of excuses to get out of anything that made her uncomfortable. The only role she could play well was the queen of self-sabotage.

"All the world's a stage and the men and women are merely players," her mother quoted, like an actress in a Shakespearian play.

"Yes, the seventeenth Earl of Oxford sure had a way with words," her father shot back.

Adelia paused mid-bite and lowered her fork to the plate, scowling at her father with a cheeky grin. "I could and will dispute that until the sun sets in the sky, if you so choose?"

"Aye, as could I, my love." He gave her a devious smile. "That is what I love about you."

"Oh, will you two please stop all that nonsense before you make my head spin." Her mother rubbed at her temples, though her eyes twinkled with playfulness.

"Well, if it's a-go, Adelia, we must make ready our preparations. Clearly Mum is ready to get us out of this house."

While she smiled, she clenched her gut at the flurry of butterflies flittering through her. England lay ahead, with God knew what else.

Chapter Two

Adelia sat in the dimly lit café, sipping the last of her tea. This was one of her favorite spots in the city. It was quiet and rarely busy—something fast becoming obsolete in Boston these days. The building itself was used as a tailor's shop for nearly a century before it shuttered its doors and sat empty for over a decade, until its current owners had opened it up a few years ago as a café. What she loved most about this old place was its dark and gloomy interior. Something about it appealed to her, with its delightful mix of modern renovation coupled with the characteristics of its old existence. As quirky as it was, she found herself able to relate with the spirited building on a personal level.

She stared off through the window, watching as people moved up and down the sidewalk on the busy street. It was like the crowds were miles away, even though a hazy double-paned window was the only thing separating her from them. She liked the perceived distance, far from anything that might trigger her anxiety.

"You are really going to England?" Kate repeated, for what must have been the third time in the last ten minutes.

"Uh huh," she managed in response as she swallowed the last of her tea.

Kate sighed. "I had hoped we would get some time together this summer. But I guess if I had the opportunity to go, I would leave you behind too." She produced a playful smirk.

Adelia gave her friend a much-deserved eye roll. "I will miss you, too, Kate."

"No, Addie, I don't mean to guilt you for leaving me, but why are you not bursting at the seams with excitement?"

"I don't know." She turned her cup. "I am excited. This is something really worth being excited about. It's just, you know, I'm no good at meeting new people. I get that thing... You know?"

Kate maintained eye contact. "You get nervous, you mean?"

"It's so much more than nervous." She turned the cup again. "I don't even know how to explain it. Whenever I am in a place that's unfamiliar, everything just feels so loud. Like I can hear a thousand voices all around me. It's as if I can't concentrate enough to drown them out."

"I had a great aunt who heard voices once. We don't talk about her anymore since she went away." Kate shrugged. "It was a touch of the madness, they say."

"I don't think it's some sort of madness," Adelia said, sitting up a little straighter. "I don't know how to describe it, other than it's an overwhelming sense of...well, being overwhelmed." That was putting it lightly, but it sounded much better than what Kate was suggesting.

Kate leaned in and touched the back of her hand. "You always push through it. You have made it this far without some sort of apoplexy, haven't you?"

It was true. Despite all the angst she suffered in new surroundings, she always managed to weather situations where running away was not an option. However, the knowledge that she could was almost as deflating. Knowing she could control herself when forced to should have given her some form of solace, but it was quite the opposite, reminding her that most of what she felt was in her mind.

"Yes, I suppose so." She set her empty cup on the table. "I guess it's just the fear of the unknown."

She had invited Kate along that afternoon to do some last-minute shopping before leaving with her father the day after next, thinking it might help calm her nerves to spend a few hours with her friend. Now Kate had brought up her batty old aunt, she almost regretted this decision. Her anxious disposition had been a part of her life for so long, it was second nature by now. Sometimes she just chalked it up to those countless hours in empty libraries as a child. Despite how much she enjoyed her time with her father, she suffered an unintended side effect of being so removed from the social aspects of life: she became comfortable being alone. Now, interacting day-to-day with other people brought a sense of uneasiness she strained to overcome. She always sensed it as it came on, with an initial flush of cold prickles, like being drenched in fine splinters of ice from head to toe. Then the noise, the deafening racket of silence, as though time and space swirled around her like the rapid beat of her heart. Just how she could be so still in the silence, yet with the brute force of a hurricane bearing down on her, was beyond her understanding, though that made it no less real. Perhaps the most difficult part was the final emergence of fear. It coated her body like thick tar, making it impossible to even move.

For Kate to call it nervousness was too kind. She had struggled with her condition for so long, and had no sense of control when it came on, never really able to identify a cause. It was a fear of everything, and a fear of nothing all at the same time. She wanted to be normal—to enjoy the life every other twenty-year-old woman should be experiencing. All the while, she wanted to be unique, special even, with some quality that made her stand out from the crowd. And even though her condition made her different from others, it wasn't in the way she desired.

Perhaps she was progressing into madness after all. She'd always hoped it was something she would grow out of, but time seemed to make it worse. It could be just a matter of time before she was walking the streets mumbling to the pigeons, like one of the old ladies in the park.

She let out a heavy sigh as they walked the short distance to Landry's shop. *These thoughts are doing nothing to calm my nerves.*

"Addie, you have lived a sheltered life," Kate said, ever intuitive to the burning inferno of her friend's thoughts. "That is really the problem. You have grown up most of your life never leaving this city for any real length of time. Boston might seem like an exciting city to other people but we have lived here our whole lives. We are numb to it now, and it is time for you to go out and discover more of the world."

"I wouldn't say my life has been sheltered. Personally, I just like consistency. I—"

"Sheltered!" Kate's look held firm certainty. "You never had a boyfriend in school. You spent every free day in dusty old libraries with your dad. You are most definitely sheltered."

"Well, I did have that one boy—"

"That was in middle school, and you would hardly even make eye contact with him when he tried to talk to you." Kate nodded once, looking through her raised eyelashes before lifting her head. "You spent most of our high school years reading Shakespeare. Shakespeare? Who would do that if it wasn't an assignment?"

Adelia glared at her for a moment, but deep down she knew her friend was right. Up to this point, she lacked any type of experience that could truly give her life direction. This trip would be difficult, no doubt about that, but it was something she must do if she wanted to break this cycle she'd created for herself. She wanted more than anything to break this pattern of fear, yet the thought of it terrified her.

"Yes, yes, you are right," she admitted, though it hurt her to say it. "Thank the Lord we are here." She gestured at the front window of Landry's.

The shop was one of the go-to places in town, at least for the middle class. It boasted a mix of new fashions and refurbished second-hand attire, and had grown in popularity over the years. She paused as Kate opened the door, marveling at the activity inside. As was to be expected on the first warm weekend in May, the place brimmed with patrons. Way too many. For a moment she considered waiting outside until it cleared, but she knew it wouldn't. The steady flow would continue all day, with no such thing as a downtime at Landry's.

Wrangling every vestige of confidence she could muster, she took a deep breath and stepped across the threshold. The establishment held all the latest fashions a professor's daughter could hope to afford. She had often overheard the other girls at the university talking about all the wonderful finds they'd come across. Being here was something anyone in their right mind would enjoy, yet that wasn't the case with her, and the tight knot building in her stomach told her she may not be in her right mind, as Kate had suggested earlier.

Consumed with surveying the endless stream of people, when she looked up to see that Kate was nowhere to be found, a sudden panic gripped her. In desperation, she made her way through the store, seeking any nook or cranny that contained the fewest people.

With whatever was left of her confidence dissipating, she felt like a tiny mouse caught in a trap, awaiting its impending doom. If there was anything she detested most about her nervous disposition, it was the feeling of utter weakness. Knowing the presence of other people around her could crack her resolve so easily was deflating. The space seemed to shrink, and she found herself slipping into the abyss again as icy prickles worked their way into every hair follicle.

She closed her eyes, hoping the cacophonic racket of her surroundings would somehow die down. It didn't happen—the sounds reverberating off the walls even more. Nearly forgetting her purpose for being here, she moved on wobbly legs to another section of the store, seeking space, clenching her jaw, and repeating to herself in her head: *Just stop it. Everything is fine.*

When she got to a small round table, she picked up a delicate pair of white gloves displayed in an open box. She traced her fingers across the soft fabric, almost warm to the touch. A few of the fingertips were speckled with soil, but otherwise the gloves were in perfect condition. She caught the faint scent of lavender oil. Perhaps it had been a perfume one of the other patrons wore—she didn't know, but its light fragrance lifted her spirit, evoking a feeling of a bright, sunny spring day that brought a wash of calm over her. It was odd how such a simple distraction almost pushed the anxiousness back into hiding.

"Those just arrived," a smartly dressed salesgirl remarked.

Adelia flinched at her unexpected intrusion. "They are beautiful," she said, her voice soft. "Worn for a spring wedding."

"Why, yes, they were." The girl leaned back, her eyes wide. "How did you know?"

"I don't know." She hoped she didn't look too confused. "I guess I just assumed."

"You must have a great eye. They would go well with any type of dress, though." She tapped the box on the table. "They are fairly priced. If you ask me, you would be crazy not to buy them."

It may have been the scent but there was something about the gloves that conjured a feeling of light and airy joy. Her anxiety nearly disappeared the moment she'd held them, and now, she almost couldn't bear to part with them as she asked the clerk to place them behind the counter for later.

As she journeyed further into the store, she searched for a few dresses she could bring along on her trip. She decided to depart from her usual style of fitted tops and flaring skirts, opting instead for something more tailored and demure. If she was determined to embrace change, then she may as well begin with her wardrobe. As she made her way to the dressing room, she stumbled upon Kate who encouraged her to hurry so she could view the outfits on her.

Her first choice was a pale-blue dress with a boatneck collar, and a long pencil skirt that hit just at her calves.

"I love it, Addie," Kate said, clapping twice. "So much better than those housewives' dresses you usually pick."

Adelia scowled at her. "I will have you know my mother picked those out for me." She snapped around and returned to the dressing room for the next dress.

"Your mother is a housewife," Kate said.

Adelia popped her head back out the door. "My mother is a career woman too."

"Part-time career woman, full-time housewife. Now, try on the next one."

Adelia huffed, hoping her friend could hear, as she pulled the next garment from its hanger. This one was a gray cotton and wool-blended traveling dress complete with a tailored jacket.

"I will probably consider buying this one too," she said, after enduring another bout of Kate's unsolicited opinion.

"It's the classiest thing you have ever put on, Addie. You are buying it, and you know it."

She had to ponder for a moment why she was friends with Kate. The girl was her best friend—really, the only friend she had growing up. Hmm, if it wasn't for the daunting prospect of trying to find new friends, I might never speak to her again.

Of course, she knew that wouldn't happen. Kate was annoying sometimes but never uttered a word that wasn't the truth. Honest friends were hard to come by. As much as it pained her to admit it, Kate would always be part of her life, royal pain or not. She was one of the few people she felt comfortable being herself around. Above all, Kate had a way of pushing her to do the things she might otherwise have avoided if left to her own accord.

She paid for her purchases, suffering pangs of guilt for indulging herself quite so much. While she wanted a complete change, it would come at more than an emotional cost.

They left the shop and made their way back down the crowded sidewalk to the next intersection.

"This is your crossroads, Addie," Kate yelled over the noise.

"Here?" she asked, confused as she took in the passing traffic and pedestrians.

"No, silly, this trip abroad. This is the point where you have to decide what your next step will be. You can stay here in Boston, among everything you know is familiar, avoiding everything that's uncomfortable, and squeak out a humdrum existence that makes all around you feel safe and secure."

"That doesn't sound all that bad, Kate." She knew full well that wasn't the answer her friend expected.

"Listen to me, will you? You can take this chance and really give it your all. You can experience so much more than you have ever dreamed, but you have to take those first steps. The ones that make your skin crawl, even just for a moment, will be the ones that give you new perspectives. You have to be willing to live like you have never lived before, if you are really serious about discovering what you are capable of doing."

"Kate, how is it you are giving me the most inspirational advice I have ever gotten, in the middle of an intersection during the evening commute? How is it that you can be irritating, and logical at the same time?" She took a steadying breath as her bottom lip quivered. "I will miss you terribly this summer."

They hugged for a long moment, the traffic bustling around them.

Kate leaned back, holding Adelia's upper arms. "Just take the leap off the edge, Addie. You will not fall so far that you cannot catch yourself." She smiled, kissed Adelia's cheek, and walked off in the opposite direction.

Perhaps it wasn't considered a means of personal fulfillment for most but Adelia found her shopping excursion with Kate to be the precise amount of therapy she needed that day. She had succeeded in finding four new dresses, a belize bag, and those divine white gloves. Something about her purchases made her feel mature and sophisticated—a necessity for a grown woman, even if her bedroom was decorated in frilly pink, more suited to a child. After today, she felt a renewed sense of confidence. She had placed herself in the most undesirable situation and was able to exert some sense of control over her feelings. That had never happened before. Then again, she had never really tried. She had wanted to spend a day experiencing something new, and although it was challenging, it had been far more successful than expected.

Spending the day with Kate, even with her painful truth and honesty, had improved her spirits. Just like in those old high school theatrical productions, she would have to play her part so well over the coming weeks if she were to start believing it for herself. There was, hidden deep within her, a personal strength she had to discover. With serious challenges ahead of her, she was determined to conquer whatever insecurities had plagued her entire life. Kate was right, she was at a crossroads now. Either she would test herself, or end up like Kate's batty aunt that no one speaks of anymore. The latter was not an option.

Chapter Three

Once they touched down at Heathrow Airport, Adelia and her father made their way to the train station. The train ride would take them about forty-five minutes out of the city to an area called Richmond on the Thames. If Adelia ever manipulated her way out of uncomfortable situations, this trip was the precise amount of karma she had earned. Every minute was unfamiliar, every second overwhelming. She was so out of her comfort zone, she almost accepted the tight knot in her stomach as something that was supposed to reside there. Her deep fear, being so familiar, was almost a comfort in a time when she had little else to rely on. However, as their journey progressed, she reminded herself that it was still more than she once thought she could do.

She glanced at her father, sitting opposite her. In all her life she had always known him to be a happy man. Yet, as he stared out of the window, watching the sights and sounds of the city dissipate into the calm of the countryside, no smile she had ever seen could rival the one he wore now. Being back in England brought him a kind of childlike joy she would never have understood had she not observed it with her own eyes.

"I think you are going to love it here, Doll," he said, releasing a satisfied sigh. "I know that you are already quite the expert in England's history, but you will still learn so much."

"I'm not the expert here, Dad. That is entirely your department." She pulled a book out of her belize.

"Yes, but staying in the palace where Richard III lived before he died at the Battle of Agincourt is really something extraordinary, don't you think?"

As she thumbed through the pages to find the marker, she shook her head. "Hampton Court did not exist in Richard III's time, and he died at the Battle of Bosworth." She gave him an expectant look, trying to determine just how he, of all people, had made such an error.

He tilted his head and smiled. "I think my point has been proven then, Doll." With that, he folded his hands behind his head and slid down to find a comfortable position for the rest of the train ride.

As the train moved out of the city, Adelia took in the simplicity of this new world. After the rapid-fire hustle of London, she felt as though she may have entered some time warp. There was a serenity to the countryside—as if it remained untouched for centuries. Yes, there were modern conveniences added over the years, yet, if one could ignore the presence of modernization, it wasn't impossible to imagine that most of this area looked as it had in the sixteenth century. She imagined the number of kings and queens who had made the same journey from London to the palace of Hampton Court. It was so intriguing to think she may well be traveling along the same stretch of land as Henry VIII or Elizabeth I. Stately homes and modest cottages peppered the landscape, with sprawling fields on country farms creating picturesque scenery.

The surroundings felt so familiar, though it had been years since she'd been here. She found herself so transfixed by the tranquility that she was surprised when the train's whistle blared as it approached Richmond Station. It didn't seem possible that forty-five minutes had passed since leaving London. She hadn't even managed to read a sentence from her book.

She let out a deep sigh as the train's brakes screeched, bringing them to a halt. While each leg of this journey had been trying, she had to admit that she was handling it better than expected. More than anything, her resolve felt stronger than ever before, and she gave credit to these beautiful, historic surroundings for helping to overshadow the constant presence of anxiety. She was excited, and she needed to cling to that to distract from her worries.

They departed the train, dodging other travelers as they moved through the cloud of steam. The old station, with its cobblestone platform, looked like something out of a Victorian novel. Boston was a place rich in history but nothing like England. Everything she'd encountered exceeded her imagination thus far, and she hadn't even made it to her destination yet.

As they reached the far end of the station, she caught sight of something truly magnificent in the distance—the ornate roofline of Hampton Court. Towering above the low-hanging fog, its red brick exterior burned through the skyline with a commanding presence. She knew the history of this place well, having grown up hearing stories of its past, and the prospect of reaching it sent excitement radiating through her like a spike of pure energy.

"I will have our bags conveyed to Grandmother's apartment," her father said as he motioned her to wait for him. She smiled at the formality of his words. "The palace is just a five-minute walk or so, up this pathway and across the Thames."

She looked down at her gray low-heeled dress shoes, which were not suited for a long walk, but seeing the gleam in her father's eyes made it impossible to protest. He was at home in this place and a complaining traveling companion would do nothing but stifle his joy. The pathway leading to the palace was paved with smooth stone, so she complied and fell in with his steps.

Anticipation swelled, even as she struggled to keep pace with her father's long strides. He was a tall, thin man—not athletic by any means. His years of scholarly pursuits had left him little time to hone his physique, yet he walked with such vigor now, she feared her legs were going to cramp. The unyielding firmness of her leather shoes rubbed against the sides of her feet, promising a blister by the time they reached their destination.

The mist felt heavy and thick. Lying along the coast, Boston had its fair share of fog but nothing of this sort. As they walked on, the faint sounds of people talking filtered through, the volume louder than a whisper. Without losing pace, she glanced around, trying to catch sight of others who may also have departed the train, but none could be seen. Who was it? They sounded so close. Maybe, as she struggled to keep up, she'd mistook the sound of her heavy breath for something else. The conditions brought on a slight disorientation, and she couldn't figure which way was which.

"Dad, could we walk a bit slower?" she yelped, hitching her belize higher on her arm.

"Sorry, Doll," he said, easing his pace. "I guess I am just excited for you to see the palace. It's the only remaining fully functional residence of Henry VIII, you know?"

"I don't mean to be a spoilsport," she replied through heavy breaths. "I would just like to get there without having to seek medical attention."

He smiled. "We will take the approach used by the tourists. You simply must see the palace from the Tudor side. There is no better way to enter than through Anne Boleyn's gate."

She struggled not to grimace as guilt pinched her for making such a fuss about the walk. Her father had a divine love for this place, filled with excitement at the thought of her being there to experience it too. When they made their way around a bend, toward a bridge, she understood why, even through the heavy fog. The looming red brick structure was so enormous, she had to pan from side to side to take it all in, and each step forward revealed a little more of its magnificence. As they crossed the bridge, she gazed down to the murky water of the Thames as it flowed by.

"Can you just imagine it, Adelia?" her father said, shaking his head as he stopped to peer over the side of the bridge. "Centuries of people have traveled up and down these waters."

"Indeed, I imagine coming upon this grand palace must have been a sight."

"Would it ever have been!" he said, almost glowing now. "The red brickwork would have been painted then. It would have been even more breathtaking than it is today. Although, I can still appreciate its weathered patina. This palace was meant to be a statement of the king's wealth. Just look at that gatehouse." His eyes widened in awe.

She nodded in agreement. The fog produced an ethereal glow around the structure, as if its outline was electrified. It brought an intensity of anticipation that filled her stomach, similar to her all-too-familiar anxiety. After the calmness of the train ride, she hated to let that resurface. Yet she had to give herself some grace. An overnight flight, coupled with the shuffle from taxi to the train, had been exhausting. It felt as though they'd been traveling for days, and a heavy weariness was starting to settle in her.

As they moved forward, details of the structure revealed themselves in slow steady grandeur. Patterned brickwork mingled with high-reaching ornate chimneys. Carved statues sat on tall pillars just outside the entrance. It seemed unfathomable that such a place could have been built as a residence for just one man. She thought back to her father's reference to this palace being built for the cardinal before the king made it his own. Such extravagance for a member of the church? This place could house hundreds of people in its time as a royal residence. It was so unlike any building she'd seen in the States. Even the oldest ones in New England were only half as old. She had seen a great many pictures of Hampton Court and none ever managed to do it justice. The structure was so large, a person would struggle to fully appreciate it without seeing it in person. Right then, she was only seeing the front façade—the Tudor entrance—with the palace itself going on for acres and acres.

"There is so much history here, Dad. Why did you ever leave?"

"I can't say I don't ask myself that sometimes, and there is so much I love about England. Still, I had dreams of going to America, I suppose, even as a young kid. When I met your mother, I knew I had to follow her wherever she went."

"And she wanted to go home?" She knew the answer. This was a story she'd heard dozens of times.

"Her parents would have never let her stay here, and I didn't want to stay without her. Just like you are now, she spent a summer abroad during her first few years of college. We had both been assigned an internship for the Heritage Society. Was the best summer of my life, kiddo. When it was over, I knew that all of my plans had changed. So, I took a teaching job in Boston, and, well, the rest is history."

"So, basically, you are saying that I will likely find the love of my life here in England?" She giggled. "I can just live your story in reverse."

He smirked. "You know, on second thought, screw this whole trip, we're going home."

She gave his arm a light push. "I highly doubt I could be as lucky as Mom here."

"Want to find your very own bookish nerd? I don't know whether to be flattered, or warn you to run as fast as you can. You will find what is meant for you in your own time, Doll. Don't rush it."

As far as she was concerned, there was nothing to rush. She had never considered herself a magnet for the opposite sex, and her high school experience reminded her that she wasn't the most attractive girl in school. If she forgot that, Kate could always be counted on to remind her that her only potential boyfriend was in the seventh grade, and that was, by all accounts, a flop.

Since the palace was not yet open to visitors, her father spoke to one of the Yeoman Warders guarding the gate. He motioned to her to follow, and the warder swung the gate open, allowing them to pass through before almost slamming it shut again. She flinched at the sound of its heavy iron bolt dropping into place. As they moved through the gatehouse, she marveled at the intricate detail above her. The ceiling was carved in beautiful designs, craftsmanship the likes of which she had never seen in the buildings back home. It was hard to think of how many distinguished and historical people had passed through this space over the years. Her skin prickled, as if fed by static electricity, and she shuddered, wondering at its origin.

"Anne Boleyn's Gatehouse," her father said. "Old Henry tried to erase her as best he could but her initials still exist in the grand hall. Even a king can't erase his past. I have often wondered if, when he died, his heart was filled with any sort of regret for his actions. It's doubtful, given his enormous ego, but one can't deny that guilt does not distinguish between social classes."

The fog took on a life of its own when they stepped into the court-yard, with visibility no more than a foot or two in all directions. An eerie stillness cloaked her, until she sensed voices close by. She stopped, scanning all around to source the origin but there was nothing, just gray mist. The voices seemed to grow with intensity, disorienting her further. It felt like a crowd of people were encircling her, and she feared she might be trampled at any second. The commotion almost made her want to retreat—turn and run—but she couldn't move, frozen to the spot, her legs heavy as the red brick surrounding her. She nearly screamed when a cold hand gripped her elbow.

"This way, Doll," her father said.

Maybe his soothing voice should have calmed her, but it didn't. A rush of heat surged through her, rising from her neck to her face. As she moved forward, guided by her father's hand, she couldn't under-stand the flood of sound that filled her ears. With the palace still closed to visitors, how could there be so many people speaking around her? Yet, even with diminished visibility, it was clear they were alone in the courtyard.

"This place can be overwhelming at first," her father said, giving her elbow a gentle squeeze, "but you will get used to it, I promise."

Even if she had tried to hide her nature, her father knew her almost too well—how she always let new surroundings overwhelm her. It was something she could never seem to escape, even all the way across the Atlantic Ocean.

"Y-yes..." she stammered. She wasn't sure why she said yes, only that it sounded like the right thing to say.

"I wanted to enter this way," her father said, "so you could see some of the majesty of this palace, but the English fog isn't cooperating so well. You can't even see the clock tower. You will get used to it—the fog. It may be difficult at first but the dampness of this climate grows on you after a while. Once you are settled in with your grandmother, I promise that we will take the tourists' tour of the palace. You will want to explore it a bit before you start working."

She nodded, still looking around and trying to collect herself. When they reached the edge of the courtyard and were able to enter the building, she permitted herself a quiet sigh of relief. Her father resumed his quick pace, allowing her only a glance of anything as they passed.

"Now, before we reach your grandmother, there is something I should tell you." He turned and looked straight at her. "Mum has a tendency to be a bit eccentric sometimes."

Adelia already had a sense of this, aware that her father had done his best to keep it from her throughout the years. His loyalty and devotion to his mother had always rendered him a protective son.

"Eccentric?" she asked, giving him a searching look. No point bursting his bubble here. "How so?"

"Well, she is a high-spirited sort. Everything that science tells us to be true...well, she believes the opposite. She has a wild imagination."

"High spirited? That's a word I haven't heard you use before. Are you trying to say my grandma is crazy?"

"Not crazy, Doll. Eccentric, high spirited. A bit imaginative, yes, but not crazy."

"Okay," she said, dragging the word out.

He turned and started walking again. "Oh, and sometimes she gets crazy eyes like Rasputin."

"Rasputin?" she called after him, an image of the famed Russian mystic dancing in her head.

He laughed. "If Rasputin wore fine English frocks and had proper tea at noon."

She had no idea how to respond, so she didn't. Leave it to Dad to divulge this information moments before we reach Grandma's apartment. Lucky I already had an idea. For a man consumed by detail, he sure has a knack for leaving important ones out when he finds it convenient. Which, I might say, is becoming altogether too frequent these days.

It had been a long tradition of the monarchy to grant Grace and Favour apartments to individuals in recognition of their service to crown and country. After her husband passed away, Marjorie Grey was permitted to stay on. Adelia found herself amazed at the prospect of living in a palace such as this. In any palace. However, the buildings that held the apartments were a stark contrast to the royal residence tourists visited, and were kept separated from those areas. They had many updates making them resemble true apartments, rather than the ornately adorned spaces the kings and queens had once resided in.

One could imagine that modifications like centralized heating, plumbing and electricity, had been expensive to install. These spaces, while modernized, were not built with these updates in mind and must have necessitated a great deal of work to bring them into this century. She surmised that residents should consider themselves lucky to have been bestowed such an honor as to live in a Grace and Favour apartment, so minor inconveniences like the constant flow of tourists nearby could be overlooked. As her father had explained it, the residents were a close-knit community. As they passed each door, she thought about all the unique people who lived here, and found it hard to imagine herself lucky enough to stay the summer. The whole idea was remarkable.

They arrived at a finely polished wood door with a silver plate that had 28A engraved on it. Her father gave it a light knock, and much to her surprise, it wasn't her grandma who answered but a younger woman in a navy-blue cotton dress. Her features were smooth, and Adelia guessed she could not have been much older than thirty.

"Good morning, Mister Grey and Ms. Grey," she said with a delicate grin. Her bright-red hair produced a stunning contrast to her emerald-green eyes. Had there been no mistaking her English accent, Adelia might have taken her for the poster child of the Scottish Highlands. The woman's fair skin looked like fine porcelain—unflawed. Her graceful mannerisms made Adelia feel gangly and awkward as she stood, threatening to break into a full sweat in her wool traveling dress.

"How do you do, Lizzie, so nice to see you again," her father said, his manner exuberant. "This is Adelia, my daughter."

Adelia extended her hand and shook Lizzie's in return. The woman's hand was as delicate and soft as her smile. She cringed inside, imagining that her own was damp from the heat still radiating off her. The occurrence in the courtyard was still fresh in her mind, and she hoped her unease would be quick to pass. With every fiber of her being, she wanted to enjoy this trip. She had put so much hope in England being a turning point for her, yet, right now, all those old feelings of doubt were lurking, threatening to overtake this moment. She sucked in what she hoped would be a calming breath, though she felt sure her overthinking was doing nothing to help matters.

"Lizzie helps Mum around the house a few days a week," her father explained. "Mum would surely be lost without her."

Lizzie let out a light sigh. "I suspect Ms. Marjorie would do quite fine without my assistance. Just the same, I enjoy her company. She is always full of colorful stories, you know."

Adelia's father reacted with a half-nervous grin, and nodded in agreement.

"Lizzie, is that Johnny and Addie?"

Adelia almost chuckled hearing her rigid father being called *Johnny*. The question came from the next room.

"Yes, Ma'am," Lizzie answered. "I will bring them right in to you." She motioned to the adjoining room. "Ms. Marjorie is just there in the sitting room. I will finish getting the tea together, then wait for your things to arrive. Go on in."

"Thank you, Lizzie." Adelia's father smiled as he led the way into the sitting room.

It was a bright space, with an abundance of daylight streaming through the tall windows, each dressed in fine English lace valances. A credenza along the wall held a vase with fresh-cut roses, their faint perfume hanging in the air. The room wasn't large but the tall ceilings gave it an appearance of being much bigger. Two wingback chairs and a matching couch, all clad in a busy floral print, were centered around a high polished sofa table.

A petite woman with light-colored hair, got to her feet, both arms outstretched for an embrace.

To say her grandma was polished would be an understatement. Her look was impeccable, from the placement of the gold brooch on her jacket lapel down to the light-vanilla blonde of her immaculately sprayed hair. Much to Adelia's delight, her grandma looked nothing like Rasputin. It was easy to see that Marjorie Grey was part of a noble line of well-respected residents here at the palace. She understood her position, and played her role without flaw.

"My darling, it's so good to see you," she said as she pulled Adelia into a tight embrace, her strength coming as a surprise considering her size. The floral scent of Chanel No. 5 filled her head. How fitting for a woman of such impeccable taste.

"Johnny, you look well, I hope your trip was good." She hugged her son.

Adelia took it all in. While it was funny, the scene held a certain tenderness. Aside from letters and gifts, she barely knew her grandma in the flesh, and was delighted to find her as warm and affectionate as she had always thought. While John Grey was a loving father, he wasn't prone to letting emotion overshadow his businesslike demeanor. He was, in all things, the consummate professional. Throughout her life, she had wondered if that was a characteristic derived from his side of the family, perhaps from his own father, a staunch military man. It was clear it hadn't come from his mother.

"You are just in time for tea," her grandma said with a smile. "Lizzie will bring it to us in just a moment. Now, Addie, do tell me all about your trip."

Her grandma's approach brought an instant ease, and she wondered how that was even possible. She felt a tangible sense of connection, as though they'd spent every day of their lives together. A real calm permeated her bones, and she had no urge to contain her breathing to stave off impending panic. She was not familiar with this, and welcomed the serenity it hinted at.

She sat beside her father on the sofa and looked at her grandma with inquisitive delight. *Dad had to be joking when he told me she was high spirited. She looks the picture of formality. Hmm, it's not a stretch to see that she and...Johnny are kin.*

As she shared the details of their flight and subsequent train ride, Lizzie came in with a polished silver tray, with pink floral-print China cups and teapot. She set it on the table, and straightened on hearing a knock at the door.

"That will be the porter with your luggage. Back in a sec." She left the room, and muffled voices filtered in from the foyer.

"Oh heavens, we don't have any sugar cubes," Marjorie said, wrinkling her nose.

"No worries, Mum, I will get them. Lizzie is busy." He leapt to his feet and strode to the kitchen.

Movement to her right had Adelia looking down to see a gray cat with tiger patterns making its way from behind the sofa, followed by a black and white one, with an orange one taking up the rearguard.

She couldn't hold back a smile. "Oh, Grandma, you have cats. How delightful."

"This is Devereaux, Cromwell, and Sir Walter Raleigh." She stretched out her hand to give Devereaux a gentle pat on the head.

"Are they aware that their human counterparts all met an unfortunate end?"

"Sshh! They must not know. It would be most distressing to them."

Adelia straightened her spine, taken aback by her reaction. "Indeed." She kept it polite, pretending to brush imaginary dust from her skirt. Perhaps it is too early in our relationship to insert humor. The sense of ease she'd felt earlier dissipated enough to be noticed.

"We have been waiting so long for you," her grandma said in a hushed voice, rubbing Raleigh's head this time. "There are a great many secrets to be revealed, Adelia, but you will have to listen." She flicked a look left and right, as though expecting someone might be earwigging from another room.

Adelia could only assume she was referring to the cats. What secrets do they have to tell? Perhaps these years of living as a widow have made her far lonelier than she's letting on.

As she looked up from the cats, she almost gasped on seeing her grandma's eyes glow with a wild glare.

Rasputin? Well, if the man wore a light-pink day suit and had a perfectly coiffed shampoo and set.

She stared for a moment, then gave a polite nod before turning to the doorway, hoping to see someone, anyone, enter the room. The

mood had changed within seconds, the atmosphere now heavy, as
though the fog in the courtyard had crept into the room with the sole
purpose of choking her. Hmm, Dad might be right about Grandma
getting a bit eccentric in her advanced years. This summer may be one
to remember, if I'm fortunate to come out with my wits intact.

Her father entered the room, carrying a bowl of sugar cubes, and,
without missing a beat, her grandma gave her a delightful smile, as if
their previous exchange hadn't just occurred. At the flip of a switch,
she was back to the warm and fuzzy grandma.

Adelia sat, dumbfounded, trying to acclimate to the change. Three
minutes in this place and she was already starting to question her
sanity. My, what a long summer this is going to be.

"I have the luggage in their rooms," Lizzie said as she entered the
room.

Margorie's face lit up with another beaming smile. "Thank you,
Lizzie." She turned to them. "I had Lizzie set up the yellow bedroom
for Addie and the purple one for you, John. I figured that, since you
will only be with us this week, the purple one will suffice for you.
Addie will surely get a headache looking at all that color after a while.
It's just too loud, if you ask me."

"That's perfectly fine, Mum. I hope you and Lizzie did not go to
too much trouble?"

"No trouble at all for me. Lizzie did most of the work. She really is
heaven-sent, that girl."

After a half hour or so of conversation, Adelia stifled a yawn, the
past 24 hours of travel catching up with her. She shifted in her seat,
trying to stretch her back.

"You must be tired from your journey, dear," her grandma said, her
tone reminding her of her mother's soothing voice. "Best you lie down

and rest for a bit. Then your father can take you out and show you around the grounds. Fresh air will do you good."

Adelia liked the idea of exploring the grounds, if the fog had dissipated by the time she woke. She didn't fancy experiencing those eerie whispers again.

"Now, Johnny, I hope it isn't a problem but I have an appointment to play bridge with the girls at two o'clock. You see, Doris is sick so it will just be Martha and Mary."

"No trouble at all, Mum." He got up and gave her a kiss on the cheek. "We will get settled and Doll and I will go out exploring."

Following her father's lead, Adelia bent to give her grandma a hug. "Enjoy your game, Grandma."

Her father led the way down the hall to her room. When her grandma mentioned it being yellow, she fully expected it to be like a child's room. Much to her surprise, it was quite the opposite. Pale ivory walls were bordered by a delicate yellow floral pattern that matched the curtains. The double-sized bed was made of white-painted wrought iron in a French provincial style. Its coverlet was a mix of fine, pale-yellow satin bordered in ivory lace. It was feminine but with a touch of sophistication. She understood why this would not have been her grandma's first choice for her father.

Lizzie drew a hot bath for Adelia, and as she soaked, the stress of the long journey faded away. After a restive nap, she woke to a room cloaked in the full sunlight of mid-afternoon. She lay in bed blinking, taking in the events of the morning and thinking of what was to come. Even though she had seen little of the place she was set to inhabit over the next three months, she was still overcome with the reality that she was here, lying under the roof of Hampton Court Palace. As she thought back to the odd conversation with her grandma, she was content that she'd misread the interaction. She was prone to misinterpreting situations. In the swirling firestorm of her mind, her thoughts were never idle, and she often read too much into things, overanalyzing to her detriment. She reassured herself that this was not an exception.

Something caught her attention through the silence. Faint whispers. Not again. Oh, perhaps it's Grandma and Lizzie. She checked her watch, surprised to see that it was nearly three o'clock. It can't be Grandma—she had a game of cards at two. All was still around her, yet people were speaking nearby, in hushed tones. Dad probably has a visitor. He'd visited Hampton Court numerous times over the years, and was well known here, despite living thousands of miles away.

She lay still, focusing hard to distinguish the voices but couldn't tell if they were male or female, or both, just that they were voices. Hmm, perhaps they are coming from neighboring apartments, or from the hallway. She threw back the coverlet, slid over to the side of the bed, and stretched. The voices had stopped. She shook it off. In such a busy place as this, one could always expect there to be people about.

As she rubbed the side of her stiffened neck, a faint swishing sound caught her attention, and she jolted her head in its direction. Just inside the doorframe sat one of her grandma's cats. Cromwell, if she remembered correctly. He was a stout little fellow, full in the middle, with an emotionless beady-eyed stare. The fact that he bore an uncanny resemblance to the real Thomas Cromwell wasn't lost on her, and she wondered if that had any bearing on why her grandma had chosen the name.

"In full transparency," she said, shooting daggers back at the cat, "I haven't forgiven you for destroying all those churches and priceless artworks during the reformation. I am not your biggest fan, Mister Cromwell."

For a fraction of a second, Cromwell shot her a look of disgust, then turned and walked back out into the hallway. Adelia sat perplexed, but brushed it aside, reasoning that the perceived standoff with her grandma's cat was just her grogginess wearing off.

The room was beautiful, and more so with the sun lighting it up. She walked over to the small white vanity and checked herself in the mirror. Dark-brown eyes stared back at her, big and searching, unlike the delicate features of her grandma. It was clear that her looks favored her mother's side of the family. She admired the light-pink flush in her cheeks. The humid air gave her skin an earthy glow that complimented her looks. She smoothed her dark waves back into place with her brush and powdered her face to refresh. While she had never considered herself to be pretty, at this moment, she wasn't entirely disappointed with the image staring back at her.

After brushing her teeth, she made her way out into the kitchen, smiling at the clack of her father's coffee cup on the table as he poured over the daily newspaper.

"Ah, Doll, are you ready for our adventure?"

She looked around the room, expecting him not to be alone. But it was just the two of them.

Despite the nod and smile she gave him, she wasn't ready to go out just yet. She could already sense trepidation at the prospect of leaving the coziness of the apartment for the large looming palace that lay just down the hall. It was far too soon to think she could conquer this lifelong affliction. That feeling of unease was so second nature to her, it never required prompting. Yet, just as she'd done over the last few days, she continued to remind herself that she was making progress.

She didn't want to jinx herself by thinking she could never fully win the battle. Even so, she was beginning to understand that true healing would not come from winning the battle but from the work it required to achieve victory. And while that work was a distraction, it was where true growth would happen. Still, if she ever did win, her fear might just shift to worrying that she may relapse someday. Perhaps it was better to never really be healed and be content to forever be a work in progress.

Her father's cup clacked again, pulling her focus to the present. Something inside told her she was about to embark on an adventure beyond her imagination. Even though that excited her, she still felt nervous about the unknown. As she stared at her father, now getting up to leave, she remembered how important this trip was to him. Even though he would only be here for a week, he wanted nothing more than to spend quality time with her. This was a trip he had dreamed about sharing with her for years, so she would have to try her best to set aside her fear, for his sake.

"Let's go explore our palace, Dad," she said, taking his arm in hers.

He looked at her and smiled. "I thought you'd never ask."

Chapter Four

From the moment they left her grandma's apartment, Adelia knew what to expect. Her father would be like a child in the toy department at Harrods. Over the next few hours, he would cover every major historical event that happened within these walls, most of which she already knew from dozens of chats with him about the period. He would be brimming with excitement as they followed the path of many royal processions, with him delving into the architectural changes from the Tudors to the more baroque style of William and Mary. And because he was a learned man of science and history and didn't believe in such hocus pocus, she had no doubt he would scoff at the tales of Catherine Howard screaming down the haunted gallery. He could also be counted on to point out Anne Boleyn's initials in the great hall with a degree of satisfaction, knowing that Henry had missed them in his quest to erase her. All of these things she'd fully expected, and all of these things came to fruition. Her father had rattled on until the last minute when the palace shooed out the remaining visitors and closed its doors.

The palace was massive in size, and her father had used his connections to secure an after-hours tour of areas undergoing routine maintenance. It wasn't a place that could be seen in one day, let alone a few hours, but her father did his best to touch upon what he considered the most notable spaces. She had never seen him so alive with excitement. He was, indeed, in his element at Hampton Court.

"Are we going back to Grandma's now?" she asked, assuming they would be meeting her for the evening meal.

"Not just yet, Doll. I have someone I want you to meet. We need to make a stop at the offices to see Doctor Brown."

"But haven't they closed for the day? Won't he be gone home by now?"

"Oh goodness, no." He chuckled. "Doctor Brown is here conducting research for the summer. Researchers never go home at closing time." His eyebrows arched. "It is unheard of."

All she could do was nod, having witnessed the countless hours her father had spent in libraries poring over musty old books.

As they passed a row of empty offices, she couldn't help but notice how big this place felt without people. Hampton Court Palace was enormous by any measure, and seemed all the more eerie with the tourists gone, leaving nothing but empty corridors. Despite the warmth of the day, a wisp of cold washed over her, bringing goosebumps up along her arms. Though she rarely found herself wishing to be around more people, right then, she wished for just that as they moved down the gloomy hallways.

She nearly gasped with delight at the pale stream of light seeping out under another polished wooden door. Her father gave it a light knock before twisting its handle. He cracked it open to peer inside, and she was relieved to see light engulf his face. The quietness of the space behind her was almost more than she could handle, and a heaviness at her back did not encourage her to turn around. She wanted to move but felt like a stone, unable to budge.

"In here, Doll."

"Huh?" Her breath caught as she was snapped back to reality.

"In here."

She smiled, his soft voice helping to ground her, dissipating the awful pressure threatening to overwhelm her.

As they stepped into the room, she glanced around. The space was much larger than expected, and...messier. It served as a makeshift miniature library, with books and manuscripts placed in neat rows on tall bookcases that stretched almost to the ceiling. The center of the room was taken up by several large wooden tables, all covered in haphazard piles of paper, as though someone had started on one project then jumped to another, and another. Movement behind a stack of papers, books, and other debris caught her attention, and she held her breath as the top of a head appeared.

"John?" the man called out from behind his paper fortress.

"Doctor Brown. I knew I could still find you here this late."

The man, with a tall slender figure, moved around the table. Adelia stared at his muddy-brown hair that had a hint of auburn, then at his light-blue eyes, glimmering behind the thin wire frame of his spectacles. He was cleanshaven and dressed in a shirt that was, by this hour, somewhat wrinkled, but she imagined it had begun the day crisp and well starched. His brown wool trousers reminded her of ones her father owned. She had heard of Dr. Brown, but had not expected him to look quite like this.

Both men exchanged a handshake, then Dr. Brown gave her a piercing look that almost pulled her off balance. In that intense moment, his eyes took on a brilliant shade of blue and she found herself staring right into them, unable to look at anything else.

"This is Doctor Brown," her father said, his eyebrows arched.

"Yes? So...young?" She cringed inside as her face burned.

"Not so young," the man corrected. "I am almost twenty-eight now."

I can't believe I just blurted that out like a silly child. The man standing before her was not old at all. Quite the opposite, in fact. And handsome. The reality that he had already achieved such accomplishments at such a young age had thrown her for a loop.

In truth, most girls her age would not have been so taken by the figure before her, but she was not most girls. To be fair, it was 1957, an era where young women were smitten with leather-jacket wearing, wavy-haired men on motorcycles. It was also a time where men would find a twenty-year-old woman who could tell you exactly where Richard III went wrong on the battlefield at Bosworth just plain weird. She had always found herself attracted to intellect over brawn, so her attraction to Dr. Brown did not come as a surprise.

"I am s-sorry," she stammered. "It's just that my dad has told me so much about you. I just assumed you were..." She grimaced as she held back the word filling her mouth.

"Oh, Doll, you're thinking of Daniel's father." Her dad hitched his shoulders up, his eyes wide open. "The Doctor Brown I went to Oxford with as a lad. Daniel is following in my old mate's footsteps." He gave the young man a proud pat on the back.

Daniel stretched his hand out to her and she shook it. His skin was just as warm and clammy as her own, which gave her a minor sense of solace in her own insecurities.

"Adelia, your father tells me you have come to Hampton Court for the summer to stay with your grandmother. You will be working here during that time?"

"Yes," her father said, jumping in before she could respond, "she will be working at the gift shop. Starts on Monday."

True to his nature, her father had failed to disclose a vital nugget of information to her. The gift shop? All this time I'd assumed I would be a tour guide, something at least a little more entertaining than working in a...gift shop. A wave of embarrassment swept over her at the realization that she was standing in front of an Oxford professor who was doing important research—whatever it was—and she, a college student, was going to be the gift shop girl. How humiliating. She had felt stupid before, but this ranked high on her list of looking like an idiot.

"I love the gift shop," he said, though she wasn't at all convinced.

She stared at him. "You do?"

"Yes, they have those lovely little ornaments with the Tudor Rose, you know?"

"You decorate your Christmas tree with Tudor rose ornaments?" She almost wanted to laugh but managed to hold it in, knowing it might seem inappropriate given the moment. Besides, he seemed more nervous than her.

He smiled. "Hmm, I can't decide if I am more of a Lancastrian or a Yorkist, so I like the blend." Her father's brows furrowed, and Daniel's mouth hung open for a second too long. "Well, Adelia, I am sure we will cross paths this summer. Please don't hesitate to call on me if you need anything...at all."

"You are most kind, Daniel," her father said. "We won't keep you. I know you have much to do here."

"Your visit is a welcome distraction, John. Really. I am not getting as much done as I would like, anyway."

Even though it was clear her father had decided to wrap up the conversation and leave the man in peace, for some reason Adelia wanted to stay a bit longer—to take the first step off the ledge, even if only to tell Kate she had done it. In that bottomless moment, she wracked her brain for a credible conversation starter. Something that did not include her blossoming career as a humble gift shop clerk. How embarrassing.

"May I ask what you are researching, Doctor Brown?" It was the best she could come up with.

A delightful smile washed over his face and, for a second, she felt as though she were staring at a younger version of her father. She knew she had asked the right question. All of his nervous bumbling disappeared in an instant, replaced by a look of confidence. All these scholarly types are much the same, liking to be rescued from their discomfort by talking about something they know inside out. Yes, Daniel, at least we have this in common.

"I am researching the death of Amy Robsart Dudley," he said.

"The wife of Sir Robert Dudley, favorite of Queen Elizabeth I?"

His eyes widened as he leaned forward. "One and the same. Are you familiar with the circumstances surrounding her death?"

"To an extent," she answered. "The Elizabethan era is a bit out of my wheelhouse, mind you."

He smiled, then glanced at her father, who returned the smile with a shrug. She could almost read Daniel's thoughts. Her father's studies were focused up to the death of the last Plantagenet king, Richard III, therefore, it stood to reason that she wouldn't possess a wealth of knowledge of the Tudor period. Still, she felt a niggle of indignation thinking Daniel assumed she wasn't inclined to learn about it on her own.

The unspoken exchange between the two men annoyed her. Truth be told, it was an era she had taken a particular interest in learning, and now she had the urge to show it.

"As I understand it," she said, "Amy Robsart Dudley met her end with an apparent fall down a set of stairs. I know there has been much speculation that it may not have been natural, given her husband's relationship with the queen."

Daniel showed his approval with a grin that lit up his eyes. "It's a futile endeavor, mind you. A mystery nearly four hundred years old in the making, but recent medical research points to new clues."

"What sort of clues?" she asked, relishing his smile as it grew wider.

"Well, if one is to believe that she died of natural causes by falling, much has been said about the fact she may have been ill prior. There has been some medical examination of the old documents suggesting that the malady she was reported to have may have been a form of..."—he coughed into his hand—"breast cancer. If that was the case, there could have been a brittleness to her bones that may have contributed to her neck being broken in the fall."

Her father moved over to a high-back chair, taking in the exchange between the two with a thin-veiled delight she didn't miss. His pride in her was clear but she sensed that some of it rested on himself. No doubt he took credit for her molding.

"If I am not mistaken, Doctor Brown, she was found with her headdress fully intact on her head. Given the construction of that piece, and the means of securing them to the head at the time, wouldn't that be unusual for a fall such as the one she took?"

"Yes," he admitted, the word drawn out. "That is a question that certainly has been pondered. It is likely that she took a minor fall, though. Just down a step or two—not the entirety of the stairs, as might have been suggested before. If her bones were made brittle from her illness, that might provide a credible explanation."

"Indeed, it could, but there are other factors that really do not add up for me." She found her confidence growing. "Why would Lady

Dudley have been so insistent that the servants of the house all leave to attend the local fair? That would not have been proper in that time period. A woman of such high nobility would scarcely be left alone."

"You know far more than I would have expected," he said. "Please, call me Daniel. Doctor Brown seems so much more fitting for my father." He smiled. "I am the younger one."

"Yes." Another flutter of heat flushed her cheeks. "I have read Sir Walter Scott's novel *Kenilworth*. The story has always intrigued me."

He flicked a backhand wave from his wrist. "Oh, don't put stock in that pish posh. It was little more than a Victorian work of fiction, and they loved shock and awe."

"Yes, but the facts are still there. Amy Robsart was the wife of Robert Dudley. Robert Dudley had his sights on Queen Elizabeth, and by all accounts she was equally enthralled by him. No one in Elizabeth's court wanted to see the two together, so there was much to gain for many by Amy's death. Either Dudley and Elizabeth could have planned her demise, or other people in the royal circle, such as the privy council, could have desired her death enough to frame Dudley and derail a potential marriage to Elizabeth by planting suspicion on him for the murder. If you ask me, there are so many other contributing scenarios that a convenient fall down the stairs seem highly unlikely."

"I think I should marry you," he said, his eyes wide.

A heavy silence filled the room, until her father shot up from the chair. "She is here for a summer job, Daniel, not a June wedding." He gave her a nod she knew too well. "Now, Adelia, I am absolutely starving. We really should get back to Mum and let the good doctor continue his work."

Even with her head still dizzy from the exchange with Daniel, she produced a polite smile and agreed. He looked at the back of his hand, his expression somewhat glum. When he made eye contact with her, heat returned to her cheeks.

"So, why are you here, Doc— Daniel?" She groaned inside at the audible sigh from her father that said he was ready to wrap up the conversation and depart. *No, he deserves retribution for not telling me about the gift shop thing earlier.* "Amy Robsart Dudley never lived at Hampton Court. Elizabeth I was far too vain to have allowed the wives of her courtiers to stay at Court."

"That is a very fair question," he said, his smile returning. "Following the trail of Amy's life is quite difficult. Some of the locations she stayed in no longer exist, and I have already scoured every inch of those that do. This country can be quite frustrating when you are looking for answers on a case this old. As places succumb to inevitable decay, precious documents can be moved to the most unlikely of places. Most of the key players in Amy's particular case would have been here at Hampton Court at some time." He held his open hand out to his paper-strewn desk. "I am hoping to find something in the archives here. If not here, then I will be onto the next place."

She nodded once, her lips pursed. "I suppose it's unrealistic to think that all letters and documents could survive the changing times. I manage to lose my term papers at least three times a week, in my tiny dorm room." She followed this with a lighthearted chuckle. "However, it always gives you hope when a Hans Holbein painting is discovered in the attic of a manor house, or when that one piece of jewelry is discovered in someone's family collection."

He held both forefingers up at shoulder level. "That's exactly the lucky break I am hoping for."

Her father cleared his throat and she shot him a scowl. "My father wishes to return to my grandma's apartment. I really did enjoy meeting you, though. I wish you luck with your work. It really does sound fascinating." She turned to leave.

"Ms. Grey, I would like to continue this conversation at another time, if it pleases you? There is a document I would like to have your opinion on. If I could just find it in this clutter." He looked around the room, his expression pained. Given the mess, it was unlikely he'd find anything.

She couldn't hold back her smile. "I will look forward to meeting you again, Daniel."

The two men shook hands, and she followed her father out the door. As they made their way back through the corridors to her grandma's apartment, she acknowledged to herself that she felt a little starstruck after meeting Daniel.

"What an intriguing man," she said.

"He was quite taken with you, too, Doll. Just promise me that you won't run off and get married this summer." He laughed. "We professors make dull husbands, you know."

She wondered just what type of man her father would want for her, sure he had strong opinions on the matter. He always had a discreet way of being overly involved in her life decisions. The fact that she was in England for the summer was proof of that.

"Did we not already establish that I am here for a summer job, not a husband?" she snapped, a tinge of independence surging through her chest.

"Yes, Doll, we did," he agreed. "Still, once upon a time, I knew a beautiful girl just about your age who was swept off her feet by a boring intellectual. Just can't seem to remember her name." He drummed his fingers on his chin.

"You have my word, Dad, I will be much wiser than ole whatsername." She laughed. "Now, let's get back. I am exhausted."

Chapter Five

On Monday morning Adelia rose early, dressing in a modest navy-blue dress with a boatneck collar. She pulled a string of faux pearls from the side drawer of the vanity table and fastened them around her neck, then checked herself in the mirror before grabbing her handbag to leave.

She had been given the first few days to familiarize herself with her surroundings, though she spent most of the time in the company of her father and grandma, not having the opportunity to go anywhere on her own around the colossal palace. Today, she was beginning her employment, and with the place being so vast, she was determined to give herself a few extra minutes in case she lost her way.

Much to her dismay, her job would not be as one of the many historical figures on the living-history tour. No, there would be no period dress, and no enlightening the public with little known historical facts. Who am I kidding? Interacting with strangers was never a strong skill for me. My assignment is to wear a pleasant smile and ring out purchases in the gift shop. On a positive note, it was a job that allowed her to blend in and draw as little attention to herself as possible. Low pressure, and she should be delighted but, deep down, she felt a bit disappointed.

Over the past few days, she'd found that the palace held a kind of magic that made her a little bolder, even if it was just once or twice—far more often than she could remember in recent history. She had been so busy, there was scarcely time to do anything but try to catch up.

Today, as she set off to begin her humble little summer job, she was reminded that, in a couple of days, her father would return to Boston, leaving her on her own. This should have scared her death but, for some reason, it didn't. Such a lack of fear, or diminished fear, was new but welcome. It felt like she was breaking free from some intangible force, able to live her life as she had always wanted.

She soon discovered that the distance from the apartments to the gift shop was like walking a marathon. With each day that passed, her appreciation developed of just how big Hampton Court was. The grounds itself covered more than 750 acres, so a simple walk in the garden was of Olympic proportions. By the time she reached the gift shop door, she felt winded and her calf muscles burned. It wasn't open yet. She'd been instructed to arrive fifteen minutes beforehand, but she'd given herself a few more in case she took a wrong turn along the way.

A bench outside the door provided the perfect spot to ease back and watch as the occasional staff member passed by on their way to their duty station. In just a few minutes, the palace would open its West Gate to a flood of eager tourists. The serenity of these walls would disappear under a rush of activity that would continue until closing time.

Sitting in the quiet, she became aware of her anxiety awakening. *No, I've been doing so well.* She shifted as a flush of heat worked its way along her limbs, spreading, inch by inch, through her body. This heat surge was coupled with a frigid coldness. Though she knew it wasn't the case just yet, the space felt as if it was crowded, with people bustling around her, shoulder to shoulder. She closed her eyes in frustration, berating herself for thinking her new life could be so easy. In reality, she had been naive to think she could just will this nervous disposition away. What made it worse was the knowledge that whatever filled her with such fear, was nothing at all. Nothing. Yet it felt so real.

She clenched her eyes tighter, her heart gripped by the fear of losing control. Her mind raced, screaming at her to run, to escape the discomfort. Don't let the fear leave you sitting here like a paralyzed, blubbering fool. People will see you. They will think something is wrong with you. You can't let them see.

But she couldn't run. That fact burned in her as much as the stifling fear. She had to follow through with her duties. I owe that to Dad. I owe it to myself. No matter how hard this is, I will have to power through it—every single gut-wrenching moment.

The prospect of the people she loved knowing something was wrong with her was far worse. She had spent her entire life camouflaging her anxiety from the world. Everyone, bar Kate, just assumed she was shy by nature. She had never wanted to disappoint her parents by having them think she wasn't the "normal," perfect daughter they had built her up to be in their minds. The sheer effort weakened every aspect of her, and she hated it like nothing else in her life.

She sat in the chaos, taking long slow breaths, doing her utmost to block out everything around and within her. To succeed, she had to dig deep, concentrating on absorbing the quiet until the warmth subsided. In that moment, when she approached a point of real peace, her focus was shaken by voices around her. Full conversations, as though there wasn't a frightened woman sitting on a bench outside the gift shop—like she didn't exist in their world. She eased her eyes open, prepared to face the fear as if it were an oncoming truck.

The hallway was empty. She scanned the area left to right, trying to pinpoint the source of the voices, to no avail. Perhaps they are coming from off in the distance—from another room? She didn't understand. These voices sounded as though they were close by—inches—which added to her confusion. During her first year in college, she had really only touched on the nuances of human psychology, yet she knew enough to know there was a fundamental difference between paralyzing fear and hearing actual voices. She straightened. Goodness, I might be crazier than I thought.

This trip was supposed to be her saving grace, her ticket out of self-induced destruction. It made her feel something she had interpreted as boldness—a strengthened sense of self confidence. Yet, from her arrival, something else was manifesting itself. She wasn't sure she trusted what that condition was or what it meant for her future. As she sat in a near daze, keys jingled to her left.

"Have you been waiting long, dear?" a tall slender woman asked.

If Adelia had to guess, she was well into her sixties, if not older. However, her well-placed makeup and fashionable hairstyle helped to mask her true age. "No, Ma'am," she answered, not knowing who she was talking to.

"Well, Ms. Grey, it is a delight to meet you in the flesh. I have heard a great deal about you from your grandmother. We are bridge partners on occasion. My name is Doris."

"Oh, what a pleasure to meet you." Adelia smiled at the familiarity of her name.

"My heavens, what a pretty girl you are."

Adelia's cheeks flushed with heat. She had never been good at accepting compliments. While she had been called pretty before, it was by her parents, so didn't count. In truth, she knew she wasn't entirely unattractive but she never seemed to be attractive enough to catch much in the way of male attention.

"Let me get the doors unlocked," Doris said, fumbling with her keys. "You will be training alongside me today. Don't get too excited, though. Working in the gift shop is really very simple."

"Glad to hear that," Adelia replied, somewhat relieved. "Honestly, I was a little nervous about today. Are you the manager, Doris?"

"Heavens, no. I live in the apartments here. I just volunteer. It gives me something to do to get out and about, if you know what I mean? I just like being around people. Breaks the monotony of retirement."

"I can understand that." She followed the lady after she opened the door and switched on the lights. With the interior illuminated, she took in the splendor of the store and all the trappings of a gift shop, with books, souvenirs, and postcards lining the shelving. She spotted little figurines of Henry VIII—the more recognizable plump version, not the young lion he'd been known as in his youth. As they passed a small metal hanging tree adorned with ornaments of the Tudor Rose, she grinned as she thought of Daniel and his admitted fondness of them.

"You have been friends with my grandma for a long while then?" she said, trying her hand at polite conversation.

"Oh yes, probably a decade or more by now," Doris replied, in a near hum. "She is a great lady, your grandmother. Quite the storyteller."

"Ah, yes, I have heard that before." She took care not to sound insulting.

"We all have a vivid imagination, dear. Some of us are just better at keeping it to ourselves."

"Well said, Doris. I agree."

"Well now, let's get you started over here at the desk. I think we shall start with something simple. We should see a flood of customers after lunch, so it's best if we don't overwhelm you to start with."

Not feeling overwhelmed at some point today was a prospect that seemed nearly impossible for her. In that moment, though, she appreciated Doris's calm demeanor.

The morning progressed at a slow pace but she learned quite a bit, which surprised her. Doris explained everything, showed her where more inventory was stored, and gave her a crash course on the cash register. As customers trickled in, she found it easy enough to keep up with the flow.

At noon, Doris directed her to the lunchroom, and after the allotted half hour, she returned to finish out her shift. Just as Doris said, the customer traffic picked up and soon she was bouncing from one job to another. The busyness didn't bother her as much as expected. In truth, there wasn't time to think about anything in depth. She rang out purchases, restocked items as they were depleted from the shelves, and assisted with any questions that arose.

Several times, Doris said how remarkable it was to have someone well versed in the palace's history. It made her easier to train, as she could already answer most customer questions on the spot. Adelia smiled at the compliment, which boosted her confidence.

At about three o'clock she glanced up from the front desk and spotted a tall thin figure enter the shop. She swallowed an unexpected tightness in her throat. His short-cropped hair glinted with more auburn than when she'd seen him in the dim library a few nights before. Trying not to stare, she followed his movements out of the corner of her eye as he walked through the store as though searching for something specific. He maneuvered around the other customers, then made a point of acknowledging that he'd spotted what he was looking for before heading toward the ornaments hanging on the metal stand. With one in hand, he turned and headed in her direction. She shifted her gaze down, pretending to examine something on the glass-topped desk, aware through her lashes of the figure approaching. When she looked up and met his gaze, she cursed how quick the smile came to her lips.

"Why, Daniel, it's a pleasure to see you again."

He stared at her, his awkwardness obvious as he fumbled for an adequate response. Something about his nervous disposition warmed her heart.

"Hello, Ms. Grey," he said, clearing his throat. Without saying anything else, he placed the small piece on the countertop and pushed it toward her.

Tiny beads of perspiration had surfaced along his hairline. He pulled at his collar, like a seventh-grade boy about to ask a girl to the dance.

"Are you sure this is the one you want? There are many others to choose from on the display."

"They are all exactly the same," he said, staring at the carved piece of wood.

"Are they? I wasn't sure if they were identical. I suppose you would know, considering you have several of them already. Would you like this one gift wrapped, or do you plan to take it home and put it on the tree straight away?" Oh, my goodness, am I flirting with this guy? She tongued the inside of her bottom lip. She had never actually flirted with someone, so she wasn't convinced she was doing it well.

She knew Daniel's type all too well, though. I bet he's like Dad in so many ways. Her father paid enormous attention to detail in the things that mattered to him most, which, more often than not, centered around his work. He was a notorious forgetter of birthdays, anniversaries, and holidays in general. She suspected that Daniel's apartment was strewn with books and piles of papers, and he probably never even put up a Christmas tree. That got her thinking. It was just the end of May after all. A bit early to start stockpiling Christmas decorations. The reality hit her and she found herself feeling a little flattered that he was here.

He looked at her with hesitation, as though he needed longer to pick up on her humor. "I...will just take it as it is." He smiled. "No need to even bag it."

"My pleasure, sir." She smiled as she rang up his purchase, the high-pitched ding of the cash register resonating through the store.

"Ms. Grey, I was wondering if there was a time that I could pick your brain about that document I mentioned the other day?"

She looked at him for a long moment as she handed him his change. "I don't see why not."

He flicked a look to his right before leaning closer. "Perhaps this evening?"

"Oh, I am sorry but I have a dinner engagement with my father and grandma tonight. I actually have something tomorrow too."

"Oh, yes, that's okay. Another time." A heaviness in his voice hinted at his disappointment.

"What about Wednesday?" she asked. "I am done here at five o'clock, though I might run a touch later, after setting things up for the next day, but it shouldn't be by much. I could stop by your office on my way home?"

"Perfect," he said, almost jumping to catch the coins slipping from his hand. "Wednesday would be great."

He stood there, smiling, and she sensed he had something further to say but didn't want to prompt him.

"Wednesday then," he said at last, then turned and walked away.

As the afternoon progressed, she found herself unable to think about anything but him. It was her first day of work and she had a great many other things to concentrate on but her mind refused to cooperate. Daniel was not what every girl would consider attractive, but for some reason he had caught her attention without much effort. She couldn't say he wasn't her type, because she had never really established what her type was. What is it about him that drew me to him? He is intelligent, and that's something I find appealing. He isn't too sure of himself, but he's not overly insecure either. And his clear discomfort in social situations is something we both have in common. Yes, he had piqued her interest, and his presence was a welcome distraction from thinking. Indeed, thinking about him came easy, even if it added a new area of uncertainty.

Doris came up to her later. "Was that Doctor Brown I saw you serving earlier?"

"Yes, he was in to buy another one of his *prized* Tudor Rose ornaments." She failed to bite back her smile.

"Tudor Rose ornaments? Interesting choice. I haven't seen him in the shop before today."

"Oh?" She leaned back. "I thought he'd purchased them before."

"Never while I've been here, and I work just about every day."

Hmm, well, he owns one now.

"He is a fine catch," Doris continued, arching her thin eyebrows. "Handsome boy, under that stuffy façade. Unbelievably smart, too, just like his dad."

"I imagine he is, but I am on strict orders from my father not to catch any illness or a beau on my summer in England."

"Fine one to talk, your dad." Doris gave her a knowing nod. "Didn't he meet your mother when she was here as a young woman?"

"Well, yes, but Dad seems to think that marrying a professor is a bad choice for anyone, particularly his daughter."

"That is a shame. In my day, snagging an Oxford professor was a real score."

Adelia laughed. "Stop it. Daniel is far too engrossed in his studies here to pay mind to me. He is only here for the summer, and I am sure he doesn't have time for courting some dumb American girl."

"Daniel, eh?"

"I—"

"Don't short yourself, dear, they all like American girls. Old King Henry would have been after the likes of you, to be sure." She chuckled. "You might have been lucky number seven."

Adelia flicked her hair back. "Wasn't it Christina of Denmark who said it best...? 'If only I had two heads.'"

Chapter Six

The next day, Adelia sat in the canteen, finishing a cup of hot tea and some biscuits she had brought, savoring the quiet contentment of the moment. Her days at the university had got her used to eating in a rush so she had to make a conscious effort to slow down and enjoy her break. The afternoon rush would be waiting for her return.

She gazed out the window, taking in the sights of the manicured gardens. Hampton Court was such an anomaly. Here sat this massive castle, half of it the remnants of Henry VIII, with the other half bearing the marks of William and Mary. A renaissance palace and a baroque palace, patched together to make one of the most architecturally unique landmarks in the country. Beyond that, the establishment was both a hive of activity and a place of quiet refuge. She had to nearly pinch herself every morning; being here was like a dream.

The scrape of a chair on the bare floor snapped her out of her thoughts, and she glanced across the table, almost gasping at the sight of Daniel Brown seated opposite her. With meticulous effort, he unwrapped a sandwich covered in brown wax paper, flattening each fold out with the tips of his long fingers.

"Do they permit professors to take lunch?" she asked, making sure her smile wasn't quite as effusive as yesterday. "I guess I always assumed you people just withered away to skin and bone in those dusty old libraries."

"Ah, one must have nourishment to keep up with those countless hours of dull reading, you know. Didn't your father ever eat a sandwich?"

"Barely." She chuckled, a flurry of memories coming to her. "When I was young, he would sometimes take me along to the university library. I always enjoyed the experience but was near famished by the time he finished. Apparently, feeding your child is not top priority when you are knee deep in the Hundred Years War." She sipped on the dregs of her tea.

"I will admit, we are a self-centered breed, we professors."

"Indeed," she agreed. "How are things progressing with your quest?"

He turned his sandwich. "This isn't my first time trying to research something that is near impossible to solve. That said, I am learning new things every day." He took a tight bite and chewed, keeping his mouth closed, which she appreciated.

"So, if you are researching the circumstances surrounding Amy's death, just what is it you hope to find?"

He swallowed, then dabbed the corner of his mouth with his handkerchief. "What everyone hopes to find. The truth."

"Yes...but in a perfect world, what would that truth be? It's possible that she simply took a fall and her neck was broken. It's possible that she committed suicide." She sat up, excited. "It is possible that she was, in fact, murdered."

"Amy's only crime is that she was married to a man who did not love her as a husband should. He had sights on the queen. The queen may have had sights on him. Amy was little more than an inconvenience to everyone around her." He shrugged one shoulder. "That had to be devastating to a woman who lived in a time where society gave her little choice but to endure such cruelty."

Adelia buried the urge to sigh. "Whether she brought harm to herself or harm was brought upon her, she really didn't have a lot of options. As I recall, she suspected that she was being poisoned at one point. Correct?"

"Correct. If she had been legitimately ill, she may have mistaken those symptoms for poisoning. She was insistent that only one of her servants be permitted to handle anything she ate or drank. It was clear that she understood her own situation well enough to think that someone may try to dispose of her by those means. In that time period, fear of being poisoned was more common than we could understand today." He took another bite from his sandwich, never breaking eye contact.

For her part, Adelia struggled not to fixate on the sandwich, regretting not packing more than a few biscuits that morning. She pulled her thoughts together.

"Still, that fear was great enough that she moved from her previous residence to Cumnor Place. She must have felt some sense of safety being under the protection of Sir Anthony Forster."

He nodded his agreement, holding a forefinger up as he swallowed. "But Forster was a dedicated servant to Robert Dudley, and it has been speculated that he could have been responsible for her death. You read *Kenilworth*. You know the rumors."

"I do, but Lord Varney was present at Cumnor on the day she died. He was another of Dudley's henchmen."

He leaned forward. "You're right, of course. Dudley had every reason to want his wife out of the picture. He had a number of loyal servants who were capable of murdering her, and probably would have if given the order. Still, there is something that has never sat right with me..." His brows creased.

"Go on," she said, eager to hear what he had to say.

"Well, Dudley was a smart man. He would have to have known that court gossip would brew a firestorm if something happened to Amy. If she died, he would surely have suspicion upon him given his close relationship with the queen."

"But he did tell people of her illness." She tapped the table top. "He also said that if he should live another year, he would be in a very different position. That is surely enough to point the finger of suspicion at him even more."

"It does," Daniel agreed. "Yet, Elizabeth's secretary William Cecil was not in approval of any match between the queen and Dudley. He even sent correspondence to the Spanish Ambassador, knowing he would tell everyone about how Amy was in fact quite well. Indeed, Cecil was a quiet puppet master, calling the shots behind the scenes."

Adelia sat back in her chair. "So, you are implying that Cecil could have been setting Dudley up, by using his own words against him? That actually sounds quite logical."

"Cecil was a loyal servant to Elizabeth when she was just a princess under the reign of her sister Mary. He had been loyal his whole career to her, yet he was so distraught over what would happen if she married Dudley, he told people he would resign his position. That would have been a tremendous loss of power and wealth for him." He shrugged an eyebrow. "Potential justification for him resorting to desperate measures."

"Poor Amy," she whispered, watching Daniel chew on another bite of his lunch. She was tempted to make another cup of tea but didn't want to break this enthralling discussion. "She was an innocent woman caught in the crossfire of all this court intrigue when, in reality, she had never even been a part of court life."

"Great point, Adelia. The further I dig, the more I have to remember this woman was a living breathing person. Yes, the mask of death is a cruel distortion. In the end, all we are is what we have become in the minds of those who remain. Our lives, our experiences, our emotions, are nothing more than interpretations. Indeed, our actions take on whatever narrative we are assigned. In life, our turmoil and tribulations seem insurmountable. In death, they take on a new meaning altogether. Where once we traveled through these times never knowing the answers, our death gives everything a whole new clarity. A lost soul becomes a sophisticated schemer, who then becomes the unwitting victim. Amy was real, and whatever fate befell her, she deserves her story to be told as it was, not as people want it to be told."

She realized her hand was covering her heart. "That's really beautiful. Amy does deserve her story to be told, as you say, accurately."

He smiled. "We are still on for five o'clock tomorrow?"

"Absolutely. I am more curious than ever now. I wish you had brought the documents with you."

"Oh, the chief curator would never allow me to do that with such a priceless piece of history. He would have my head."

She laughed. "I suppose there have been enough poor souls who met that unfortunate fate here over the years. Hampton Court doesn't need another ghost."

"Pfft! No such thing as ghosts. Tomorrow then?" He smiled from ear to ear.

"Yes, I will come to you as soon as I end my shift."

He wrapped the remains of his sandwich and got up. "I enjoyed our chat, Adelia. Until tomorrow."

Doris passed him as he left. She walked over to the table. "Was that Doctor Brown?"

"Yes, he was having his lunch."

"Here, in the lunchroom?" She scratched at her right temple.

"Yes," Adelia said, drawing the word out. "Isn't this where all the staff eat their lunch?"

"First time I've seen him here." The older woman looked around. "Hmm, perhaps there is something here now that wasn't here before. Wonder what that could be?" She drummed her forefinger on her chin, beneath a mischievous smile.

After returning to work, Adelia set about unpacking boxes from a new shipment, cataloging it all into the inventory ledger, then pricing each item before restocking the shelves. The work wasn't what anyone would consider exciting, but it still passed the time. As she worked, she found herself thinking about how Daniel was spending his summer. All her jokes about him spending his days stuck in his dusty library aside, she felt a tiny bit jealous of him. He'd insisted that his work would probably not get him any further than those who sought answers before. Odds were that might be true, yet what if his research did lead to some long-uncovered facts that revealed something new? Even if he never did find the answers he was looking for, the work he was doing had to be fulfilling, unlike the meaningless task of stocking postcards and gift-wrapping porcelain cups.

Passing one of the bookshelves, she caught sight of a book chronicling the reign of Queen Elizabeth I. Hoping to glean some insight into how the death of Amy Robsart Dudley was perceived at court, she placed it by the cash register. Another look at contemporary accounts could only help boost her confidence on the subject.

She returned the next day to continue her training with Doris. Like clockwork, Daniel appeared again in the lunchroom. He shared his work for the day, asking her opinion, which she was happy to give.

"What do you think Amy was like as a person?" she asked. "I mean, history shows us so little of who she was in real life."

"True," he agreed. "She was unfortunate enough to have been born a daughter. Sadly, it is not uncommon for there to be next to no documentation on the lives of women in that time, even very prominent women like say...Anne Neville."

"Now, that is a name that intrigues me." She leaned forward on the table.

"Yes, I recall that you are well versed in the War of the Roses. So, what interests you in the daughter of the kingmaker?"

His bright-blue eyes almost drew her closer, and she had to blink to break the magnetic connection. "What would not interest me about Anne Neville? Despite the fact there is little historical record about her life, what does exist tells of an extraordinary one, to say the least.

I suppose it's the same thing that interests me in Amy Robsart. Here were these women, born into lives entirely predetermined for them. They lived and breathed each day in the most turbulent times in history. I can only imagine the thoughts and feelings these two women must have had. They may not have been able to ever truly speak their minds about their situations, but that doesn't mean they did not have an opinion." She sighed. "If only we had a window into their lives for just one day."

"Yes, wouldn't it be interesting to know what her life was like married to Richard III, with his withered arm and hunched back."

She stared at him. "Now who is the hypocrite?"

He frowned. "Whatever do you mean?"

"Wasn't it you who said not to believe all of that Victorian...I believe 'pish posh,' was the word? Something created for shock value? You know full well that Shakespeare's portrayal of Richard III was more propaganda to please the Tudor queen than reality. I don't believe there is any proof that Richard had a withered arm or hunched back."

He raised his fingers from the table top. "I don't disagree. They say Shakespeare's portrayal of him was simply to show his inner evil manifesting itself as a physical deformity. Like the portrait of Dorian Grey."

"Superstition," she barked back with a dismissive shake of her head. "Same people who burned poor souls as witches for putting a curse on their cows."

His eyebrows arched. "There was that portrait painted of Richard with one shoulder higher than the other."

"Again, propaganda. Everyone knows that painting was altered after his death in an effort to keep public perception of him low. It was all an effort to keep Henry Tudor's subjects on his side. I am not saying I don't think Richard did some very bad things. Ultimately, he was a man of his time. I am just saying I don't see evidence he was the villain history has painted him to be."

Daniel nearly spit out his tea as he laughed.

"What's so funny?" she asked, far from impressed, and feeling somewhat belittled. I can't believe he's making fun of me. She shrank back into her chair. He was so smart—perhaps she had let her guard down in thinking she could keep her end of the conversation up.

As if reading her thoughts, he reached across the table and touched her hand, a zing of energy coursing into her wrist.

"I am so sorry, Adelia, I should not have laughed." He pulled his hand back. "I just wanted to see if I could stir you up a little, to see how passionate you were on the subject. I actually agree with you one hundred percent about Richard III. I think he descended into darkness as his ambition grew. I don't think he was always the bad guy history portrays him as."

She released a quiet sigh of relief but berated herself for allowing her insecurities to come to the surface so fast. And she loathed how obvious they had been to Daniel. Time to move things on.

"Do you think Robert Dudley actually loved Amy?"

"Yes, I do," he said. "Like Richard III, I believe his ambition led him in a different direction somewhere along the way. Sadly, it was the women of that period who paid the highest price. Even so, there is plenty of evidence that mutual affection existed between them for some time. I think it was Amy who stayed devoted and he who discarded her in the end."

"I guess I feel a little guilty sometimes. I spend so much energy worrying about what I am going to do with my life. It's so easy to take for granted that these women didn't have any chance of making a life decision for themselves. They were almost entirely dependent on whatever self-serving plan someone else had for them. It seems so unfair for me to be so selfish."

He gripped the table with both hands and stared at her. "What are you talking about, Adelia? You are hands down an accomplished historian already." He ran a forefinger in an arc across the table top. "You will finish college and go on to be one of the most esteemed professors in your field. I have no doubt about that at all."

"I am not going to college for history, though." She glanced behind, glad to see they were still alone. "I am studying psychology."

"What!" He blinked several times, his brows arched.

She could almost hear his brain working in overdrive. "I...am majoring in the study of psychology."

"Look, I don't mean to be rude, but why would you not be studying history?"

"I don't have to study history just because my father is a professor."

He leaned back, glaring at her. "I don't care if your dad was the Fiddler on the Roof for an occupation. You don't have to do anything just because your dad does it. I am saying you should be studying history because you are damn good at it." He leaned forward, resting both elbows on the table, his hands open, palms up. "I would work beside you any day at Oxford."

"Thank you," she said, flattered to think someone so esteemed would think of her in that way. "I guess I still don't know what I want to be when I grow up." She allowed a light chuckle. "I just don't want people to think I would only pick history because it's what my father wants. I do actually have an interest in psychology too."

"Believe it or not, I understand much better than you think. When I was younger, I had a notion that I would take a completely different path to my father. I thought I was too modern for the old conventions of Oxford. To be truthful, I went out and experienced a few failures. You see, I am not really great at most of the stuff other guys are good at doing. Before long, I just had to learn that there is nothing I love nearly as much as studying the history of this country." He shrugged, one side of his mouth curling up in a half smile. "I am good at it, and I would be good at it even if my father wasn't."

She nodded, liking what she'd heard. "I guess I hadn't thought about it that way before."

"What I am trying to say is people will always have expectations about what you should do with your life. You shouldn't force yourself to do something you're less passionate about just to prove them wrong. You have to pursue your own dreams." He turned his cup.

"Look, if that is what others thought you should do, fine. But if it's not...?"

"It is difficult at times," she said. "I guess I have always felt like I'm not who people think I am."

"People rarely are what we think. We all have things better left concealed to prevent risking the judgment that comes with revealing our true nature. Despite what you might think, every person comes neatly packaged with flaws. Whatever you think those flaws might be, they are part of you." He moved the cup to the side and clasped both hands together. "If there is one thing in life I have learned, it is that you cannot sit around and wait for life to get less difficult before you start living it."

"Oh, so, life doesn't get easier?" She dropped her shoulders, the move exaggerated. "That sure doesn't give me much hope, does it?"

"No, I guess that sounded rather cynical. I am sorry." He laughed. "Truth is, life doesn't become less challenging as you get older. However, the more you experience, the more knowledge you have to navigate those challenges. That makes it a little easier, or so I'm led to believe."

She found herself smiling back at him, and while it was nice, she wanted to continue with this serious, honest thread. He was so different, and she had never found it so easy to be as open to anyone else. "I have always been an overthinker. I can talk myself right out of a good idea, if I let fear take over. It is a perpetual awkwardness I have battled my whole life." She clasped her own hands together. "That's why I have always had an interest in psychology. I want to have the tools to figure myself out."

"Again, I can relate better than you know. If you are interested in psychology, and you're as knowledgeable as you are with history, why not merge those two together? There is not an event in history that did not take the inner workings of the human mind to come to fruition."

She knew he was right. Part of her rebellion against undertaking a career in historical studies was rooted in the fact that she didn't want people to assume she had done so because of her father. She loved and respected him but wanted to make her achievements on her own. Seeing that Daniel was able to carve out his own path, despite his father's being similar, sharpened her perspective. Perhaps I can find a way to merge my two interests into something that is uniquely mine. Daniel said he'd be glad to work with me at Oxford. What a far-fetched notion. No, that is far too great a goal to even consider. Isn't it? While distinguished universities such as Oxford had moved into the 20th century, their pace was still way too slow. The presence of female professors was still minimal at best. Daniel could never fully understand the barriers women such as she faced in the academic circles he traveled. There would always be doors closed to her that would be open for him. She could spend a lifetime trying to explain it to him but, until he lived that inequity himself, he could never really understand.

Even so, she was glad he had come into her life, if only for a brief time while she was here for the summer. In just a few days, he had managed to give her a level of clarity about herself that had evaded her before. She was drawn to him in some way—there was no doubting that—but she wasn't sure why. Conversation with him came so easy—it was like time didn't exist—and because of that, she was nearly late returning to work.

Just as the day before, she found herself consumed with thoughts of him. So much so, she knew she needed to pull herself together or she might end up losing her job in the first week. What was this hold on her his friendship evoked? He was nearly eight years older, yet it felt as though they were the same age. The man brought out an undeniable desire to take a risk. There was a certain irony in that notion. Daniel was by all accounts a man in control of his surroundings. He may have suffered awkward moments but he appeared to have a firmer grasp on his mannerisms than she possessed of her own. Maybe that was the one area where her youth got the best of her—never really allowing her enough experience to make the right move in a given moment.

It took effort but she managed to push such thoughts from her mind. With her focus regained, she set about replacing items that had been sold yesterday. After about an hour of this, two women approached her, whispering back and forth to each other. She met their enquiring looks with a polite smile as she moved around a display table. Their whispering unnerved her, reminding her of all the voices she had heard since arriving at the castle, but she tried to focus on the task at hand until she thought greeting them might encourage them to move on to another area of the store.

"Can I help you ladies find anything special?" she asked, as though she had worked in the gift shop for ages.

"You're just perfect," the thin blonde woman said. "Isn't she just what we need?" she asked her friend, smaller than her, who nodded in response, smiling from ear to ear.

"Excuse me," Adelia said, "I'm not quite sure that I understand."

"Your figure, your hair," the woman explained. She turned to her friend. "She has a tiny neck too." They both nodded in agreement.

"I am sorry, I'm still not following you."

"We are in a bit of a muddle, you see. Our Mistress Boleyn has quit and we are in desperate need of a replacement."

"Mistress Boleyn?" Adelia asked, just short of scratching her head.

"Mary?" She almost took offense at the suggestion that she resembled the king's mistress. She caught herself glancing down at the V-neck of her dress, hoping it wasn't cut too low.

"Anne," the smaller woman corrected. "We are in quite a bind. You would be doing us a great favor to serve as her fill-in until we can find someone to replace her. Of course, you will have to do a bit of work on your accent, but that is just a minor detail."

Adelia struggled to hold back her excitement at this prospect. At best, she might only be needed a day or two but she didn't care. Not only was she taking on the chance to do something far more entertaining than slogging through the day in the gift shop, she was to play the role of Anne Boleyn no less.

"When can I start?" she blurted out. She had no doubt she would regret this commitment later but, for now, she was too consumed by the prospect of doing something more worthwhile than stocking shelves.

Chapter Seven

When her shift ended, Adelia could hardly contain her excitement as she hurried down the hall toward the library room that served as Daniel's study. No sooner had she made a few yards when she heard Doris calling out to her from behind.

"I wanted to catch you before you got too far," Doris said, her breath labored. "I heard the news that you will be taking leave from the gift shop for a while."

"Yes," Adelia said, trying not to sound half as overjoyed as she was at the prospect of getting out of the gift shop. "It appears that I will be playing the role of none other than Anne Boleyn. That is to say, until a proper replacement can be found."

"I will be terribly sad to lose you, but this is certainly an opportunity that you should take. I have no doubt you will be perfect for the role. It is a role that requires great courage, but I firmly believe you are up for the task."

Adelia nodded, unsure of just what Doris meant by her statement. It was clear that the woman had little insight into the real Adelia, the one so carefully hidden behind the pleasant smile of a humble gift shop girl. Though a little guilt-ridden, she gave herself a mental pat on the back for keeping up with her own false image.

"Your Dad left this morning?" Doris asked. "He doesn't even know the good news yet."

"Yes, he had to get to the train station quite early, but I made sure I was up to see him off. I am sure he will call once he is back in Boston. I will share the news then. I know he will be more than thrilled."

After exchanging a few more words, Doris turned to head in the opposite direction, and Adelia continued to Daniel's office. Glancing down at her watch, she saw that she was more than half an hour late, and she quickened her pace. The corridors took on their usual silence now the doors to the palace had been closed up for the night. As she walked along, wondering what historical nuggets Daniel's document contained, she swore she heard faint music. She realized that she knew the tune from passing through the palace over the past few days—a song composed by the younger Henry VIII. The direction of the music was unclear; it could be coming from every empty room she passed. At times it sounded like it may be drawing closer, and the next second it felt further away.

The muffled sound of laughter echoing off the walls stopped her in her tracks. Most unusual. She moved on but stopped again when she caught an unexpected smell. The palace had an odor she could best describe as layered and ancient—a mix of old wood and some special concoction used to clean its many fragile surfaces. Her tummy rumbled as she focused on the scent of food—rich, decadent food: roasted meats and sauces, reminding her that lunch had been some time ago. Convinced there must be some after-hours' event taking place—a banquet perhaps, with minstrels playing period music—she quickened her steps even more. The last thing she wanted to encounter was a crowd of people.

She walked on into the depths of the palace until she reached the long dark hallway containing the administrative offices. When she knocked on Daniel's door, she barely waited for his response before opening it. He just about had time to smile before she blurted out that she would be starting tomorrow as Anne Boleyn until a permanent replacement could be found. She was so breathless with excitement, she found herself gasping at times. Even as she spoke, she was aware of the surprise on his face at her enthusiasm. But she couldn't help herself. She was talking to him like he had been her best friend for a lifetime. Though everything about this moment was out of character for her, she wasn't afraid, or even shy—just bursting at the seams with exhilaration and needing to share it with someone.

"I am so happy for you, Adelia," he said when she finished. "This is a fantastic opportunity. Have you ever done anything like this before?"

"I was in a Shakespeare production back in high school," she answered, not revealing that she was a tree in a forest. A silent tree at that. In her defense, she had memorized just about every other character's lines, dreaming of the day she might have the courage to audition for a lead role herself. And then to play that part. That day had never come, until today.

Snapping back to reality, she remembered why she was here. "I am sorry, Daniel. This is not about me, but thank you just the same for listening to me prattle on about my new position. What is it you wanted me to look at?"

For the first time since entering his office, she scanned her surroundings. One of the tables that had been covered in books and papers was now dressed in a tartan plaid tablecloth, with a beautiful array of cold meats, cheeses, and bread slices across it. Two plates, along with a glass carafe containing sparkling water, were placed at one end.

Doing her best to hide her disappointment, she motioned at the table. "I am sorry, we were supposed to meet now, right?" She glanced about. "If I interrupted you, I can come back at another time. Really, it is no trouble."

"I...I thought you might be hungry," he said, his nervousness clear as he wrung his hands. "I figured that you might not have time to eat after work."

She stood stunned for a moment, looked at the table, then back to Daniel, caught off guard that someone would go to such lengths for her. It was something that had never happened before. She became self-conscious when she realized he was reading her. Oh goodness, have I come across as rude in my reaction? Hold on, is this actually a...date? She had never been on an actual date before, and didn't know how to react. One thing she was certain of: she couldn't just stand there and say nothing.

"Thank you, Daniel," she said, cringing inside when it came out close to a whisper. She worked up a smile. "This is the nicest thing anyone has ever done for me."

He gave a half smile, no doubt wondering if he'd been out of line arranging such a thing. His insecurity was on full display now, and, for once, she found herself focused on someone else's discomfort instead of her own. Her deep anxiety often made her self-absorbed and, as a result, it was rare that she considered someone else's discomfort, but she could see all the signs in Daniel. She found it comforting knowing she wasn't the only person who suffered such vacillation.

"Shall we eat, first?" she asked, placing her handbag on a nearby chair and walking over to the table. She wanted to relieve his self-doubt. Her fake confidence seemed to work, and he slid into the chair near hers.

When he reached over and poured water into two mismatched glasses, she pretended not to notice his hands trembling. This man is adorable.

"Just where did you get all of this food?" she asked, setting a slice of bread onto her plate. He handed her a fork and slid the platter of cheeses toward her.

"The palace kitchens. Each day, they have food left over from the demonstrations. I didn't have time to make a trip into town, so it was the best I could do."

"I think it is just marvelous." She took a bite of her bread and cheese, covered her mouth as she chewed, then swallowed. "Yummy. Now that I think about it, I really am hungry."

As a satisfied grin lit up his face, she tried hard not to focus on the magnificent touch of auburn in his hair, loving how it looked in this light. His gorgeous eyes drew her in just as much.

"Tell me, Adelia, how have you found living at Hampton Court so far?"

"I could ask you the same." She chuckled. "It is the most magical place, though I have not even seen half of it yet. I guess I just never imagined myself here. It is as though this palace has flipped some switch in me."

"It has that effect, doesn't it?" He placed a cluster of grapes on his plate and popped one into his mouth, his cheek muscles rippling when he chewed on it. "I think all the castles in England have that sort of magic. You can just feel the change in the atmosphere. You would love Ireland and Scotland too."

"I hope to get the chance to visit them someday. I suppose you have been to a great many places."

"I have never traveled much farther than the British Isles," he said, with a hint of disappointment in his eyes. "I have been to just about every imaginable place across them, mind you. Scotland, Ireland, Wales, England. They all have a vibrant past and present. I honestly couldn't tell you which one I prefer more."

"I can't help but be jealous of you." She smiled. "I have never been one to travel much, but it is something I have always wanted to do."

He arched his eyebrows. "You didn't get to travel much growing up?"

"We would take trips in the summer when I was younger. Those were few and far between, though." A swirl of memories came to her. "My father did much of his research in the summer, so his time was limited." She took another bite of her food.

"Now that you are an adult, do you plan on going out to see the world? Backpacking across Europe is the fashion of these free-spirit types these days."

She didn't miss the teasing quirk at the edge of his mouth. "I am not really a free-spirit type. I reluctantly admit I am a homebound type. While I am always curious about the world, I lack the courage to actually go out on my own to discover things."

"Really?" He looked at her with disbelief. "If I am not mistaken, you did fly across the ocean to spend a summer in England. It seems to me you might have a bit more adventure in you than you think."

She wiped her mouth with a napkin. "Honestly, if I hadn't felt the pressure to please my father, I probably wouldn't be here. I have always been uncomfortable with new things. In truth, I was terrified of coming here at first." She somehow felt better being able to admit her hesitancy, and sensed that, even though they didn't know each other well, Daniel understood.

"You seem to be getting along better now," he said, his tone reassuring.

"That is the part even I don't understand. It was like, from the moment I walked through the front gates, my whole world changed." Her excitement caught her by surprise but she didn't want to stop. "I am still nervous by nature. That probably will never go away. But now it feels different." She gave him a slight shrug. "I can't put it into words."

"As you say, Hampton Court holds a kind of magic. Perhaps it is not for us to understand. I am probably the last person on earth who should say this but, as best you can, live in the moment here. Don't dwell on the past. Don't dwell on the future. Just take things as they come."

"Life would be far simpler." She placed her napkin on her plate, still not certain if she had just had her first date, or if Daniel really was just a caring person by nature. Both might be true. Something akin to a giddiness dwelled in her tummy, coupled with a feeling of being naive to all things that involved the heart. It was unfair that a woman of her age should be so in the dark about relationships. Having never dated before, she couldn't help missing every obvious sign. Doris had picked up on it. If this was a first date, she could not have imagined it being any more romantic. If it wasn't, well, at least the cheese was divine.

"Thank you again, Daniel, the food was perfect. I didn't mean to take time away from your project, but I do appreciate you feeding me. I am a terrible listener when I'm hungry." She laughed.

"Oh, yes." He held up a forefinger and swallowed what he'd been chewing. "I want you to take a look at something. It is a copy, mind you, but it will do just the same."

He got up and moved over to a desk scattered with papers. It reminded her of her father's study back home. In her experience, men with brilliant minds were not tidy people. She was well accustomed to hearing "Just let me find that paper. I know it's here somewhere."

To her surprise, he located the document with ease. He laid it on the desktop with a delicate touch and pulled out the old wooden chair for her to be seated. As she sat, he pulled over another wooden office chair, its steel casters squeaking across the floor. When he took his place next to her, she caught the smooth fragrance of his cologne. It was pleasing, and a nice departure from the aroma of dusty old books a room like this was better known for.

When a shiver ran through her, she wasn't sure if it was his closeness or just the scent of him. It felt foreign, as though that giddiness in her tummy had quadrupled. Despite the unfamiliar sensation, she decided that it wasn't an unwelcome one. It even felt good, though she doubted she would be able to concentrate if it persisted.

Daniel handed her the sheet of paper, a much-needed distraction from the surge of emotions she was trying to decipher. She looked down to see neat Elizabethan text. It was a letter of sorts. A short one but, judging by Daniel's enthusiasm, it had to be something important. She scanned the script, pleased that she was well versed in the language of that era.

"It's a letter to a tailor or a seamstress," she said. "The author is asking that they take the black velvet fabric she provided to make her a gown. It says here she wants a collar similar to the dress he'd made her before." She stopped, hand over her heart. "Oh my goodness, it's signed by Amy Dudley." She looked at him, amazed that his eyes had taken on a more radiant hue, if that were possible. "How marvelous of a find is this?"

"I know," he agreed. "It was written just a fortnight or so before her death. What do you make of it?"

While he had a way of making her feel at ease, there was no disputing that she felt wholly inadequate on an intellectual level with him. He had spent a great deal of time studying this subject and she could only draw from what little she'd read in a few books, one being a work of Victorian fiction at that. She hesitated, aware of the old insecurity creeping in.

"I don't know what insight I can share with you, Daniel. You are so much more well versed in these things than I. At best, I can only offer a female perspective."

"In case you haven't noticed, Adelia, I am entirely lacking in female perspective. Just share your thoughts with me. I want to hear them."

She allowed a slight smile, reassured by his words. The fact that he was interested in her opinion was something she found flattering. She focused back on the letter.

"Black velvet was extremely expensive for the time. Not a fabric available to a commoner." She raised her hand a few inches. "Naturally, Amy was not a commoner, so she could easily afford such opulence."

"Go on," he said.

"Black velvet was not exactly a fabric used for a simple day dress, though, so it only makes sense that, even as a woman of noble birth and plentiful resources, Amy would desire such a gown for a truly special occasion." She traced her fingertip down the page. "It says she wanted a collar made like the one she had before. She would have felt it was attractive on her. Why else would she want something similar if she didn't think it was flattering?"

He tapped the table top. "You see, I would have never gone in that direction. What else?"

"It has been suggested that perhaps she ended her own life. If she took such an extreme measure, given the deeply religious sentiment of the time, she would have faced damnation of her soul and not been permitted to be buried in the consecrated ground of a church. I just don't see it as a likely option. We throw the term 'God fearing' around quite loosely today, but it would not have been the same then."

"As you know," he said, "she did demand that every servant leave the house that day. Perhaps she wanted the place empty for that reason?"

"That's odd behavior, to be sure, but the tone of this letter doesn't say that to me." She crinkled the paper between her thumb and forefinger. "Women don't order new frocks if they have some dire intention in mind. Neither would she have ordered a gown if she were ill enough to think her days might be numbered." She had the strong urge to close her eyes as she held the page. Strange feelings spread through her, reminding her of the day in Landry's when she held the white wedding gloves. It was an odd mix of emotions, though she wasn't sure what they were at first. She forced herself to slow down, focusing hard, taking in the essence of the letter with pinpoint precision. Then it came to her, as if a door had been opened.

"There was an excitement in her when she wrote this letter. Something really good was about to happen."

"You get that?"

"Yes. She wanted this dress for a reason. As if wearing it would give hope of better days to come."

"Well, she had been away from her husband for over a year. He was just forty miles away at Elizabeth's court. Perhaps she was hoping for a reunion with him."

She opened her eyes to see him staring at her and had to look away, caught off guard. Something about the way he'd been studying her was unnerving, as if he had some genuine interest, like he wanted to puzzle her out as much as he did Amy. Even though he seemed to treat her as his intellectual equal, she was positive they were not.

For the little time she'd known him, he had always been a kind and respectful sort. If he considered his intelligence superior, he was not the sort to flaunt it. Was Doris right about it being infatuation? She couldn't be sure. Her lack of experience in dating would always hold her at a disadvantage in deciphering these things. The only thing she was sure of, was that she liked being in his company. While Lizzie, her grandma's helper, had always been friendly, she was far too busy to engage in anything more than the expected pleasantries. Since arriving at the palace, Daniel was the only person close to her age she had to converse with, and each time she saw him, something about him made her feel a little more alive. She tried to refocus on the task at hand. Come on, Addie, you're here for a purpose.

"He had been such an ass to her. Dudley, I mean," she said, so fast, she could barely believe herself so brash. It was as if, deep within, she knew a hint of shock value would obscure the strangeness of the moment.

He nodded in agreement. "She surely would have heard whispers about his relationship with the queen. Maybe she thought she must pull out all the stops to win back his affection?"

She pondered that for a moment. "William Cecil himself once wrote in a correspondence that the match between Amy and Robert had been a carnal one—a love match. It is safe to say there was an equal measure of affection between them at one time."

"Ah, but what looked like a love match, likely was not in how we understand them today. Women who were born into nobility knew full well that making a match of political or financial gain was essential to their futures. Amy was born in a time where arranged marriages were common. She may not have expected to ever find love in its true sense. We know she was set to inherit a great sum of money and land upon her father's death, and Dudley would not have been blind to that fact."

"No, he would not," she agreed. "Still, Cecil scoffed at the match in his letters. He must have found it irresponsible on one of their parts. To me, that suggests affection between them. Funny how finding someone you really cared for was regarded as inconvenient or irresponsible."

"As fate would have it, Dudley would be imprisoned in the Tower following Lady Jane Grey's, albeit brief, ascension to the throne. That's where he became close with Elizabeth. Afterwards, he was stripped of his title and inheritance by Mary I, so he and Amy had to live off her inheritance after both her parents passed. Keep in mind that, even though it was Amy's inheritance, it was considered her husband's, as women rarely retained rights to their own property."

In that time, Adelia knew that what would be called impoverished, would still have been quite wealthy by today's standards. She couldn't hold herself back. "And despite her continued devotion to her husband in his most trying days, he still sought to discard her when the queen took favor on him. Oh, maybe she thought she should spend extravagant amounts of his money, just to spite him." She almost laughed.

"Maybe," he said, nodding as he smiled.

She lifted the page and took a quieting breath. "I don't get the sense that this dress was about Robert, though."

"No?"

"No. I sense that she loved him and her devotion was still there, but it had changed somehow."

"How so?" he asked.

"How could it not?" she responded, aware that her voice had risen. "Look, Amy stood by this man, and he cast her aside in quest for something better. She might have cared for his wellbeing but I don't sense that she could have loved him as she once did. As you say, despite the age in which she lived and the customs that were expected to be accepted, she was still a living, breathing soul, complete with emotions that would leave her open to being hurt. He may have owned her as his property but he did not control her heart."

"You see," Daniel said, his grin broader than before, "there is something to be said about a female perspective. A historian can only go by the facts that are presented in what documents survive. What I wouldn't give to have my hands on all the ones that didn't. But it's your insight, your inferences, that give life to this mystery. That's the missing key. I told you a psychology degree could be of some use."

"All I am saying is that human nature is timeless," she replied. "We have to think of it that way. The infant mortality rate was very high in that time period. A great many children did not live past the age of two. Of course, that doesn't mean mothers did not grieve as mothers would today. The loss of a child is a pain that transcends any era. Amy's desire to be loved by her husband would have been much the same. To live a life as a lonely existence with no hope would have been the same loneliness that you or I would feel if we were in the same situation."

He nibbled his bottom lip for a moment, casting his gaze across the paper-strewn table. "To be lonely is something that sneaks up on you." He sighed. "It makes you question everything you are doing, and everything you have not done."

Adelia leaned on her elbow as she thought about that. She believed his words came from experience. One she shared, too, although she was far too uncomfortable to admit it aloud. She, like Daniel, had a million things to keep her mind occupied. A never-ending number of things she could be doing, but wasn't. No doubt they could both chalk that up to being self-absorbed in their own worlds, though loneliness was also a factor. Back in Boston, she had become so complacent in being alone that she rarely reflected on how such isolation crippled her ability to do all the things her heart desired most. Being alone felt comfortable but being lonely was defeating in so many ways. What was all the knowledge in the world if one didn't have someone to share it with?

As if sensing the need to lighten the conversation, Daniel moved on to other topics. They discussed what living in Hampton Court would have been like back in its heyday, and how much of a treasure it was to the country that it had survived all these years. After making a pot of tea, Daniel shared some of his favorite places to visit as a child, and Adelia told him what it was like living in Boston all of her life. Words between them flowed with ease, and before long, several hours had passed. She shifted in her chair as the weight of the day caught up with her. It had come out of nowhere. Maybe due to the stress of being so emotionally involved in this discussion. She leaned back, stretching her muscles with a heavy sigh.

"It's getting late. I suppose I should go back to my grandma's apartment. I have a big day tomorrow." She rose to her feet, pulled her gloves from her handbag and slid them on.

He almost jumped up. "Let me grab my things. I will walk with you."

"No, Daniel, it's out of your way." She lifted her handbag. "I will be fine. Besides, it's nearly nine o'clock. You have to get up in the morning too."

"I absolutely know that you will be fine, Adelia," he said, his tone matter-of-fact. "I would like to walk you home just the same. We can walk through the palace and I could show you some of the places that are strictly off limits to the public. I know a few of the warders fairly well now. They will allow us access."

She reacted with a soft huff. "Well, in that case, I will permit it."

No more than a couple of minutes into the all-access tour, she remembered just how intimidating Hampton Court was when its halls were not filled with the buzz of tourists. All the corridors were dimly lit with emergency lighting, making it difficult to discern the sumptuous patterns of wall hangings and gilded woodwork. The shadows in the corners seemed darker and denser than normal too. As they walked, some unspoken darkness hovered at the edge of her senses. Even areas she had visited before felt unfamiliar—larger, and looming, as if threatening to swallow them up like tiny flies.

She inched closer to Daniel, hoping the uneasiness would subside. The atmosphere had changed, like the air was suspended and muted. Even as he shared bits of history, much like her father had done on the earlier tours they'd taken, his hushed tone only added to her anxiety. Despite how much she enjoyed being in his company, she wanted the excursion to end so she could be back in the bright cheeriness of her grandma's apartment.

It was clear that Daniel didn't notice her unease, wrapped up, as he was, in his element. Sharing his knowledge was second nature to him, and she had no doubt that he made an exceptional professor at Oxford.

They rounded a corner, coming to the base of a curved stone staircase. She stopped, looking up at the structure as it disappeared around a wall. Her feet felt weighted, as though they had become part of the stone floor. She tried to nudge herself forward, to no avail. The stress was too much, and she felt as though she could cry, without understanding why. This was unlike the usual nervousness she experienced in uncomfortable situations. It was more of a raw emotion deep within her chest.

"What is it, Adelia?" Daniel demanded. "Are you well?"

"I..." She hung on whatever it was she couldn't quite articulate. Words jumbled as she held back the salty sting of tears.

"Are you frightened?" he asked, with clear concern in his eyes.

"No," she said, shaking her head. "I am...sad." Just saying it came as a relief, and she was glad she'd managed to interpret her feelings. She should be embarrassed, but she wasn't. As she stood there, it was like there were worried voices around them, containing a fear that was more rooted in a deep concern. She held her breath as she listened. Yes, there was mourning in this place, and, somehow, she was able to feel it radiate through her, as though it were her own burden to carry.

"Do you know where we are, Adelia?" Daniel asked, his voice slow and clear.

She shook her head in a foggy confusion and took another look at her surroundings. The staircase was dim and gray, giving no indication of their location. "No," she muttered, her voice weak.

"This is the Silver Stick Staircase." He reached for her hand. "Have you ever heard about the Silver Stick Staircase?"

His hand on hers sent a rush of warmth through her cheeks. It brought a flash of remembrance, and the voices surrounding her faded. She had heard of this place. It was significant, but the specifics escaped her. Her mind couldn't quiet itself long enough to fully process what Daniel was telling her, and it took extra effort to focus on his words.

"This staircase leads to the apartments of Queen Jane Seymour. Henry's third wife."

The details came to her in a wave of visuals. "That is where she died of childbed fever."

"Yes, she succumbed to puerperal fever less than a fortnight after the birth of her son, Edward VI. Adelia, what is it that you are feeling?"

In the turmoil of her emotions, his question felt almost insensitive. She knew in her heart that he meant no harm in asking. He was naturally wired to want to know everything about things that surrounded him, wanting some empirical explanation she couldn't give. She struggled to reason with herself that she should not be annoyed with him, but all she wanted to do was run as fast as she could and as far away from this place as possible.

"I don't want to go up the stairs, Daniel," she managed to say. She slumped, feeling as though she had been drained of life.

"No," he agreed. "I think it's best we do not go."

She tried without success to smile. "I think I should just like to go home now." Her voice sounded like a fragile child and she wrinkled her nose in annoyance, still wobbly on her feet.

"Yes, I think that's best." He glanced about. "I know a shortcut."

She jerked back. "Daniel, not through the haunted gallery."

"There is no such thing as a haunted gall—" He pursed his lips and nodded once, placing a supportive hand behind her elbow. "No, we won't take that route tonight."

By the time he delivered her to her grandma's door, she was starting to feel like herself again, but the embarrassment of what had occurred was setting in, the humiliation of her actions making her want to run. Escaping had always been her only goal when she felt her self-control slipping away.

She nodded at him and entered without so much as a word, leaving him standing bewildered in the hall. Under normal circumstances, she would have considered her actions as rude. Truth be told, she had no idea what she would have said had she lingered a moment longer in his presence. She didn't understand what had just happened to her, any more than Daniel. What explanation could be given to something so...unexplainable? All she knew was that she wanted nothing more than to hide in the soft safety of the yellow bedroom, and the first act of that was to close the hall door in Daniel's face.

Chapter Eight

A delia rested her head against the closed door, allowing the coolness of the solid wood to ease the warmth that had invaded every inch of her body. From the corner of her eye, she noticed the light in the sitting room was on.

No doubt her grandma was perched on the couch, awaiting her return. They had been in each other's company little more than a week, and despite the oddness of their first encounter, it was already apparent that the two were much alike. It had become the custom for them to enjoy a nightly chat before going to bed, which Adelia loved, welcoming getting to know her grandma better with open arms.

With her father having departed that morning, it would just be the two of them for the remainder of the summer. She adored her grandma, despite her prevalent eccentricities, though after their many chats, she now found these qualities rather endearing. The woman was a delightful and colorful character—a breath of fresh air to a girl who was way too serious for her own good. Every day she spent near her brought those vibrant characteristics more to light. Though her grandma managed to keep an active social calendar, there was still a hint of loneliness about her. Something in the way she greeted Adelia each day with so much warmth said she enjoyed having her company. And she always had some outlandish story to share—far-fetched tales Adelia welcomed. With so little contact between them for most of their lives, she now welcomed the chance to become better acquainted, even if their conversations left her fretting that her grandma's eccentric disposition might be hereditary.

Tonight was different, though. She lacked the energy to even pretend to want to converse, preferring to avoid the inevitable interaction. But she knew it was impossible. As she set her handbag and gloves on the foyer table, she took a deep breath, bringing up the most convincing smile she could muster.

Her grandma beamed with delight on seeing her, wanting to know all about her day. Exhausted, Adelia recounted her opportunity to play the role of Queen Anne Boleyn. Even though she doubted that her grandma was interested, she shared how she had helped Daniel with the document after work. Her grandma surprised her by listening to every detail. However, when she recounted their walk back to the apartment, and the interrupted tour, her unease welled and she fidgeted in her seat. Her grandma, intuitive as always, leaned forward to look her square in the eye.

"Did something happen, dear? Something with Doctor Brown?"

Adelia realized that she thought Daniel had acted inappropriate towards her in some way. "Goodness, no, Daniel was most amiable—I assure you, Grandma. During the tour, I found myself feeling a bit out of sorts, I guess. I was...dizzy, I think. Oh, maybe I'm just overwhelmed by the activities of the day. I'm not used to such excitement back home, is all."

"What do you mean by out of sorts?" Her grandma maintained eye contact. "Tell me everything, dear."

Adelia smiled at the manicured older woman across from her. For the first time, she realized that, for all her grandma's eccentricities, she was most likely the only person on the planet with whom she could confide these feelings and not risk being branded a lunatic. The easy comfort in her presence encouraged her to reveal every detail of what she had been feeling since the day she stepped off the train in Richmond on Thames. Her grandma listened with diligent interest.

"Grandma," she said when she finished her story, "tell me there is some rational explanation for this that doesn't include me being mad."

"There is a rational explanation, darling, there is. But what is rational to you and I may not be so to others who don't have the gift."

Adelia straightened as she stared at her. Gift? What on earth does she mean?

"Close your eyes," her grandma said, her voice soft and soothing. "Listen to the sounds around you."

Despite a natural hesitation, she did as she was instructed.

"Now, my dear, listen."

The slow hum of the fan filtered in from the other room. Birds stirred outside the window, fluttering as they bathed in the last rays of the setting sun. She almost flinched then at the sound of her own rapid breath—something she hadn't considered listening to. What is this all about? Has Grandma lost it? Is she really insane? Maybe I shouldn't have disclosed so much about my thoughts.

"You have to focus, my dear. It won't come to you unless you are ready to hear it."

Did she read my thoughts? "What exactly is going to come to me, Grandma? I don't understand what I am supposed to be hearing."

"Just listen. I know you can do this."

The familiar shadow of panic loomed at the thought that she was now supposed to possess some mysterious gift she had no idea about. She released a sigh of frustration and decided to give it a more honest attempt this time. With a gentle breath, she focused beyond herself and took in the silence behind the background noise. For a moment, she just listened, allowing potential distractions to flitter away as she steered her focus into deeper layers.

Then, without warning, faint whispers came to her. She focused harder, and as the seconds passed, the sounds became louder, sharper, until, even though they were alone in the room, it felt as if they were seated within a large crowd. The back of her neck tingled. What am I hearing? How is this even possible?

She snapped her eyes open, sure she would see people around them, but it was only her grandma, giving her an expectant look. "Grandma, what is happening?"

"I knew you had it, darling. It is something only the women of our family line possess." She tapped the coffee table with the side of her forefinger. "Through the years I have often wondered, but I sensed it from the moment you stepped through the door last week."

"Yes, but what is it?" Her face tightened as fear crept through her. "Somehow, it's vaguely familiar but I don't know why."

"Haven't you ever felt overwhelmed in a public place?" Her thin eyebrows arched.

"I...have always felt overwhelmed in social settings. That's nothing new. It wasn't like this, though."

"Oh, but it was, my dear. A crowded room is all the more crowded for those with the whispering gift."

"The...whispering gift?"

"You see, we women of the Babington line have a special gift. It's been passed down for so many generations that no one really knows its origin or with whom it may end. That is why I am so very pleased to know that you have it too. It enables us to read the energy of a place,"—she drew her hand in an arc to take in the room—"just as someone watches a movie in a theater."

"Read the...energy?"

"Yes, my dear. For us, time exists in layers. The past and the present are occurring almost simultaneously. Past events of a space replay on a continuous loop, while the present occurs right before our eyes. Those who are readers are given a mere window to observe. We hear everything like a gentle whisper, always playing in the background. We can feel the emotions of those we observe."

Adelia took a shaky breath. "Grandma, are you telling me that I am listening to the past when I hear these voices?"

"Are you frightened, dear?"

"Out of my wits, yes, but somehow consoled by knowing that I am not crazy."

Her grandma met that with a delicate laugh. "Well, people will surely call you crazy if you share it with them. Believe me, they will."

"Wow." She shook her head, remembering so much. "I guess all of these years I just assumed that I was an anxious sort. It got the best of me when I was out in public. Everything seemed so loud. I couldn't bear it sometimes. It's been this way as long as I can remember, but through the last few years it has only gotten worse."

"Let me guess—you would make a thousand excuses not to partic-ipate in the smallest of things?"

"My goodness, yes." For the first time in her life, she felt validated knowing that someone other than she shared the same experience.

"You thought you were just a daydreamer when your imagination took over and your mind started showing you images that weren't there? Conversations that couldn't possibly be taking place around you?" She conveyed this with a flutter of her hands.

"Actually, I thought it might be the start of some sort of lunacy. Maybe I was just manufacturing those voices in my head."

"Ahh, but you were not, Adelia. You are a reader, like me, and like my mother was too. You can see, hear, and feel what others cannot. In time, you will learn to control it better, but there is nothing to fear, even when the truth that comes to you is at times frightening." She gave a slight eye roll. "Not all who wandered in the past had the best intentions."

"I guess that explains the sadness I felt at the staircase tonight." She recalled the stifling emotions she'd experienced.

"As I said, at times you will find that your senses are extremely acute. We are at the mercy of whatever decides to come through. Be it happiness, sadness, or even pain—we do not control the energy we read." She shifted forward, giving a knowing nod. "A word of advice, my dear, you will do well to avoid the scaffold at the Tower of London."

Adelia allowed it all to sink in. Just thinking of Hampton Court Palace itself, there was enough dark history to consider. Perhaps it had not seen such gruesome deaths as the Tower of London but there were many years of intrigue and deception within its walls. Court life was a risky business, and it was rare that a person could stay on the right side of a monarch for their entire life. When one was in favor, immense wealth and privilege could be gained. Perhaps that's why so many found it worth the risk. Yet falling out with the king or queen would certainly mean a tragic end for a courtier. Even if they managed to stay in the good graces of the monarch, they would still have to maneuver around all the other nobility, who might become jealous and find a way to bring about their downfall. Hampton Court was so steeped in centuries of dramatic history that she couldn't even try to imagine everything that had taken place there. The opportunity to better know these stories intrigued her, but she understood what her grandma meant about everyone's intentions not always being for the better. How easy it would be to lose yourself in the past—in the stories and drama that unfolded there. She knew herself well enough to understand that she could become so wrapped up in the stories of others, she might use it as a means to avoid her own.

Her grandma asked her to close her eyes again, to focus on the space around her.

Taking further direction, she acclimated to the noise, straining to pick out just one voice from the crowd. Many conversations vied for her attention at first, but little by little she filtered them out until she could make out everything that was being said. She marveled as she took in conversations by servants that must have taken place centuries ago. Her mind spun like the skirts of ladies in a crowded ballroom, turning this way and that to pick up on the energy of anyone she might recognize from her historical reading. This day may well be the most trying of her entire life, yet she couldn't contain her need to know more and more.

"This can't be possible," she blurted out as she snapped her eyes open.

"You know what you heard," her grandma said, her expression stern. "What is it that you can't believe, dear?"

"It's j-just..." she stammered, her face strained. "Forgive me for struggling to wrap my head around the fact that what I just heard was someone who lived centuries ago. It is so hard to believe, yet, somehow, I know you are telling the truth. It's as if I am more confused than ever but it all makes perfect sense."

"Give yourself some time, Adelia. This is not a revelation that is easy to accept. There is still much that you have to learn about the whispers, but your acceptance of this profound gift must come first."

"What if I don't want to hear the whispers? Can this be shut off?"

Her grandma looked at her with an incredulous look, her entire face wrinkled with disbelief. "As new as this is to you, I think you already know that answer."

"Don't get me wrong, the whole notion of hearing the past is intriguing. Up to this point, if all of my so-called issues have really been the whispers, I don't know that they have been particularly helpful in the grand scheme of things."

"That," her grandma said with a laugh," is precisely why we have to work on getting you better versed in your abilities. It is not all bad, as you will see. Personally, I find it more entertaining than anything that comes out of that accursed box over there." She pointed to the television set in the corner.

"Can I hear what people are thinking and feeling now? Like, would I be able to know what you think?"

"No, the gift is not so refined, my dear. I find it nearly impossible to see the past of someone who is still on this earth. I look at the body as the protective vessel. Once we pass, the soul is released as another type of energy." She held her hand open in front of her, as if weighing the air. "That is the energy we have the ability to read. It seems that only once the soul has left the body can it be heard."

"What if I wanted to read the energy of a specific person? Like Queen Elizabeth I?" She leaned forward, eager to know.

"There are times when you can sift through all the energies to find something specific." She tapped her chest. "I find that is the most diffi-cult, though. The energies we read come on their own terms—they do not bend to our will. These are stories that want to be told. Just why is not always clear. It is as though the events chose us to be privy to them. Yet, I find if you want to narrow down to a specific person, you must be in the space they occupied to do so. Remember, past events replay as they were when they happened. A place like Hampton Court has changed so much through the years, and you can easily find yourself disoriented when things look different to how they were."

"So, I can see these things too," Adelia asked, elated.

"Not so much that you see them with your eyes, as with your mind's eye?"

Adelia looked at her for a long moment, visualizing symbols of the third eye she'd come across over the years.

"It's like a daydream, you see," her grandma continued. "As though you can imagine things with perfect clarity, even if they aren't really playing out directly in front of you for you to see with your own eyes. They are there, though, just in their own time. You do not exist to them."

"Okay. So, what do I do with this ability?" Is it actually all true? It has to be—I've heard the voices.

Her grandma smiled. "There is no right or wrong when it comes down to it." She grasped Adelia's hand. "I don't know why we have this ability, any more than my mother knew, or her mother before her. Everyone has some ability to read energy. We are just more fine-tuned in our senses, I guess. We feel the energy around us, just as others do but, somehow, we have the ability to interpret it differently, at a much deeper level. Where someone else might feel an odd sensation, we can pick up pure emotions. Emotions that, for some reason, were just left in that space years ago."

"But I can't change anything? I can't actually talk to people?"

"No, my dear, you can't. The people we observe are living moments in their own time. We do not exist there."

"So, what am I supposed to do with this ability? This gift, as you call it. Why do I have it? What is its purpose?" She wrestled with all she was expected to understand but held off further questioning, fearing her grandma might be overwhelmed. Perhaps she had been just as excited when she discovered her gift long ago.

True to her nature, though, the woman smiled, her eyes kind and reassuring. "We are not fixers of the past, Adelia. We are...casual observers. What comes through to us is like an excerpt from a story. Maybe it is something that was missed long ago. Perhaps it was some event that the soul wants discovered. I don't know, dear. It is something I have had all my life, and even I cannot fully explain everything."

Like so many other things in her life, Adelia was left with more questions than answers. Somehow, though, amidst the confusion, she felt a sense of peace, maybe at finally understanding some fragment about herself she had spent so long fighting. She had always held a self-loathing for the way she was, criticizing herself for never fitting into the world around her. Now, for the first time in her life, she understood that she was different for a reason. That difference might not be something she fully grasped but, in time, she might come to embrace and accept it in her own way. She almost smiled at the realization that being different did not feel quite so bad anymore.

The longer she sat and talked with her grandma, the more she reflected on countless things that had happened in her life. Events she had been baffled about, or never gave much thought to, now made perfect sense. All those thoughts and feelings that once came crashing to her in waves, were now told in hidden stories. The muddiness of the world could be washed clean, if only she took the time to listen. That night, *different* took on a whole new meaning, no longer signifying something negative. It was a gift, a second sight, a sensitivity to everything that passed within a space both seen and unseen.

Grandma is right, though. This is not a gift I can easily share with others. It is something I should keep concealed, lest people might think I have the same wild imagination they see in her. She has never been one to keep her gift entirely concealed, and for that she has been branded an eccentric old lady. I, on the other hand, have spent my life concealing my true self from the world, or who I thought my true self was. Truth be told, I've had twenty years of practice in being someone I wasn't.

She sat up at the sudden realization that she'd been hearing the whispers for as long as she could remember, but it had never been clear just what was happening. Right there, she had no idea what her ability to read the energy of the past would bring but she was certain, if required, that she could hide it from anyone in the present. Thinking back over her past few hours with Daniel, she saw that she hadn't got off to a good start, allowing him to see her react to how she perceived her environment. She would have to be more guarded from now on.

Chapter Nine

Though nervous, Adelia was eager to begin her new assignment as the queen, a character most in-demand for the tourists. Given the short notice, her training had been brief, to say the least, with a short test of her accent and knowledge of Anne Boleyn, after which she'd been shuffled to the dressing room and dressed in her costume. They expected her to study her lines and pick up the moves as she went, until a proper long-term replacement could be secured. Being well versed in history, perhaps more than most who had played the role before, was a major plus for her. She felt confident she could answer questions and improvise as required. Short-term or not, she was determined to give it her all.

As she stood in the presence chamber that morning, she ran her hands down the tight bodice of her dress to the kirtle-of-gold stitching, meant to resemble cloth of gold. The fur-lined sleeves gave the impression of fine ermine that would have provided the warmth needed to survive harsh winters in the cold and drafty palaces of Anne's day. Though her dress was a reproduction, it was historically accurate, with every detail of embellishment perfect. Her hair had been braided and placed under the stiff French hood, with loose strands tucked in behind the black fabric veil at the back.

Once dressed, she took in her image in the mirror. Being so immersed in her character made her feel confident and beautiful at the same time. Still, it was hard to imagine dressing so elaborately on an everyday basis in the Tudor era, though she knew such high-ranking women had many servants to assist. Even with the grueling preparations, it had been more fun than expected.

Today, they would start where the king and queen greeted distinguished guests. The room had elaborate tapestries adorning the walls but was sparse in the way of furnishings, allowing plenty of space for visitors. She could only imagine the English nobility and foreign dignitaries who had graced these floors through the centuries. As she looked around, she found it hard to believe that she was here, dressed as Anne Boleyn. It was like a little girl's dream and, for a moment, she nearly forgot that she was scared out of her wits. She'd rehearsed her lines at every opportunity, and every detail of the tragic queen's life played like a song in her head. Even her grandma had assisted, listening to her recite the words, until she could have played the role herself.

On recalling her grandma's words about reading energies, she considered trying to listen for signs of the country's most famous queen but dismissed the idea out of hand. Her head was swimming with far too many apprehensions about the day to even try to focus on such a daunting task.

Then a familiar feeling came over her when she spotted a man entering the room. Not just any man but the king himself—Henry VIII. He was dressed in a velvet, jewel-encrusted doublet, with his fine silk hose held in place by jeweled garters. Every detail, down to the reddish cast in his beard, was perfect. His broad waistline was in near-perfect symmetry to his wide shoulders. He was an enormous man, playing a character large in both stature and personality.

As the palace had not yet opened to the public, only a few other people were in the room. He zoned in on her right way, and began a disturbing saunter in her direction. As he approached, she couldn't help but see a slimy snake-oil salesman about to make the biggest sale of his life. He stopped inches away, standing in what any reasonable human would consider her personal space. His breath tickled her skin, and she rocked back on her heels to gain distance.

"And you, my lovely lady, must be Anne Boleyn." He took her hand and planted a wet kiss across her knuckles. She shuddered inside, wondering where she could wipe it off without being seen.

"Pleased to meet you, sir," she said, in a stiff but polite response. "I am Adelia Grey. And you are?"

"His majesty King Henry VIII," he announced, his tone sharp. "I was born for this role, you see. Any other name that was given to me at birth was just temporary."

She raised a brow. "Okay then, *your Majesty*." She pondered this creature, seeing a man who had gotten too into his role. Now I know why the last Anne Boleyn resigned. She doubted he had the ability to discern between the man who drove his little four-door car in the staff parking lot and that of the king who lived more than 400 years ago.

"Your Majesty," she struggled to choke out, cringing at the absurdity of the sound, "I have been studying my lines and—"

"No need," he cut in. "I will do the majority of the talking here. You see, in this time period, women were more the silent type. The public may have a question or two for you, but, primarily, it's the husband who has the say."

"Forgive me, sir, but, as I understand it, Anne Boleyn didn't play the role of the silent type so well."

He responded with a revolting smile. "As you will recall, dear lady, she lost her head for it."

"Yes, I do *recall* that was the case," she hit back through gritted teeth.

"Now, dear lady, let's not start off on the wrong foot. Remember, you waited over seven years to share my name and my bed." He nudged her side in an attempt to be clever, his elbow pushing into the stays on her bodice and almost winding her. In such a brief time, she'd decided that this king's impersonator was almost as vile as the one in the history books.

Throughout the afternoon a sort of competition arose between the queen and king. She imagined it resembled what their interactions might have been like in Tudor times. Every time Anne went to speak, Henry interrupted with his booming voice. Each time Henry went to take center stage, Anne wooed the crowd with diversions of her own. In his frustration, Henry tried to enrage her further by groping her around the waist and allowing his hands to trail when the crowd's focus was on other players. She flashed him repeated looks of disgust, which did little to deter his actions. When the audience was distracted by the entrance of an actor playing Cardinal Wolsey, she flinched at the unwanted brush of the ill-mannered king against her skirts. She snapped around to face him, the heavy golden pomander that hung from her belt swinging through the air. The metal ball, filled with flowers and herbs, made direct impact with the over-embellished codpiece, nearly knocking him to his knees as he tried his best to keep his composure. The shock in his eyes told her he'd got the message. By the time the place cleared out, there were no words between them, just side-eye glares and huffs as they departed in different directions.

Like the real-life queen, she had to be assisted out of her dress when work finished. Besse, no more than a year or two older, helped her unfasten and untie the sections of her costume so they could be stored for the next day.

"So how did it go?" she asked, laying the kirtle over a chair.

"Great for the most part, I guess. If only I didn't have such a pompous ass to be married to."

Besse giggled. "That is what I like about working here. Everything *is* historically accurate."

Adelia looked at her for a second, then burst out laughing. "Oh, you are so right. Perhaps whatever his name is was really born to play the king."

"Gerald. His name is Gerald. My mum said she went to school with him. Sounds rude but he wasn't very popular as a lad. Guess he found a little power and it went straight to his head."

Adelia rolled her eyes. "Boy, has it ever."

As she finished dressing, she found herself almost disappointed that she couldn't channel Gerald's energy. It might be nice to have ammunition to use against him while she played the temporary role of the queen.

Over the next two weeks, she made a point of avoiding Daniel, taking care to keep clear of areas they'd come across one another before. She needed time to process what had transpired in her life, and still held doubts about how he'd perceived their last encounter. On the one and only occasion she'd spotted him, she ducked into a corridor, reminding her of the way her mother evaded the woman she called the "neighborhood gossip" whenever she caught sight of her in the grocery store. As far as Adelia knew, he hadn't tried to find her either, though she couldn't be sure.

She spent her days engrossed in her role as Anne, and her evenings learning more from her grandma about her inherited gift. In a short time, her abilities had grown exponentially and her grandma had begun to teach her how to make her focus more specific. They'd visited various places within the palace: the stables, gardens, and courtyards, and in each one she was challenged to be more intentional in her purpose.

"If you listen, the whispers will reveal," her grandma declared, with gentle reassurance.

Setting aside her innate need to control her environment was difficult at times. Yet, as she did, it amazed her how fast she could catch on to something that was so complicated. With each passing day, she saw herself growing in both her abilities and her confidence.

One Sunday she rose early and dressed in a simple pale-green dress. She had not ventured out into the palace or its grounds much lately, and working nearly every day didn't give her a lot of time. Today, she decided to visit the Chapel Royal for the Sunday service. And though she had not been to church in what seemed like ages, attending a service in the opulent chapel was far too exciting to pass up. The chapel had been in continuous service for more than 400 years, and she followed small groups of the palace's residents as they navigated the halls of dark wood paneling until she came to the hallway known as the processional route, the one monarchs had followed on their way to the chapel, with swarms of the court's nobility in their wake.

The corridor known as the Haunted Gallery lay just ahead, so she stepped to the side to allow other people pass. She had made a point of avoiding this place. To this day, stories of the image of a shrieking Catherine Howard, Henry's executed fifth wife, persisted. Legend had it that after being charged with committing adultery, she broke free from her guards in an attempt to reach Henry in the Chapel Royal.

She ran down the gallery, screaming his name, but was apprehended and returned to her confinement, ultimately facing death at the Tower of London. Visitors still report seeing or sensing her apparition as that fateful day replays itself.

Adelia knew these stories well, and something in her didn't want to feel the anguish of a queen who was little more than a teenager when she was brutally beheaded. Catherine would have been well aware of the fate that awaited her after charges of treason were made. Her supposed last-ditch effort to sway her husband was one of utter desperation, and Adelia didn't want to experience that turmoil just yet. Catherine's story had always been one she found particularly sad. A young girl, close to her own age, had been paraded as a potential replacement for the failed marriage between Henry VIII and Anne of Cleves. The aging king was both morbidly obese and suffering from a foul-smelling ulcerated leg. Not something a mere teenager would find appealing as a love match. Yet she was likely drawn by the promise of living life as a queen, and all records of the time show that Henry doted upon his young wife. Like his previous wives or mistresses, Catherine's family was eager to secure the favor that would accompany such a match. It is unlikely that she had a say in the matter, her fate being sealed the day she caught the king's eye.

Regardless of the social pressure placed upon her, Catherine was still an inexperienced teenager. She was lighthearted and reckless, as her age should have allowed her to be, but this was Tudor England and the stakes were high, leaving no room for mistakes. However, she did not take heed and soon found herself smitten with another man. In the end, her indiscretions, however innocent or severe they may have been, were discovered.

Henry was devastated by the news. Even so, the injustice was that, being king, he wielded unquestionable power. Where modern men might just suffer their broken heart and move on, he was not that sort of man. He had far too much ego to admit that he could ever be undesirable as a husband for such a young girl. In his anger, he became the same tyrant that so many other women in his life had known. Catherine was beheaded not more than three months later.

In every presence Adelia had encountered so far, she'd felt a moral obligation to hear their story—to feel the events through the people who lived them. In time she would want to hear Catherine's story, too, but not today. She just didn't feel ready yet. As she stood in the corridor, she fought to maintain control, pushing Catherine and all the lore from her mind and closing herself off to the slightest emotion.

She stepped out of the shadows and fell in behind an older couple heading for the haunted gallery. They turned and walked through a doorway, its large wooden doors like sentinels, and she found herself at the end of the long narrow corridor. Its walls were covered with a vibrant-green damask fabric that hung from ceiling to floor. The color reminded her of the popular wallpaper that adorned Edwardian homes. Beautiful portraits lined the walls, and she recognized nearly everyone from the books her father had back at home.

As the couple moved along, frustration niggled at her because of their leisurely pace. She wanted to reach the chapel entrance as soon as possible but still grasped the opportunity to take in everything she passed. Her breath caught as she approached a massive portrait on the wall. It was Henry, the larger-than-life king, depicted in all his royal splendor, painted by none other than Hans Holbein the Younger. As an artist, Holbein had a skill for painting lifelike images that almost sprung from the canvas with their realism. He was equally an intelligent man, not opposed to being more than complimentary to his patron. Adelia stared up at the imposing figure, cringing at the thought of her dreaded co-worker Gerald. Both Henry and Gerald left

a sour taste in her stomach. So caught up in the portrait, she'd failed
to notice that the couple, who had been moving at a snail's pace, had
now departed.

Glancing from side to side, she became paralyzed with the realization that she was alone in the haunted gallery. She eyed the ornately
carved stone archway with fervor as she inched her way closer, her
legs heavy, as if she were wading through deep water. When at last she
reached it, she looked back at the empty corridor, surprised that she
hadn't heard a single noise or felt any emotion. Had she really set her
mind on controlling these emotions, or was the legend of Catherine
Howard just a told story? She wasn't sure either way. Her grandma's
words came to her: "The whispers come to us on their own terms.
They do not bend to our will."

As she entered the Chapel Royal, her mind went in a different
direction. Above her, stretching to what felt like several stories, was
the most beautiful ceiling she had ever seen. Henry VIII had commissioned the elaborate carved ceiling in the 1530s. It was one of the
few things that remained untouched during the English Civil War,
only because of its unreachable height. She stood there in awe as
she took in its gothic medieval style, with its ornate timber carvings
covered in gold leaf. The framed panels, painted in a vibrant blue,
simulated the clearest of starry nights. Pendants hung throughout,
depicting the heraldic symbols of the Tudors. All through the chapel,
the Tudor rose, a mesh of the red Lancastrian rose, and the white rose
of the House of York adorned the carved plaster and timber decor.
The Beaufort portcullis, another badge of the dynasty, was presented
everywhere in the intricate craftsmanship.

An altar stood at the far end of the chapel, with a beautiful wooden
screen covering almost the entire wall behind it. It had been commissioned somewhere around the late seventeenth century. She remem-

bered her father telling her that the heart and other organs of Henry VIII's third wife, Jane Seymour, were buried behind it.

The space was so captivating, she almost jumped when she bumped into the edge of a pew. Nobody seemed to notice. Maybe everyone was as awed as her. The pale light of electric candles illuminated the chapel's dark wooden interiors, and rich tones colored the oak wall panels and pews, adding to its ancient extravagance. A patterned marble floor tied together all the regal elements.

As she slid into one of the pews that line the walls of the main floor, she noticed the royal pew at the other side, elevated to allow its royal occupants a modicum of privacy while still being able to see every inch of the chapel. Today there were a fair number of attendees for the service, and they filled most of the common pews, although the royal one remained empty.

England had experienced a great deal of religious change during the life of this chapel. How one favored the views of the Catholic or the Protestant faith could bring about the downfall of an entire family dynasty. Favor was granted through loyalty to the sovereign, who was viewed as anointed by God. Whether or not both faiths worshiped the same god was an insignificant matter, so long as you were in line with the religious views of the king or queen, whoever that happened to be at the time.

Adelia stood as a hymn of praise was sung to begin the service. The song wasn't one she'd heard before, so she stood in quiet respect, soaking in all the wonders the chapel held. She thought about the changes this space had undergone. Like Hampton Court itself, there were visible signs from many different centuries, with each monarch leaving his or her mark. This sacred chamber had undergone remodels, near destruction, and repair in its long existence. For every original artifact that still existed, no less than ten more had been destroyed—lost to time forever. The thought that she was looking at the same things so many other notable people had gazed at over the years, amazed her. Despite the wars and destruction of the world, the fact that some things had managed to survive all of that turmoil was nothing short of remarkable—proof that humanity could always endure to keep some things intact, regardless of its destructive nature.

Modernization, too, was a necessary evil. It would be impossible to preserve every building in its original design, though it was disappointing knowing that some of the most splendid things ever created were gone forever. What price would modern-day scholars be willing to pay if Anne Boleyn's famous "B" necklace was discovered? Since it is believed Henry had any portrait she may have sat for as queen destroyed, what would an original painting of hers fetch if it were discovered? What would one give to discover letters that Anne herself sent to the king? Would the public's perception of her be changed for the better or the worst? Maybe some things are best left as a mystery.

Her mind wandered back to Daniel and his quest to discover what happened to Amy Robsart Dudley. Artifacts could be lost but not nearly as easy as the memory of lives. One could bury the heart of Jane Seymour behind an altar, but the travesty was never knowing just what emotions that heart felt in its short time on earth.

She admired Daniel's keen interest in Amy as a person. He wanted to know what her inner emotional state was during all the stages of her complicated life, and could see the injustice she had been dealt, both in life and in death. His quest was clear: to find evidence to ensure that she was remembered with dignity and respect. Most people only saw her as the unfortunate wife of an unscrupulous husband, Robert Dudley. Daniel had seen her as something more: a unique person who had years of speculation thrust upon her story. He wanted to clear away the misconceptions and help to paint her in the light of a living breathing woman. Adelia respected his quest, and was pleased that she'd played some role in helping him understand Amy's point of view. It wasn't often that a woman was asked to assist in the research of such a respected scholar as Daniel. And it was no small accomplishment for her sex. Even if she'd failed to shed light on what happened to Amy, she now felt a stronger connection to the story. Impossible as it may be, she hoped Daniel would find something—anything—that would give Amy her due.

As the small group of attendees took their seats, a member of the clergy began the sermon. Adelia felt a tinge of guilt knowing she had never been a regular churchgoer back home. Now she thought of it, this was one of the first times she'd attended a service without teetering on the edge of a panic attack. When she took a moment to observe herself, she realized that she was as calm and relaxed as she'd ever been, as though her presence here was meant to ease her weary mind. And her mind had been weary these past few days.

Concentrating on her new assignment at work had been tiring, and thinking of Daniel and their last time together had taken what energy remained. It felt good to have a quiet mind for a moment, even if she hadn't heard a word of the sermon for thinking. She sat back and allowed herself to wallow in the serenity of the space.

She shifted when a cold breeze grazed her bare arms, causing tiny goosebumps to erupt across her skin. The central heating and cooling that had been installed at Hampton Court for visitors' comfort still wasn't fully efficient. It was difficult to perfect, given the enormity of the place. She wasn't sure where the breeze had originated—maybe an open window somewhere—but it didn't matter. As she rubbed her arms, the cold feeling was replaced with a warmth that felt like static electricity deep within her skin. She flinched when her vision blurred, and watched with amazement as the colors of the chapel changed. It was as though someone had peeled back the layers of varnish and paint, and replaced them with a new palette of color.

Muffled voices came to her, some speaking in Latin, which she'd learned from her father years before, and others in what she knew to be the Tudor-era dialect. A *Catholic* Mass? A *Protestant* service too? The room now unveiled before her looked different than the one she had entered. And the voices sounded like echoes in an empty space. Blurry images resembled people in size and shape, but no distinct features were visible. She shuddered, knowing without doubt what she was experiencing. This was the first time she'd been around so many people when the whispering came through. She could no longer see the chapel she sat in nor the people who were within arm's reach, and she hoped she gave no physical indication of her discomfort or awe. All she could see was the dim interior of the chapel as it had existed in the past. With the Latin sermon and dialect, the time period couldn't be disputed.

Am I the only one seeing this? Can those around me, in the present day, notice anything? All she could do was sit still until the *whispering* subsided. She exhaled a held breath and let the energy flow through her as it willed. There was nothing else she knew to do.

One by one the feelings came, like gusts of wind before an impending storm. An infinite sadness existed here, along with a sense of real longing. The energy was not from just one person. Countless hours had been spent here in prayer, from so many people. Had one been Catherine of Aragon, Henry's first wife, praying for God to bring her the heir her husband so desired? Adelia imagined the sorrowful words she must have spoken to God during the many years Henry sought to divorce her and marry Anne Boleyn. Maybe it was Anne Boleyn praying, too, for the male heir that would secure her place as queen—the one that never came—despite her giving birth to Elizabeth, who would go on to become one of the greatest monarchs in British history. Poor Anne hardly made it to Elizabeth's toddler years before being beheaded by her own husband.

The tales she'd heard from her father swirled through her head—one of them about Jane Seymour's organs being buried behind the altar. She looked up to the massive stone altar adorned with rich cloths and silver plates. The sadness could have been that of Jane, or even Henry as he mourned her unexpected death after the birth of their son Edward. Then there was Anne of Cleves, Catherine Howard, and Catherine Parr, Henry's other three wives, whose lives had been forever altered by having the unfortunate luck of marrying the English king.

Every reigning monarch since Henry's death in 1546 had also been part of the palace's history, and each of them would have visited the Chapel Royal during their rule. There was way too much history, and far too much desperation in the atmosphere to pinpoint the source. It was a collective energy, composed of many different needs, yet all desiring divine intervention for their desperate requests.

She sat in silent reverence, allowing the voices their time before they faded into the blurred softness. Then her vision returned with crystal-clear clarity and she knew it was over. The chapel was back to its colors of the present. Her heart was calm, and her body temperature was neither too cold or warm. Just right. The whisperings had given her a glimpse of the past, but its purpose was unclear. If there was a message to be taken away, she hadn't grasped it yet.

That these souls of the past had chosen her to be their vessel was, indeed, a gift. She only wished they had chosen a more convenient time. That was something she would have to get used to. Then again, emotional firestorms had never picked a convenient time to surface, so she was probably better adapted than she gave herself credit for at navigating these things. Her mind always sought definite answers for everything. It wanted concrete specifics in the most mundane of occurrences. Yet the whispering didn't seem to want to allow her such privilege. It came and went on its own terms, invading whatever moment it saw fit to emerge. She just had to accept that was the way of things. Her constant need to control would not change anything. She doubted she was ready to take things as they came; she had honed the intrinsic nature to want to fight off such feelings. It would take time, and she had the rest of the summer, at least.

No one in the room had any idea what had just transpired. They sat, listening to the closing of the service, not even noticing that she was there. She was thankful for that, never relishing being the center of attention.

On her way back to her grandma's apartment, she sharpened her focus on her own life. Deep down she still wondered about Daniel. How is he progressing in his research? Have I crossed his mind at all? Even in her intentional avoidance of him, she still thought of him, often playing out what their next meeting would be like. Will it be awkward and uncomfortable? Should I act as though nothing happened that night? Is he avoiding me? Goodness, does he think I'm an overly dramatic American girl he has no time or inclination to indulge?

She glanced around in case anyone should notice her grimacing at herself. I wouldn't blame him for not understanding. How could anyone, besides Grandma, actually understand?

A swell of questions kept coming to her, all about him, and she had to accept that she thought about him far more than was healthy. She wanted to focus on herself during her time here but Daniel had some-how managed to weave himself into the fabric of her being without even trying.

The more she considered that he might not want to see her again, the more she desired to seek him out. She took a look at her life—how nothing was ever really left to chance, or how every single moment was part of a grand design, each action meant to build upon the next—knowing that, someday, when her soul left her body, her story might play out for others, as stories from the past did for her. The prospect of that was humbling. Her story thus far was not nearly as intriguing as those she had listened to. Those lives that took shape in front of her seemed superior to her own. Most of all, she wanted a story to tell, even if it wasn't intriguing. She also longed for emotions that, for once, didn't bring her pain and loneliness, but she wasn't sure how she could achieve the happiness she craved. All around her, wonderful things were happening: events that had changed everything in her life. Still, there was something missing. If Daniel was that something, she had to know.

Chapter Ten

A gainst her natural instincts, good sense, and all other logical reasoning, Adelia decided to devise a way to seek Daniel out. Her shyness would not allow her to just go to him, so she'd have to find a way to stumble into him, as he had done with her. She almost laughed at herself as she schemed it out. Hampton Court Palace was such a large place, two people could work in it their whole lives and never cross paths. She struggled with how to make the meeting not seem planned, and determined that she needed to make herself available in areas he frequented. So, for the next few days, she did just that. On her breaks or after work, she wandered about, as if aimless, hoping to catch sight of her target. However, by the third day, she had all but given up hope. Maybe she needed to accept that he didn't want to be found.

When she finished an early shift, she donned her regular attire and set out to find the fruit carts in the garden, glad to be getting away from her egotistical co-star. She had selected a pale-blue chiffon summer dress, perfect for the muggy afternoon. Her grandma had often mentioned how good the grapes were that had been harvested from the palace grapevine, said to be one of the oldest in the world. She'd been assured that they were some of the finest she would ever taste, so she decided to buy some so they could enjoy them together. It would be a nice surprise for her grandma. It felt good to have an errand—something to pass the time away, and a break from obsessing about meeting Daniel.

The summer sky was bright and clear, though it had been a day of intermittent showers. As she turned onto a hallway leading to the exit to the gardens, she stopped dead at the sight of Daniel talking to a man she recognized as the palace's chief curator. They hadn't seen her, and excitement fizzed in her tummy, soon replaced by the weight of apprehension. What is going on? I spend days trying to meet him, yet bump into him the first day I'm doing something else. Should I catch his eye with a little wave? She snapped her arms behind her back. No, best not to interrupt his conversation. She had no doubt his meeting with the curator was important, so it was best to continue on as planned. If anything, she didn't want to come across as desperate. She clamped her handbag to her side and headed for the exit.

"Adelia!"

She grimaced, then slapped a half-smile on before turning around, almost caught off guard at the way her heart was jumping about.

"Daniel," she said, keeping it pleasant, struggling not to smile as much as she wanted to. She was pleased that she'd opted to wear her summer dress. Her grandma had raved at how complementary the color was on her. She hoped the good woman was being truthful.

"H-how are you?" he asked, stumbled over his words. "I have not seen you around here lately." He straightened his shoulders as he glanced at the curator walking down the hallway. "You look great. I mean, you look well..." His brows creased with a pained look.

"I am well, and you? Have you been able to make progress on your work?"

"I have," he answered. "That is not to say I am any further into solving anything, but I am learning to look at things a little differently." He leaned forward. "I have been meaning to tell you that you really did help me."

She held her handbag over her tummy with both hands. "I helped you?"

"Yes, well, your perspective on that document—it made me think a little differently, I guess, is what I am trying to say."

She couldn't help but relate to his constant stumbling over words. Little she tried to say came out right either. It was one of the many things they had in common.

"I am glad to hear it," she said.

He glanced about, then looked at her. "Where are you off to?"

"I am on a mission to secure a container of grapes for my grandma."

"Ah, those are really good. I am sure she would appreciate them, but I am afraid they don't start harvesting them until September."

"Oh, I hadn't thought of that," she said, disappointed. "I guess I will have to find her something else."

His smile lit his eyes up. "There is a lovely flower cart with fresh-cut blooms from the garden."

She smiled back and nodded. "Flowers it is, then."

"What are your plans afterwards?"

"I thought I might make my way to the Wolsey Rooms. One of the girls I work with, Besse, said I should look at them. Evidently, they are interesting."

"You haven't seen the Wolsey Room yet? I am surprised. I agree with Besse, that it's something you should definitely see."

"I don't really know what is so interesting about it, but I have some free time so I thought I would explore."

"Are you opposed to some company?"

"Are you asking to come along?" she asked, trying not to smile at the idea.

"Well, yes," he said, matter of fact. "I suppose a stuffy recluse of a professor in a brown tweed suit is not ideal as a fellow explorer, but I do make a superb tour guide, if I do say so myself."

"Oh, I have always had a soft spot for a nice brown tweed." She stifled the urge to giggle. "Come along if you like, but we have to get the flowers first. I don't want to forget them."

"Understood, but you should know that the Wolsey Room will be closed at this time."

"Oh no." She looked back the way she'd come. "How did I get that wrong?"

"Not to worry," he said, "I know the guide in that area, so I should be able to get us in for a quick visit."

She almost clapped. "Excellent, Daniel. Okay, let's be on our way."

He raised his hand to his forehead in a kind of salute.

"Bit much, that," she said with a chuckle.

He laughed. "Yeah, probably."

The sky was crystal blue, with a light breeze giving welcome reprieve from the heat. After a quick visit to the flower cart just outside the garden, Daniel motioned to the direction they would need to go to reach the Wolsey rooms. As he shared some of the things he'd been working on over the past few weeks, Adelia marveled at the lack of awkwardness between them. It was as if no time had passed since they'd last spoken. She kept the conversation going by asking pertinent questions, to which he always reacted with enthusiasm. In truth, he had not gotten any closer to solving the great mystery of Amy Robsart's death. There was no great expectation that he would, but that didn't dampen his excitement. The act of delving into the matter suited him just fine.

She imagined that all researchers felt the same as he did. To hear about a document was nowhere near as exciting as having the original in your hand. Holding something that had been created centuries ago held its own sort of magic. There was a magic in watching him too. Here was this super-intelligent creature—so accustomed to shutting himself away in the confines of a dark, dusty library—throwing his head back and laughing at something she'd said. Perhaps she didn't have the ability to read him the way she could the past inhabitants of this place but his energy was still intoxicating to her. Just being in his presence when he let go of all the stuffy formality made her feel fearless. Never in a million years would she have let her inhibitions go like this in Boston. Daniel was older than her, true, but it didn't feel that way in the slightest. As she watched him, enamored by his every motion, his words became so faint she could hardly make them out. It was then she realized that she just might like him a little more than her father would have preferred.

For a woman of just twenty years, who had spent her entire life lost in a sea of emotions, this might be the most beautiful one she had ever experienced.

"Are you listening?" Daniel asked, snapping her back to the present.

"Yes, absolutely," she replied with a smile, knowing she hadn't heard half of what he'd said over the past ten minutes. She walked along with him, embarrassed in herself about the thoughts running around her head. He probably didn't feel the slightest thing for her in return. Although, she couldn't help but wonder if maybe a little part of him did. She had the sudden urge to smack her forehead, for no other reason than to push these childish thoughts out. No, Adelia, not a good idea. Explaining *that* to Doctor Brown would be a challenge.

As they walked, she was aware how he watched her with quiet determination, no doubt trying to decipher what she was thinking. She could almost feel a bead of sweat forming on her forehead as she smiled at him.

"Tell me about these infamous Wolsey Rooms," she said, thankful she knew how easily these intellectual types were to redirect.

"As you know, Hampton Court was actually built by Henry VIII's closest confidant, Cardinal Wolsey, right?"

"Right," she answered, smiling to herself. Works like a charm.

"Well then, when Henry and Wolsey fell out—"

"When Wolsey could not secure the annulment from Henry's first wife Catherine so he could marry Anne Boleyn." She nodded once to him, encouraging his agreement.

"Exactly." He gave her an appreciative smile. "So, Henry confiscated the palace from Wolsey and the rest is history. Prior to that, though, Wolsey and Henry were very close. I like to think of Wolsey to Henry as I do William Cecil to Elizabeth I. They were their most trusted advisers, yes. However, both Cecil and Wolsey were constantly working behind the scenes controlling things."

"The puppet masters, as you alluded to previously. But neither Henry or Elizabeth really understood just how much they were being controlled."

"Precisely. That is a great way of putting it. So, the story behind the Wolsey Room is that it was a space where Wolsey might take someone, like a foreign ambassador or someone of nobility, to plot and scheme out of earshot of others. It's not a big space really, just heavily lined with wood paneling. Perfect for whispering all the details of some court intrigue."

"Sounds absolutely scandalous," she said, unable to hold back a smile. "I do love a good scandal."

"I thought you loved tweed?" he joked.

"I like tweed and scandal." She raised her eyebrows for a moment. "Both in moderation, of course."

"Of course," he said, his smile full of mischief.

They walked through some of the older portions of the palace to the chambers that once held the cardinal's private apartments. Much had been changed over the years to suit the tastes of whatever monarch reigned at the time, but a great deal remained of the cardinal's original designs. It was clear that he was not a humble man of the cloth, but a wealthy and powerful figure at the center of Henry's court for a long time before their falling out. The original designs of Hampton Court were proof of that wealth and power. No expenses had been spared to make this place the show-stopping palace it was meant to be.

As they moved through each corridor and room, Adelia tried to comprehend what such fine details would have cost in the present day. With WWII only ended a decade or so, this sort of opulence seemed so wasteful. Countries were rebuilding from the effects of the war, with families still recovering, and the sheer amount of money spent building and decorating this palace was inconceivable in the context of today.

In general, it was difficult to fully understand the layout of the palace. So many rooms had adjacent chambers where nobles would have greeted their visitors, never allowing them into the confines of the private apartments. The palace had so many additions and recon- structions throughout the years, it was challenging to imagine what everyday life would have been like for those who resided within its walls. Wolsey had been a man of importance, so all the formality of royalty was bestowed on him as well. His private apartments were enormous, and elaborately decorated to display his prominence within the court.

She bit down on a hint of disappointment as they neared the entrance to the infamous Wolsey Room. Strolling along with Daniel had been most enjoyable, and she almost dreaded getting back to business. At the entrance, she saw there were other visitors inside, conversing with a young tour guide who answered their questions and gave details about the life of the cardinal, a trusted advisor to the king before his fall from favor.

The two of them lingered near the doorway as the visitors filtered on to other areas of the palace. When they were the only ones left, Daniel approached the guide and greeted her with a smile. She looked surprised by his presence but greeted him with a cheery hello. Adelia was sure by their interaction that they'd met before.

"I just wanted to show my friend the Wolsey Room, if it is possible? She works here, too, and while I know it isn't open to visitors at this time due to restoration work, if it were possible to pop in for a quick look around...?"

"Absolutely, Doctor Brown," she said, her heavy eyelashes fluttering as she beamed. She flicked Adelia a look that made her feel as though she were being sized up right there on the spot.

As she followed Daniel into the room, she glanced back at the guide, whose assessing glare hadn't changed. She returned the look, regretting it straight away. That girl is so pretty, I might just despise her.

They entered a small room that looked like a chamber meant to be a passage into a formal greeting room. Heavy wood panels stretched midway up the walls, and despite the centuries of age, each was so polished it gave the impression they were freshly installed. A stone fireplace was set into one of the longer walls, so simple in its design it almost looked out of place in the opulent room. From the top of the wood panels to the ceiling, vibrant murals depicted Christ and his disciples—images quite fitting for the private apartments of the famed cardinal. However, nothing in the room could rival the breathtaking ceiling. Both Adelia and Daniel stood in awe, taking in the masterful craftsmanship that hovered over them. It was so beautiful, it commanded silent scrutiny.

The sculpted plaster ceiling consisted of a series of connecting hexagons, each containing artfully carved scroll work. Its breadth was covered in gold leaf, giving the already stunning room an added layer of overindulgent excess. Adorning the sea of gold were Tudor roses painted in a bright shade of red with white accent. No doubt painstaking hours had gone into each and every one. The room, albeit small, was beautiful in its own right, but when matched against the grand size of most other rooms in the palace, this felt more like a closet than a greeting space, as it had been used for in the past. If one were claustrophobic, they would not linger too long in its close confines.

As Daniel had said, these rooms had been used by the cardinal and a great many others as a secluded place to have frank discussions about the business of court life, far from the prying eyes and ears of those who might not be trusted. The air felt heavy and thick on her skin. It was as if she could visualize the particles around her, rich with burden and secrets. The sensation of worry pulled on her like a weight.

The room held an almost deafening number of whispers, reverberating off the walls, sending chills through her that made her shudder. So many voices came through at once—each one muffled in a hushed tone. The small space was drowning in apprehension, and it was clear that a great many dealings had occurred here. Whether by Cardinal Wolsey himself, or those who came after him, powerful plans had been hatched within these walls.

She recalled the old saying "*If walls could talk.*" Now that she had become attuned to her ability, she wished others could know what truth that statement held. Her grandma referred to this ability as a gift—one of reading the energy—yet, each day as it grew stronger, it was so much more than that. What would this experience have been like if I'd never been told the truth? These feelings, senses, would have shaken me to my core. I would have thought my mind was damaged in some way—that these voices were figments of my imagination, or some malady I couldn't have brought myself to admit.

So much more about her life made sense now, even though she had been hurled into a state of confusion trying to process what she knew. Today, the world, in all its shadowy corners, was intriguing, not scary.

"What do you hear?" Daniel asked.

She studied him for a moment. "I'm...not sure. Voices from the other room?"

He tilted his head. "There is no one in the other room now."

She knew that, of course, but there was no rational way to explain what she was feeling and hearing, least of all to Daniel. He was a man of black and white facts. Gray area did not exist in his world. Things were or they weren't—there was no in-between. She couldn't be honest with him. After all, this was the first time they had spoken since the last encounter that had no doubt left him questioning her sanity. She was content to enjoy this time with him, having no desire to muddle it with talk of her ability to hear ghosts.

He continued to stare at her, as though sensing her dishonesty. She worked up a smile, giving no hint of anything other than what she said to be so. He moved around the room, trying to make it seem as though he wasn't watching her from the corner of his eye, but she knew better. The man was terrible at being sly. He was far too matter-of-fact to ever be good at it.

Unlike in the past, these whispers did not subside when she was distracted. They were way too powerful here. Had they been in a normal tone, she doubted she would have been able to hear Daniel at all. All she could do was try her best to push them into the background and focus on what was going on around her in the present. But there was something different about these whispers. Something new. A sense of danger, like whatever was happening around her was forbidden in some way. She thought back to some of the advice her grandma had given her over the past few weeks, and focused her attention on details in the room in an effort to quell the flurry of voices around her. Daniel stood to her left, studying a mural. It was remarkable how he couldn't sense a thing, while she felt as though she was standing in the face of a hurricane.

"That's enough of this stuffy old house," he said, stepping over to her. "Let's go outside for a bit, shall we?"

She all but laughed at him referring to the enormous palace as a mere house.

"Is it still raining?" she asked, glancing out one of the enormous windows after leaving the Wolsey room. Even on a bright summer day in England, one could expect a pop-up rain shower. Today was no exception, with the grass outside glistening in the sun from a recent downpour.

"Are Americans afraid of rain then?" he asked, one cheek dimpling from his sardonic grin.

"I should say not," she shot back. "Especially not us New Englanders."

"Well then, let's take a chance. The old hedge maze looks beautiful after a summer shower."

She couldn't keep herself from smiling. Daniel had flipped from being a guarded, obscure creature, who dwelled in dark dusty libraries, to a spontaneous fearless being she hardly recognized. His starched shirt was unbuttoned at the collar, and his chestnut-brown hair lay haphazard across his forehead. Even his eyes had changed, holding a new light she hadn't seen up to now, captivating her more than before. The rigid, formal man she knew was somehow replaced by this reckless risk-taker, whose behavior only confirmed what she'd suspected for a while: she liked him, a lot. It felt like a high school romance—so fitting for two adults who never found the opportunity to have one while they were in high school. An inexperienced giddiness bounced between them, and it was by far the sweetest thing she had ever felt.

All her thoughts flittered away the moment he took her hand. She remembered that flash of electricity pulsing through her, but this time was different—more intense—euphoria and utter nervousness meshed into one consuming emotion. Is this infatuation? Does love feel this way? Whatever the answer, she had never experienced the intensity of this emotion before.

She walked alongside him, at a loss for words, her mind foiling all attempts at forming an articulate response. As was always the case with Daniel, the desire to not let this moment end too soon consumed her.

"You have been to the maze, right?" he asked.

She almost jumped at the opportunity to reply to something non-challenging. "Yes, my father took me through when he was here. It's very impressive."

"A similar one has existed here for hundreds of years. The maze has always been an important part of the palace, you see. Unlikely as it may seem, it was a place of palace intrigue, just as much as the Wolsey Rooms once served. Beyond that it was also a place of courtship. Henry courted Anne on these grounds. Dudley courted Elizabeth here, too."

Something inside her swayed with the romantic notion that she was trekking through the same playground where Anne and Elizabeth had given their hearts into the care of their respective lovers. Right then, she couldn't help but wonder if she was doing the same thing. Had this been Daniel's intention by bringing her here?

As they walked, she was struck by how lush and green the foliage looked with the shimmering glaze of recent rain. It was just as Daniel had said it would look. The pathway consisted of small pea gravel, still wet, and the heels of her shoes sunk into it, to the extent that it took some effort to stay up on her toes to keep from sinking further. It didn't help when Daniel's pace quickened with each step.

"I still think I should marry you someday," he said, somewhat breathless as he led the way deeper into the maze.

"Are you in the habit of proposing marriage to every girl you encounter?" she asked, doing her best to keep up with him.

"No, just you. You're the only one I have proposed it to. Twice now, as I recall. I rarely encounter any other girls." He shrugged. "My nose is always in a book."

"Well then, perhaps I should take this as a compliment. Absurd an offer as it is."

"Absurd!" He stopped, released her hand, and turned to her, his eyes wide.

"Yes, Daniel, it is absurd to propose marriage to someone you don't know." She struggled to make eye contact with him as he faced her with his beautiful wide smile.

"Even if you are sure that she is the girl of your dreams?" he asked, not giving her a moment to respond before turning away and walking on.

"I... I am not even sure how to respond to that." She set off after him.

"Then don't," he said over his shoulder. "You will just come up with some cheeky comment and spoil the whole mood."

She scowled as he laughed but kept following him. The maze twisted and turned and, more than once, he led her into a dead end, only to proclaim that he'd turned the wrong way before setting off in the opposite direction.

By the time they reached the center, she was delighted to see two stone benches in the small circular space. Without thinking, she hastened over and plopped herself down on one, glad for the opportunity to give her feet a rest. She lay the bouquet of flowers down at her side, then closed her eyes and let out an audible huff.

"Are you tired already?" Daniel asked, even though he was breathless.

She opened her eyes. "No... Well, yes, but that's not it."

He tilted his head. "What is it then?"

"I forgot that it rained earlier." She shifted. "Sitting on this wet bench was not the best choice I have made today."

"I suppose not," he said, chuckling as he walked over and sat beside her. "There. Now we are both guilty of poor decisions today."

She gave his arm a playful nudge.

He smiled, closed his eyes, and took a deep breath. "I come out here sometimes just to think." He shrugged one shoulder. "It calms me, I suppose. It is my quiet place of refuge."

"What sort of things do you think about?" She hoped he didn't think her intrusive but he had a way of keeping himself just beyond her understanding. He was a complex person, to say the least—shy and reserved, and in full control of his emotions. Yet, every now and then he said or did something that revealed his vulnerable side. Maybe it was loneliness. He'd mentioned it that time in his study. Maybe, deep down, he possessed the same uncertainty as the rest of the world. If he had uncertainty, he always managed to keep it hidden. The longer she knew him, the more she wanted to chip away at his well-crafted façade. She wanted to know him, in a way she knew no one else. Just who would this man be if he was unveiled? Something about this moment told her she was closer to that goal than she had ever been. She just had to push him that bit further.

"A great many things," he answered. "Far too many to recount, I am sure."

"Do you ever think of me?" she asked, not sure she really wanted his answer. Yes, she wanted him to respond in the affirmative, but she wasn't prepared if he didn't. She almost wanted to retract the question the moment it left her lips.

He looked at her, his eyes glinting blue beneath the lenses of his thin-framed glasses. "I think of you often." His wisp of a smile matched hers. "I think of you too much, if you ask me."

Flattered and somewhat stunned, her breath caught and she coughed into her hand to cover it. "What precisely is too much?" It wasn't like him to be sentimental, and she expected him to explain that the time he spent thinking of her served as an unwanted distraction from his work. A light mist of rain tickled her eyelashes.

"In the morning, when I wake, I wonder if Adelia would like this shirt. When I walk into my office, I think how much nicer that space would be if Adelia were there helping me sift through my piles of papers. When I eat lunch, I think it would be so much more enjoyable if Adelia were there to talk to. I wonder what you're doing every minute we are apart, but most of all, I wonder if Adelia thinks of me even half the amount of time that I think of her."

She stared at him, and he held her gaze in return. During their initial meetings, she had grown accustomed to him looking away from her when he was uncomfortable, but this time was different. He searched her eyes for the same answers she sought in him. Her natural inclination was to just smile, maybe even give out a little nervous chuckle, but that didn't seem fair when he'd just revealed something that had taken a great deal of courage. She had asked her question with the sole purpose of dragging him from his comfort zone, and by all accounts she had been successful. Yet, Daniel was oh so clever. He had asked her a question in return—one that required an honest answer.

To fill the ensuing silence, she picked up the bouquet and turned it on her lap. "I think about Daniel at my morning tea. I wonder if he will take it with milk and sugar today or just plain. I think about Daniel when I pick out my dress for the day, wondering what color he likes best. I think about Daniel on my way to work, hoping that somehow our paths will cross and I can see his face before I start my shift. There is not a room in this whole palace that I don't like better when you are in it. I think about Daniel entirely too much, but, to be honest, I don't mind."

"That changes everything, I suppose." He moved a wisp of her damp hair off her face.

Her mouth hung open for a moment too long before she pulled herself together. "What does it change?"

"Everything," he repeated.

She leaned back and stared at him with what she hoped he took as a playful rebuke.

"Do you dance, Adelia?" He took her hand and pulled her to her feet.

"N-no," she stammered, perplexed by the question. She dropped the flowers onto the bench.

"Just try," he whispered, wrapping his arms around her waist and drawing her to his chest.

"There is no music," she protested.

"There is, you just have to listen."

Something about that reminded her way too much of her grandma. His breath was warm on her neck, contrasting to the cool droplets of rain on her face. Goodness me, this is the craziest thing I have ever done. This simple recluse from Boston is standing in the middle of the maze at Hampton Court, wrapped in a near-stranger's arms, swaying to the patter of summer rain and the pale hum of tiny insects hiding in the hedges.

The drizzle soaked into the chiffon of her dress, and she could hear her mother complaining that all those water spots would ruin that beautiful garment. However, at this moment, she couldn't care less. Being in Daniel's embrace made her feel reckless—fearless even—as though she could float up a thousand stories high without feeling one single shred of anxiety.

"You are special, Adelia," he whispered into her ear. "There's no one in the whole world like you."

"Daniel, there are millions of girls in this world. I hardly think I am all that special." She could almost hear her insecurities spilling from her lips.

"To me, there is only you." His Adams apple bobbed as he swallowed

She didn't respond. As he'd said earlier, she didn't want to do anything to spoil the moment. She just went with it as it was, allowing herself to get caught up in what had to be a dream, even if it felt so real. For a second, she wondered if he would kiss her. It seemed the only thing in the world that could complete a moment so perfectly designed.

"Tell me your secret," he whispered.

She froze, goosebumps erupting across her shoulders, as if a sudden breeze of icy air had descended upon her. Her skin felt hollow and cold, despite the humidity of the day. She pulled her head back from his shoulder, positive her face showed the sheer panic spreading from her stomach.

"What?" she asked, that one word the only thing she was capable of articulating.

"What is it that you see around you?"

She glanced around, near frantic. "The...maze?"

"That is not what I am asking," he said, patient yet stern. "Quit being so literal."

"Okay. I see you."

He sighed. "You and I both know that you see more. I don't pretend to know what it is, Adelia. I am only saying that I want to."

She hoped he couldn't see the flurry of thoughts racing behind her eyes. Clearly he had picked up on something she'd tried so hard to conceal. Can I trust him with the truth? There is nothing in our interactions so far that says otherwise. It would be nice to have someone other than Grandma to confide in. Yet, how can I share news of my ability when I don't fully understand it myself? How would I even begin to explain?

In her life now, feelings swirled through her that were not her own. Voices and conversations surrounded her that were from hundreds of years ago. She had known men like Daniel her whole life, and there was no way he would believe such an ability existed. He would do his best to explain it away, believing that her knowledge of Hampton Court had caused her imagination to run wild, maybe even that she wanted to possess some secret ability to read the past. No, the truth that she had inherited a gift, passed down through generations, would never fly for him. Just as her grandma had warned her, no one would believe such a thing, least of all Daniel.

"I have no secrets, Daniel," she said, conveying as much certainty as she could muster.

He nodded once, more to himself than her. "You have no secrets, or just one you don't want to share with me?"

"Both," she answered, fixing him with a steely glare.

"Is there anything between us, Adelia? Anything at all?"

She hadn't expected that, and stared at the ground, searching the corners of her mind for the right response. I want to tell him everything. I want to tell him nothing. I want to know that I can trust him. But the cold around her kept her frozen in place, perhaps trying to tell her that it wasn't the right time. "He won't believe you," she kept hearing over and over in her head.

"I am not afraid to say it, Adelia. I am crazy about you. You are all I can think about night and day. Am I alone in this?"

She looked up at him and became lost in the softness of his eyes. A wave of warmth seeped through her, all but melting the frigid temperature of her skin. She had thought of him so many times since they'd met, and now, the realization of just how much began to sink in. As she went to speak, something just behind him caught her attention, and her throat tightened at the sight of a figure standing there, staring at her with deep black eyes, and with such seriousness, she couldn't distinguish whether it was fury or pleading.

"You can't do this!" the raven-haired woman shouted.

She was dressed in black velvet that made her eyes look all the darker against her porcelain-white skin. There was only one woman from the past she knew to possess such dark eyes. The figure was hazy, as though the slightest breeze would disperse her into nothing more than particles of dust. Adelia stared hard at her, not sure if she was being seen.

"You cannot do this," the woman shouted again and again.

As Adelia continued watching, studying each detail, she realized that the hedges surrounding them had vanished, replaced by a field of fresh grass and wildflowers, with the palace standing clear in the distance. She wanted to reach out and touch her. They were so close, it wouldn't have taken but a step or two to do so. Yet she remained frozen in place.

"You cannot do this," she repeated back to the figure.

"I already have," Daniel said.

She blinked, realizing she had been so transfixed by the woman that she'd forgotten Daniel was there. Has he any inkling who is standing mere inches from him? She read nothing in his face—his whimsical smile replaced by a stone-cold, unfamiliar seriousness.

"I have been a fool, Adelia. For that I am sorry. I got lost in the moment. Lost in you. I believed there might be something between us, but I was wrong." His shoulders slumped. "I was wrong to ask so much of you. I am so sorry." He turned and walked away.

Just as she went to call after him, to tell him he hadn't been wrong, something moved behind her.

"It is done, Anne," a man said, his voice strong.

She turned, trying to pinpoint the source, but there was no one there. When she snapped back to face the woman, her face went cold on realizing she was alone, standing there in the center of the maze. Daniel had departed so fast she couldn't even be sure which direction he'd fled. The icy sensation on her skin subsided, and she stumbled back to the stone bench before sitting on its cold wet surface, struggling to catch her breath as tears streamed down her cheeks.

Their moment that had been so perfect had been destroyed so fast. Daniel was gone, and most likely for good this time. She had managed to royally muck things up. It was clear as day that she felt something for him—something far stronger than simple friendship. Despite her complete lack of experience with men, she had no doubt this was something she'd never felt before. Yet she had spent a lifetime trying to hide who she really was on the inside. Even before she knew of her gift, she had wanted nothing more than to please the people around her by being what *they* wanted her to be. Fear prevented her from revealing her secret to Daniel. Fear of what he might think. Fear that he might turn away from her if she trusted him. All that didn't matter now. He had turned away from her anyway.

"A gift," she muttered to herself, thinking back to what her grandma had called it. "More of a curse," she spat into the rain, her words carried on a wracking sob. She thought back to this maze being Anne and Elizabeth's place of courtship. A place of romance? Far from it, when you considered that neither of those relationships ended well. How foolish she had been to forget that glaring detail.

Now, more than ever, she would spend her life being plagued by something she could never reveal to others. Sometimes she wished she was back to thinking she was just an overly nervous creature teetering on madness. At least that was something people would believe. She had lost all hope of ever making things right with Daniel. He had allowed himself a rare moment of vulnerability, only for her to rebuke him without even trying.

Her heart was heavy, burdened with a sense of sadness, the likes of which she had never known. She had experienced loneliness most of her life, but never quite this much. No one in the entire world could ever understand the emotional turmoil that swelled in her chest. The face of the black-eyed woman replayed in her mind. Her grandma had said it was rare to actually see things, that the gift was more of a feeling. After today's incident, she had indeed passed into a new space. The images, though hazy, were incredibly real.

She dried her eyes, then scooped up the bundle of rain-soaked flowers. Her clear objective now, to find her grandma. There was so much more she needed to know.

Chapter Eleven

Her grandma gasped on seeing her walk in the door, drenched to the bone. Without a word, Adelia thrust the bouquet of soggy stems toward her. The elderly woman's tender smile did little to soften the worry she knew was etched on her face.

"My goodness, Adelia, what has happened to you? Come here, child, let's get you into something dry."

"I need to ask you a question." She struggled to catch her breath as she followed her grandma down the hall to her room.

"Yes, yes, what is it, dear? Let's get you changed and we can talk all about it." She disappeared into the bathroom for a moment and came out with a fluffy white towel, which she wrapped around Adelia's shoulders as they continued on to the bedroom.

"Have you ever...seen something?" Up until this point, she'd not disclosed every occurrence that had transpired over the past few weeks.

"You will have to be more specific, dear. A woman of my age has seen a great many things." She smirked, her eyes full of mischief.

"I mean, have you ever seen someone? Someone from the past?"

"Oh, that's what has you all in a fuddle, huh?" She chuckled, then became still. "Have you seen someone?"

"Yes, I have. Today, at the hedge maze."

"I see. It is extremely rare to actually see someone, at least in my case. I find that it happens more when I am most unguarded."

"Unguarded?"

"When I am so focused on my own emotions, I find the energy around me is stronger. My guard is down. I am weaker, if you will. Energy has a way of taking over." She drew her hand around, as if showing her examples of such energy, then opened the wardrobe door and took one of Adelia's dresses out—a deep emerald-green one.

"I saw someone today," Adelia said, smiling at her grandma's tender, maternal attention. "Daniel and I went to explore the hedge maze and, right there before me, I saw a woman dressed in a black velvet gown. Sixteenth century, I would guess."

"You could see her clearly, you say?" Her grandma turned her back and approached the window.

Adelia slipped out of her wet dress and patted herself dry. "I could make out her features, but she was hazy, almost blurred at the edges, if that makes sense?" She put on the dress from the wardrobe

"It makes perfect sense." She turned, walked to Adelia, and adjusted the collar of her dress. "Was your mind preoccupied? Perhaps with Daniel?" She smiled, her brow raised.

"Yes." Her cheeks warmed. "Daniel wanted to show me the maze. I guess, if I have to be honest, I like to spend time with him too. I don't honestly know why. He is so much like my father."

"Is Daniel being like your father a bad thing?"

Adelia raised her brow this time. "In a romantic sense, yes!" She took a breath and sighed. "Daniel can be dry and stuffy at times, and is entirely too wrapped up in his work most days." She patted at her wet hair with the towel. "A girl like me could be easily pushed aside if some new archaeological discovery was made. I know this all too well. Still, when I'm with him, he makes me feel appreciated, as though he respects my knowledge, regardless of my being a woman."

"Who on earth ever convinced you that being a woman does not warrant your intelligence being respected? I sure as hell hope my son never instilled such a belief in you. He will hear from me, he will."

"No, Dad has never been like that. In fact, he has always prided himself on my general knowledgeability, even if he presumes that he is the sole reason I have attained it." She almost laughed but managed to hold it back. "I just felt comfortable around Daniel...until I screwed it up."

"Oh, Adelia," her grandma said, rubbing her shoulder, "it really couldn't have been all that bad."

"It was. Believe me, Grandma, it was worse than that."

"Well, let's sit down and you can tell me all about it. Perhaps we can work through this predicament together. You know, I have found myself in a few over the years, and they always worked themselves out. You will see." She sat on the bed and patted the space beside her. Adelia sat down, feeling like a foolish girl who was recalling a bad day at school.

She had to admit that retelling the day's events to her grandma brought her comfort. Now her father was gone, she was the only person she could confide in these days. As she recounted every detail, she realized that in just two months she would be back in Boston and would no longer have her to talk to face to face. That filled her with a mixture of sadness and dread. *Can I navigate these experiences without Grandma's reassurance? I've grown to depend on it so much during my stay.*

When she had arrived in England, she'd convinced herself that this was going to be a summer of self-discovery, where she focused on her life and what her future would hold. All those things *had* come to pass, yet now, three months didn't feel like nearly enough time to finish her task. She wanted more time. More time with her grandma—time she'd never had the luxury of as a child. She wanted more time with Daniel, too, although she knew the closer she got to him, the more difficult leaving would be—if they ever become close again after today. It felt like every minute of her vacation to date had been somehow accelerated, and time was running out far too fast.

"I know I said people will not believe you when you share your gift with them, my dear. Most of them will not, it's true. Still, there will come a time in your life when you meet someone who is worthy of sharing it with. You must heed your heart." She leaned closer, her eyes widening. "You will have to take a risk sometime."

"Jump off the ledge," Adelia said, repeating Kate's wise words. "You won't fall too far."

"Exactly. Only you will know who the right person is. Only you will know when the time is right."

"Thank you." She drew her grandma into a warm embrace.

Her grandma gave her an extra squeeze before leaning away. "I must say, I am shocked that your abilities have grown so strong in such a short time. It took me far longer to refine my skills." She pursed her lips for a moment before nodding to herself. "Now that you have progressed into seeing those who walked here before us, there is something you should know."

Adelia stared at her, not sure she was ready for another revelation. Now I know where Dad gets his penchant for leaving out important details.

"As you know, we read the energy of past events. We can hear the voices around us, and feel the emotions that were once present. However, when you progress to the point that you begin to see visions of the past, emotions become stronger. Where there was pain and suffering, you will feel it just as they did. Where there was joy and happiness, you will feel that as well. At that level, it can be very difficult to discern your own emotions from those of the people you channel. Do you understand?"

Adelia gripped her bottom lip between her teeth. "Hmm. I can lose sight of my own emotions and my own reality by taking on theirs?" Even as she asked the question, she already knew the answer. There were so many times in her memory where she had not been able to justify her feelings. Now, more than ever, she could stop blaming every irrational emotion on herself. Just as in the chapel, she was a mere vessel to whatever the whispering revealed.

"Precisely, my dear. You must learn to put your guard up carefully. You must learn to push the emotions of the past into the background so as not to lose yourself in their lives. Don't get me wrong, sometimes taking on what belonged to someone else can be empowering. In a place like Hampton Court, you cannot forget that suffering was part of everyday life. It's not a life you can ever fully grow accustomed to, because it's not something you have ever known."

Adelia smoothed down her dress around her lap. "I suppose, if that's the case, there isn't a place in this world I would be safe."

"I am sorry, darling, but no. Anywhere you go, there will be past events that will come through to you. You will have to be diligent in keeping yourself distanced so you can preserve your present." She reached both hands to the back of her neck and unclasped her string of pearls, a teardrop-pearl pendant attached to the front. "I want you to have this," she said, her tone endearing. "It was given to me by my mother. It's very old, you see. Just how old, no one knows for sure, but it has been in our family for years."

When the necklace was attached around her neck, Adelia clutched the tiny pendant in one hand.

"It suits you," her grandma said, brushing a strand of hair off Adelia's face. "When your gift leaves you feeling lost, this will remind you of who you are, my dear. This necklace has passed through many generations with the gift. It holds the energy of your ancestors, and will help you to find the answers when the waters are murky."

"I understand." Though she doubted the necklace held any true power to guide her, she understood all too well what her grandma was saying. There would never really be rest for her in the future. The more refined her gift became, the more she would have to work to ensure it remained a part of her, yet not allowing herself to be overtaken. She would always have the need to remember just who she was. This ability was still new, yet with each passing day it felt stronger. She was growing accustomed to the familiar sensation of it coming on, and losing the fear she had once possessed. Now, it was a part of who she was, and more than ever, she must learn to both control and protect herself, from the emotions of the past as well as the judgment of those in her life.

I will never be safe. Though that notion should have filled her with apprehension, it didn't, and she found that strange. Knowing that her work would never be finished gave her a sense of purpose. There would always be the next thing to challenge her from within. She had been searching for this sense of purpose all her life, even if she hadn't realized it existed in her all along.

"I can't quite shake the feeling that our gift must have some purpose, Grandma. What I mean to say is, you have had this incredible power your whole life yet never discovered its...point?"

"I have nothing to hide from you, Adelia. You said it yourself that you have been hearing these whispers since an early age, and yet you could not decipher why."

Adelia nodded in agreement, owning all the truth in her grandma's words.

"At times," her grandma continued, "I have felt that the whispers have come to me with a strong sense of purpose—some message that I should derive. I have long held the belief that nothing is by chance, and everything is by design. Perhaps the intention was that I use that knowledge in my own life. Whether or not I have interpreted the message correctly, I cannot say. At best, it's always an educated guess. All I know is that your abilities are far stronger than mine have ever been. What purpose lies ahead for you, I have little doubt you will discover in due time."

When Adelia returned to work the next day, it was with renewed determination. No longer would she fight to push the whispering into the background. I must learn to let it flow within me—to face it head on as the thoughts and emotions come. This was a gift she would possess for her whole life, and it was time to strike an emotional balance between her own energy and that of others. She would take on each day with an acceptance that she could be in control. Indeed, she had a sense of duty, not just to her ancestors but her descendants as well.

Once again, she dressed for her day with the assistance of Besse, who she looked forward to seeing each morning. Besse recounted the events of her weekend, making Adelia a little jealous because it was clear that the local girl had an exciting social life. A college student herself, Besse had a busy schedule and was never at a loss for things to do—her experience a stark contrast to the isolated one Adelia had back in Boston. As she listened, she quite enjoyed living vicariously through the English girl's stories.

Once she was dressed, she made her way to the great hall, where she would be stationed for the day. Her thoughts still raged over the incident with Daniel yesterday. Is there any purpose in trying to make things right between us? I've managed to screw things up yet again, and he will see that my constant drama isn't worth it in the end. Maybe he has determined that already.

Always early, she paced along the polished wooden floor, the sharp clack of her heels echoing off the high ceilings and walls. She rehearsed in her head what she would say to Daniel if given another chance. Just as she reached the end of the room, a chill coursed over her skin. At first it surprised her, considering she was covered in layer upon layer of heavy fabric, but then she realized that it wasn't a draft. She hesitated, knowing she was still the only one in the room but not feeling alone.

With a slow and steady turn, she prepared to face whatever shared the space with her.

Her mouth fell open at the sight of the petite woman standing before her. She turned the page of a small prayer book, her dark hair peeking out of a delicate French hood, with a black veil hanging at the back. Her fine gown of black velvet was adorned with jewels, and a long string of pearls was tucked into her dress's low square collar. Beautiful fabric lined the inner portion of her sleeves, which matched the exposed kirtle at the front of her gown. Her attire was so elaborate, it could only be afforded by someone of the highest social ranking.

As the woman moved about, Adelia knew she wasn't looking at someone who worked in the palace. No, while this person belonged in this space, it was from long ago. She sized up every feature of her slight physique, and marveled at how similar they looked, but that was where it ended. This woman possessed a powerful character, was cultured, not easily intimidated, and sure of herself. The energy that radiated from her conveyed a woman full of ambition, confident of achieving any goal she set her mind to. These were traits Adelia couldn't begin to imagine in herself, though her desire for them was almost intoxicating.

If it wasn't for the slight haze surrounding her, she would have sworn this was a living being. The color of her skin was so true, with a light-pink flush in her cheeks. Her face was diminutive, her nose narrow, her big brown eyes so dark they seemed almost black. Adelia knew she was watching none other than Anne Boleyn, moving about in her own time and space, oblivious to the costume-clad voyeur scrutinizing her every move. This woman glided through the room, the queen of England, married to one of the most powerful men in the world. While Adelia had no sense of what year this could be, she saw no concern or worry in Anne's face, so assumed she had no sense of what was to come. At this stage in her life, she knew what her future held, and death on the Tower Green had no part in that.

Anne turned another page of her book, and when she smiled, Adelia could almost feel the love she held for her husband. She had fought so hard to secure him, and there was no room for doubt that he loved her equally.

Adelia's breath quickened, and she lifted her palm to her chest, focusing to clear her mind. To be here at this moment was like a dream. Millions of people through the ages would have done anything to experience this. To see this tragic queen in all her magnificence was nothing short of breathtaking, and yet it felt so intrusive. Watching her like this wasn't something she had chosen. Like every sensation or voice thrust upon her, it was just part of this ability she had inherited. There was no natural way to explain any of it to someone who had no experience of it. The stronger these energies became, the more she realized that this gift, passed down through generations, was continuing to develop. It wasn't just the energy and voices that had grown in strength, the visions were becoming much clearer too.

She cursed to herself at the sound of voices from the other room. As they grew louder, Anne faded into a hazy blur, but even as the vapor dissipated into nothing, Adelia still felt the presence linger, or maybe it was a memory thing. She thought back to all the descriptions of Anne she had heard through the years. So few portraits of her had survived, and those that existed were assumed to have been painted in the style of all Tudor-era works of art, with the tendency to over compliment the subject. Yet, as she replayed in her mind what she had just witnessed, she marveled at the unconventional beauty Anne Boleyn possessed. She was delicate and attractive, true, yet it was her inner confidence that took her physical appearance to a higher level. That radiant inner strength came through in such a flood that it made her the type of person the inhabitants of a room might stop to admire. Perhaps the way she became queen was unconventional, even by sixteenth-century standards, but it was clear that she had taken to the role with a natural grace.

Adelia couldn't help holding on to the vision she had just experienced. Did Anne really want to be queen? Had she known her fate, she might have chosen another path? Yet, what other opportunities would have existed for her? History played its part in painting her as a scheming mistress—one who had upset the entire country for her own ambitions. But was that really accurate? Once chosen by the king, there was little a woman could do to refuse. The pressure from her family would have been immense. They would have been more concerned with their own political elevation at court than Anne's feelings. Had she refused Henry, it is likely her family would have shunned her as well. Women of that time had no means of supporting themselves. At best, she would have been sent to a convent and spent the rest of her life as a nun. The woman couldn't be blamed for taking such a gamble. If she won the game, there was a promise of great wealth and status, with a life many women of today might dream of having.

Beyond the scant options Anne Boleyn had at her disposal, Adelia sensed she had a deep affection for Henry. One could not forget that he was a handsome and dashing man in his prime, who just about any girl could fall head over heels for. His determined courtship of Anne must have been flattering, so much so she would wait over seven years to marry him—allowing the prime of her own life to pass.

Each of Henry's six wives had stories of their own, but why Anne's continued to come through was something she couldn't fully understand. Maybe it was because she herself was playing the role of the tragic queen. She thought back to what her grandma had said about the whispers and how the messages might play out in our own lives. Like Henry and Anne, her and Daniel's relationship was proving more than a little complex. The spark between them seemed to be overshadowed by so many barriers. Did the whispers mean to tell her that darker days lay ahead? Love, no matter how glorious it begins, is never without risk. While there was no chance of losing her head on the Tower Green as Anne did, she wasn't impervious to a broken heart. Either way, she didn't feel too burdened by Anne's presence. Just as Daniel had said of Amy Robsart, Anne was a living breathing person who deserved to have her story told as it was lived.

Chapter Twelve

I f ever a person had found Henry VIII a difficult man, they should try working with the bastard. Each day was growing more trying as Adelia struggled to keep from being upstaged and overshadowed by Gerald and his constant quest for the limelight. He brought out a devilish being in her that was hell-bent on using every last bit of sarcasm she could muster. Torturing this man had become her prime distraction, and she couldn't help but notice how the other staff delighted in their relentless sparring. She knew she should feel bad, and even a tad immature at aggravating the man so, but she didn't, and that was fine with her.

She'd struggled to focus on her duties that day, and hadn't even bothered to change out of her costume when her midday break rolled around, disobeying protocol on purpose. Her lavish outfit was expensive, and no doubt the palace curator would be unhappy with her later. She didn't care. All she wanted was to see Daniel. In truth, she was filled with the unyielding desire to make things right between them—so much, she was willing to be vulnerable, if required. He had wanted to know her secret, and, after serious consideration, she believed the time had come to clue him in. If he rejected her, then so be it. She had spent the past few days in pure misery at the thought of how they'd left things in the maze, and no amount of his rejection could be worse than her current level of torment.

Dressed in the full regalia of Queen Anne Boleyn, she made her way through the hallways and tapped on the door to his study. On hearing his call to enter, she twisted the knob and walked in. He glanced up from his papers, which made her heart skip. His hair looked disheveled and the collar of his shirt hung at a lazy angle, as though it had given up the struggle to stand upright. She adored the way he looked—like a man who hadn't slept any more than she for the past few days. This might be a sign that he still feels something for me.

All her hopes were dashed when he dipped his head back to the folio in front of him, never so much as uttering a word to her. She considered just turning and leaving but thought it too late to do so. No, she would only make a bigger fool of herself. She stepped further into the room, pretending not to notice his blatant attempt to ignore her. It wasn't as if her being in full costume didn't at least warrant a puzzled look from the man. Whatever she'd expected, this came nowhere near it.

"Do you...believe in ghosts?" she asked, a hint of hesitancy in her voice.

He continued to stare into the pages of the folio, as though her presence was nothing of importance. She supposed she deserved that much, having left him humiliated just a few days ago.

"Do you?" he asked, his tone conveying a complete lack of interest.

She closed her mouth to prevent herself saying something he would deem foolish. Here, in the grandest of palaces, she stood opposite a most-learned professor of medieval studies, spouting about, of *all* things, ghosts. What an idiot she must seem to him right now. However, she had to say something to move things forward.

"I...don't suppose I do. That is to say, I have never seen one... Well, not in the sense of a meandering figure cloaked in a white sheet, saying boo, or anything. I just wonder if I don't like the idea of ghosts, more than I believe in it." She seated herself in the high-backed leather chair across the room, fixing her gown to prevent unnecessary creases.

She had to admit to herself that she wasn't being honest. It couldn't be denied that she had seen a person from the past, who was no longer living. But if one were to be particular about details, she didn't see ghosts in the modern definition of the word. Today's perception of ghosts depicted them as haunting a given location, seeking retribution for the wrongs they'd endured in life. Not in her case, though. The people she sensed were replaying their daily lives, caught in the fabric of time. For all she knew, what she took as the present was really the past. Perhaps someone else was reading her own energy, peering into the window of this tense moment now. If that were the case, she hoped they weren't filled with half the trepidation she felt as she looked at Daniel. Facing him was far more excruciating than expected.

"How do you know you have never seen a ghost?" he asked, still thumbing through the pages of the leather-bound volume.

She stared at him for a long moment. His lack of engagement and his infuriating monotone voice made her want to scream at him. Is he intentionally trying to show disinterest, or is he so drawn to the contents of that folio he can't tear himself away long enough to make respectable eye contact? She groaned inside when she thought of it, because that wasn't against his nature.

"I am certain that I have never seen a ghost, but I have seen other things." She straightened in her seat, preparing for more of the same attitude.

He turned a page. "You're certain you have never seen a ghost? Because you haven't encountered a form covered in a white sheet in the hall at the stroke of midnight?"

"Now you're just making a joke of it," she shot back. "I asked the question in seriousness. Just forget the conversation." She pushed herself up from the chair, the bulk of her heavy skirts hindering it from being a smooth maneuver. Despite her struggle, she took great care to keep her frustrated expression locked in place.

Right before she was about to turn away, he raised his gaze to meet hers, and smiled. She blinked, unsure why the lighting in the room seemed different all of a sudden. His eyes looked so much more vibrant than how she remembered. Just how many shades of blue can a pair of eyes take on?

"You look just like I imagine her," he said.

"Who?" she asked, grasping for the logic in his comment.

"The Lady Anne. If ever I saw a ghost, surely one stands before me now. The fiery Mistress Boleyn, willful and stubborn, has returned home. Head intact, mind you."

"You are making fun of me," she snapped. "Thankfully, my break is nearly over. I'd rather go back to being manhandled by Henry VIII out there than spend another minute being the object of your ridicule."

"Manhandled?" He scowled. "What are you talking about, Adelia?"

"The king. Well, Gerald, actually. He can get a little too into character with his courting." She snickered as she smoothed the fine damask print of her skirt, recalling the several well-placed elbows he'd received over the last few weeks.

"That is completely unacceptable, and it will be stopped."

"Whatever shall you do, Doctor Brown," she asked, unable to hold back a mischievous smile, "send him to the Tower? What a turn of events, Henry VIII is to be the one beheaded on the Tower Green. Karma, I suppose."

He nodded, eyebrows raised. "That would be a much-deserved twist." He closed the folio, which she was glad to see. "Tell me, Adelia, what ghosts do you suppose are here in the palace?"

She knew he didn't believe in ghosts, and had no doubt he was just humoring her to continue the conversation. Even with her original intention sidetracked, she decided to respond, but not before sitting back in her seat.

"Hampton Court has hundreds of years of history. So many profoundly interesting monarchs have walked these halls. That energy still exists here."

He nodded again. "Truly, what is the likelihood that every king or queen has a ghost lurking about here?"

"Well, this is the place they lived, Daniel. Where else would their ghosts go? Would you suggest a holiday in Bermuda?" She almost laughed but made do with a smirk.

"There are well over two billion ordinary people in this world. Wouldn't it stand to reason that there might be a far greater occurrence of just regular ghosts than that of famous people?" He sat back and looked at the ceiling, his splayed hand held out, palm up. "This place was filled with far more servants than it ever had nobility. Why do all ghosts have to be famous people?"

"I suppose you have a valid point," she said. "Ordinary people could be a ghost just as easily."

His face lit up with a cheeky smile. "Of course I have a valid point. It does have a certain ring to it."

She rolled her eyes at him in silent resignation.

"What did you see, Adelia?" he asked, his tone more serious.

"I did not say I saw anything," she chimed, though she knew it wasn't convincing.

"I do not pretend to understand it." He got up and pulled a chair over to sit opposite her. His face was level with hers now, and he looked at her with such intensity she could do nothing but stare back. It was by far the most uncomfortable she had felt around him, only it wasn't really a discomfort, as such, more a sense of every nerve ending pulsing, as if he'd activated her at a depth no one else had ever touched.

She shifted back in her seat, breaking eye contact. "If I told you what I saw, how could I know that you would believe me?"

He grabbed her hand, the warmth of his touch all but melting any resistance. This was different than in the maze. Here, any notion of reservation had vanished. For the first time, she knew he could be fully trusted.

"There is always a chance that I will not," he said, "but you and I both know there is something extraordinary about you." He leaned a little closer, his grip firmer. "I can sense it, even if I don't know how to put it into words. You have to trust me enough to help me understand."

"I do." She looked him straight in the eye, easing her hand free. "I just don't know if I understand it well enough to convince you."

He smiled. "Try me."

She didn't hold back her own smile as she looked down at her hands, fidgeting in her lap. "When I was a child, I used to be the nervous sort. I was a loner for the most part. I guess I always assumed that was just the natural side effect of being an only child. As I grew older, I realized that my nervous disposition was just part of who I was."

"I can definitely relate to that," he said, his voice soft.

"I hated crowds. I hated empty rooms. Everything around me felt chaotic. Loud. It progressed to the point that I worried something was really wrong with me. That this nervous disposition was something more." She took a steadying breath. "I could feel emotions that didn't make sense. I heard conversations that were not actually taking place. I was convinced that I was sinking into some sort of madness, and spent every waking minute trying to conceal my struggles from my family. When I came here for the summer, I was so full of hope that this was going to be the break that changed me."

"Has England changed you?" he asked, his look one of gentle concern.

"From the moment I stepped into Hampton Court, something was different." She glanced about. "All around me, I felt crowded. I heard things that didn't make sense. I could see people who should not have been there. It wasn't until I shared this with my grandma that I finally understood."

Daniel blinked several times, then leaned in, searching her eyes, maybe for any sense that she might be joking. She watched as realization of her truthfulness washed over him.

"I can feel the energy of what's happened here in a way that is difficult to understand, even for myself." She smoothed her hand across her lap, though no wrinkles existed. "Yet, the more I stop and listen, to fine-tune my comprehension of what's happening, it's clear that I've been able to do it for a long time." She shook herself from the grip of his gaze. "I know it sounds crazy, and I won't blame you if you don't believe a word I am saying."

"But I do believe you, Adelia," he said, taking her hand again and squeezing it a little tighter than before. "I sensed it that day at the staircase. I cannot pretend that I have ever been the sort of man to believe in things that can't be rationally explained. Yet I saw the fear and sadness in your face. I knew then that you have some ability to understand what I cannot."

Her heart swelled. "You don't know how glad I am to hear you say that. I am sorry that I couldn't bring myself to confide in you that day in the maze."

He patted the back of her hand. "I am honestly glad you didn't. I don't think I was ready for it. No, my head was in the clouds that day, but I still meant everything I said."

She didn't know how to respond, overcome with the relief that she had at last shared something she'd never spoken to another person about beyond her grandma. It was like a great weight had been lifted off her, freeing her of the burden she'd carried for so long.

"Are you okay," he asked.

She smiled as she nodded. "I am, thanks. So, where do we go from here?"

"I want you to take a trip to Oxford with me?"

"Oxford?" She stared at him. "I meant in our relationship, not location-wise."

"I know it's a lot to ask," he said, as if he hadn't heard her. "We would need your grandmother's permission, of course. I don't know why but I think you could be a real help to me there."

She decided not to pursue the matter of their relationship. "What is it you want me to help with?"

"I would like us to visit the old site of Cumnor Place. It's where Amy died. She is buried in the church there too. Saint Mary's. Perhaps we can put this ability to work."

She almost scowled. "I am not psychic, Daniel. Perhaps all I possess is nothing more than a woman's intuition."

"No less powerful," he said. "Though, I believe you and I both know that you are downplaying it."

Now that she had grown to know him better, she liked how he never allowed her to dwell in self-pity—to feel inferior. He might accept that, through the ages, women were viewed and treated as less than their male counterparts but he refused to take that perspective himself. For that, he had earned her respect.

"I would like to see it, I suppose," she said, a flurry of details swirling through her mind.

"Where will we stay? How will we get there?"

"There is an inn in town where you can stay, while I will sleep at my place. I can have everything arranged, if you are willing to go?"

"I think I am willing. I will just need to get a few things in order beforehand. I can talk to my grandma tonight." She almost clapped as she smiled. "This sounds exciting."

"A trip to Oxford sounds exciting for a woman who lives at Hampton Court Palace?"

She looked at him beneath her brows. "It's temporary lodging, Daniel."

"Yes, of course." His expression turned solemn. "I guess you won't be here in England forever."

She watched as his beautiful eyes darkened, as though impacted by the realization that, at some point, the summer would end and they would return to the lives they once knew. That same realization caught her a little off guard too.

Having arrived at work early, Adelia donned her costume and made her way to the Great Hall. She had arranged to work the entire weekend before heading off on Monday to Oxford with Daniel. They would only be gone a few days but a sense of duty saw her making an extra effort to ensure that her shifts were covered. It came as a relief when Besse agreed to play Anne Boleyn until she returned. By all accounts, she knew the part far better than most. Adelia hoped this would be an opportunity for Besse to eventually be considered for the permanent position.

Instead of the traditional receiving room they used, the location for today's performance with the king and queen had changed. The palace staff did this from time to time, and the new setting was sometimes a welcome change that helped break up the monotony of the job. Adelia had always liked the Great Hall, with its enormous timber ceilings, ornate plasterwork, and vivid tapestries. Today, she was clad in a sumptuous black-velvet gown, with a kirtle that looked like cloth of gold, trimmed in a fur that resembled ermine. She pulled the morning newspaper from her sleeve to catch up on her reading before her shift began. As she thumbed through its pages, she did her best to block out the sharp clack of shoes on the wooden floors of the hallways outside the room.

One of the great wooden doors at the far end of the hall creaked, drawing her attention. Gerald entered the room, and while he was clad in his usual royal attire, something was different about him today. She studied him for a long moment, sensing a quiet presence she had never noticed in him before. His shoulders were slumped, no longer holding the proud poise he usually sported. It was obvious that something was bothering his Royal Highness. At first, she didn't care enough to ask, yet, as she continued to observe him from the corner of her eye, her moral compass got the best of her, as it always did.

"My Lord, something troubles you?" she asked, getting right into character. "More importantly, is there anything I can do to make it worse?"

He mumbled something under his breath, barely giving her the courtesy of a glance.

"Very well then." She sighed as she turned her focus to the tapestries lining the walls. It was the same technique she had used numerous times over the past few weeks in her attempts to avoid conversation with this detestable man. Why she had felt compelled to care about his feelings all of the sudden was beyond her. If he didn't want to talk, well then, all the better.

An uncomfortable silence reigned for the next couple of minutes, and she almost cursed herself for getting to work so early. She glanced at the clock, cringing that there was still another ten minutes before the palace opened to visitors. It would be nearly half an hour before they made their way into the Great Hall. Never had minutes passed at such a slow pace.

"Why can't this be mine?" Gerald asked, his voice cracking.

She turned to him, not grasping what he was getting at. "I'm sorry?"

He slouched even more into himself. "They have decided they want to offer you the chance to stay on permanently as Anne."

"This displeases you, my Lord?" she asked in a mocking tone, burying the urge to clap with delight at the committee's decision. For once, it was she who stayed in character.

He released a long sigh that bordered on a groan. "I am not saying that you're not doing a good job. You are probably the best Anne Boleyn I have ever worked with."

Her mind flicked back to when Daniel had given her a similar compliment. "Thank you, Gerald," she said, lowering her gaze, regretting her brash behavior earlier.

"It is just that, playing Henry is the only thing in my life I have ever been good at. I have never really accomplished anything else. I know

it seems selfish but I just wanted something that was mine for once."
He slumped into himself again. "You wouldn't understand it."

"Actually, Gerald, I think I do."

He stared at her for a moment, then shook his head. "No, you have
everything going for you. You have the family name. You have brains
and talent. You will probably go on to be some great intellectual like
your dad. For heaven's sake, you have that Oxford professor following
you around like a puppy. I have none of that, Adelia." He slapped his
sides. "All I have is this."

She leaned back, looking at him beneath her brows. "I hardly think
Daniel is following me around like a puppy."

He shot her a look that screamed *Seriously?*

She softened and smiled, acknowledging that there was a tiny shred
of truth to what he'd said. "Gerald, I think I understand more than
you know what it is like to want to have something in life that is all
your own. Playing this role is your moment, and I have waltzed right
in here and taken it away from you. I assure you, I see that now."

He groaned this time, but it came with an affirmative nod. "You can
take the job if you want. You have earned your place."

"But so have you, Gerald. You are such a good Henry Tudor that,
sometimes, I forget that I'm not standing near that pompous ass
myself."

His brow creased. "Wait... Is that an insult or a compliment?"

She grimaced, lifting her opened hand in front of her, like Hamlet
holding Yorik's skull. "I rather meant it as a compliment, but it might
have come out as...something else." She stepped forward, slipping her
newspaper back into her sleeve. "What I mean to say is that you are
fantastic in this role. I'm not going to be here in England for more than
another month, Gerald. I go back to college in September. I couldn't
take the job even if it was offered to me."

He smiled to himself. "You really think I make a good Henry?"

"You are the best Henry. Actually, I take that back—you are stronger and more courageous than Henry VIII ever was. He would never have had the bollocks to admit when he was feeling insecure. He surrounded himself with acolytes who would tell him how marvelous he was all the time." She shrugged one shoulder. "At least you can be honest about yourself."

"Yeah, I suppose you're right," he said, his eyes brightening, a clear signal of his spirits lifting.

She took another step forward. "Look, Gerald, all this competition between us was just me being cheeky, I assure you." She glanced at the huge doorway. "Might we agree to a truce between us? It's exhausting, if I am being honest."

"Mistress Boleyn, it is no wonder Henry fought for seven long years to have you." He smiled as they each extended a hand to cement their settlement.

"Yes, but it didn't take so long for him to behead me, did it?" She laughed.

Somehow, each passing day was bringing about more closure. Setting things right with Daniel had felt good, but this armistice with Gerald was even more fulfilling. As the remaining days of her vacation ticked away, she was at last starting to feel that she could leave with no regrets.

Over the next few days, she spent just about every spare minute with Daniel. The second she finished work, she rushed to meet him and they spent the afternoon exploring the palace or sitting in its beautiful gardens enjoying the summer heat. He shared so much about his life in Oxford that she nearly felt like she had lived there herself. His excitement at the prospect of showing her his hometown was effusive. Talking to Daniel had always come easy to her, and she'd never felt such a connection to someone in so short a time. If there was such a thing as being destined to meet, she was sure it applied to them.

In an angry world, where a woman her age should be concerned with topics of far more importance, she still found herself plagued by one question: Would Daniel ever kiss her? She was sure he had come close once or twice. She couldn't deny she had nearly mustered the courage to do it herself that day in the maze. Deep down, she had yet to determine whether he actually wanted to, and maybe that was the reason he hadn't. Affection, even shallow infatuation, was such a weighted emotion. It was an inescapable fact that one person always felt stronger than the other. For her, the ever-present question remained: Was it she or was it Daniel?

Chapter Thirteen

On the day before their departure, Daniel arranged for them to have lunch in the gardens of William and Mary II, facing the Baroque additions to the palace. He said he chose it because the king and queen had commissioned it during their reign, and he needed to distance himself from the Tudors for the afternoon. He wanted to take a break from the dark interiors of the palace and get a little sunshine for a change. It sounded like a good idea to Adelia too. Though she thought she would never say it, she'd had enough of the Tudors for a while herself.

As they sat on one of the stone benches, she took in the splendid scenery. Beautiful flowers bloomed in the manicured borders and beds, and neatly pruned Yew trees peppered the landscape. The beautiful brick façade of the palace was decorated with crisp white stone appliques and carved columns—a refreshing change from the dim shadows of the other side of the palace. It was the perfect summer's day. Ideal for a picnic in the gardens.

Daniel unwrapped the sandwiches he'd purchased from one of the many café carts on the palace grounds. He checked the contents of one package, then handed it to her. "Tell me about life in America. It must be so exciting."

"It is odd to me that you think my life in Boston would be exciting, when you are surrounded by all of this every day." She motioned to the palace in the background, thinking back to the fairy tales of her childhood. To have grown up your entire life surrounded by castles was still something she couldn't wrap her head around. The air here was infused with a romantic quality.

"Don't get me wrong," he said, "I love it here. There is always something to discover, but I can't help thinking that where you live would be equally as exciting."

She lined her sandwich up for her first bite. "I guess America has a great many things to discover but, to be honest, I am a self-made recluse in my ordinary life. I don't really do exciting things."

"I just can't picture you being a recluse anywhere," he said. "You have far too adventurous a spirit."

She chewed, thankful she hadn't bitten too much off. Once she'd swallowed, she dabbed her mouth with her napkin and looked at him. "England has been an awakening for me, to be sure. I haven't felt the same since I came here. Do not be fooled, though, it is all a carefully crafted façade. I am far more like Hampton Court Palace than you realize. I can be dark and gloomy on one side and warm and inviting on the other. It's something I have spent a great many years trying to fight."

"What are you really fighting?" he asked.

He seemed to always have a genuine interest in her, and she found that both flattering and unnerving. She had never been good at talking about herself, much preferring to avoid the subject as a rule. Still, he had a way of making her feel safe, and she trusted him more than her mind told her she should allow herself to.

"Myself mainly," she answered. "Since as far back as I can remember, I have been afraid of just about everything. I don't know why. I never had anything traumatic happen to me that I can recall. It's just a lingering fear of a million different things—no rhyme, no reason."

He wiped crumbs from his mouth. "Everyone has fear at some level. I don't think it is a foreign emotion for anyone."

She liked the softness in his voice. His words had come as a bit of a surprise. He seemed to have a pretty solid grasp on the world around him, his nervousness around women excluded. "You don't seem to be afraid of much."

"You are wrong about that. Carefully crafted façade, as you say." This came with his mischievous grin. "When I was little, I had this ridiculous fear of ghosts. That's why I don't like to talk about them very much these days. Brings back old memories, you see."

"Ghosts? You had a fear of ghosts? I don't believe that for a minute."

"I did. I'm being serious. As a kid, my dad dragged me along to old castles and the crumbling ruins of abandoned abbeys. He would carry on about the horrific things that happened to people there and do so in great detail. Try being a seven-year-old looking down into the abyss of an oubliette and not have the shit scared out of you. More than once, I would come home and refuse to turn off the light at night, fearing some long-dead monk had followed me." He turned his sandwich. "England is ripe with ghost stories. There is no way to grow up without hearing each and every one. I spent all of my childhood thinking every cold breeze was the spirit of some crusty old earl waiting to take me into the underworld. I say there is no such thing as ghosts because, deep down, I hope that I'm right."

"There is no such thing as ghosts," she declared. "But..."

His eyes narrowed. "Must you explain further?"

"I must," she said. "The energy we had in life does exist after death. It isn't really a ghost, it's simply just us existing in the same space in another time. Our own time. My grandma explains it best. The past and present exist in layers. Like shards of fabric stacked on top of one another."

"So...you are absolutely sure a monk won't follow me home?" His expectant look, though joking, was also serious.

"I am pretty sure, Daniel. I think you can take ghosts off your list of things to be afraid of."

He leaned away from her, his brows furrowing. "Then, wouldn't it be just as easy for you not to be afraid of a million other things?"

She squared her shoulders at him. He was so good at taking anything the average person found perplexing and making it all make perfect sense. She supposed she should admire that quality. However, since this quality in him always worked against her, she rather despised it.

"It really isn't all that easy for me. I would go through these phases. Some might call it an anxious disposition, but that has always felt like far too simple an explanation. A stroll down the street. The sights. The sounds. People and cars moving all around me. It was a nightmare for me. All too much to absorb, and soon I would find myself retreating into any solitary corner I could find. I know it sounds absurd, but whatever grip the fear had on me felt so real. It wasn't just a mental impact—it became physically debilitating too. Before long I started to avoid anything that made me feel that anxiety, or anything I *thought* might make me feel that way. Eventually, you wake up to find that your inner turmoil has managed to dominate every aspect of your life."

He gave her hand a gentle squeeze. "I can only imagine how difficult that was for you."

"I think the most difficult part is not that you find yourself unable to do the things every other perfectly normal person can do. What you do to yourself is even worse. You never feel whole. Each time, you spend hours and days beating yourself up for your inadequacy—telling yourself over and over that there must be something terribly wrong with you. Most of all, not being able to do basic things makes you feel weak. You spend so much time and effort trying to hide it from everyone you know. Before long, you look at yourself as a liar too. There is no direction that you can turn where the emotions aren't waiting for you."

She left her sandwich in her lap, almost breathless after the words had spilled from her. Before this, she'd never really been able to speak so frankly to anyone. Her words came to her so freely that, for once, she almost understood her condition. Like she had finally been able to explain the way she felt to herself. After getting the words out, she marveled at how light her soul felt.

"It has to take a great amount of courage to face that every day," Daniel said, his tone making her feel like he understood exactly how she felt.

"Being well versed in internal emotions, courage is probably the one I have the least familiarity with."

He nodded. "That is exactly why life is so exhausting. Courage takes a lot of energy. It takes so much to live and more to die. You have to have courage to overcome the dark parts of your soul—the things you don't want everyone else to see. Yet it takes daring to admit that even those dark places are part of your growth as a person. Sure, they can feed your insecurity, but they can also push you into a greater place if you allow yourself to use them that way."

She nudged his elbow, the action gentle. "I'm tired of talking about me. Tell me about you. How did you get here?"

"On foot," he said, his tone flat. "We walked together."

"You know what I mean." She gave him a shove this time.

"It's a long story. Are you sure you have the time?"

She glanced at her watch. "I have precisely four hours until I'm expected home. Plenty of time for you to thrill me with your epic saga."

"Goodness, where do I start?" He wrapped the remains of his sandwich. "My mother died when I was about ten. Since then, it's been just my dad and me. He is a hopeless roamer who spends most of his time exploring old buildings or locked up in his study. Back then, he would drag me along just about everywhere. I didn't always want to go, but, if I hadn't, I probably would have grown up as some feral boy living in the woods."

"No offense but you don't strike me as the kind of man who could live off the land. You wouldn't be able to keep your shirts so starched and white."

He chuckled. "I do take pleasure in a starched shirt, so I will not take offense at your observation."

"I am sorry to hear about your mother, though, and I apologize for interrupting. Please continue."

"Well, from the time I was just a young lad, my father was sure I would go to Oxford and major in historical studies. You see, your path and my path are not so different. Both of us had expectations thrust upon us. Yet, I was a rebellious sort as a youth. I didn't want to be anything like my old man. I wanted to do things entirely my own way. In high school, I was more concerned about hanging out with my mates than I was in my studies, and my marks were poor, to say the least. After school, I thought maybe I might travel for a while. I wasn't convinced I would ever be cut out for college life. I worked and saved some money, but I never had enough to get further than Scotland. By all accounts, I was shaping up to do absolutely nothing with my life. This might come as a shock to you but I am not really cut out for the bad-boy existence."

She had to smile. "It doesn't come as a shock to me. I am still trying to process the idea of you being so rebellious. I did not know you had it in you."

"Don't ponder it too hard," he said. "I wasn't any good at it, I assure you."

"So, what changed everything?"

"Yes, I was just getting to that. After a bunch of failed adventures, I decided to visit the West Yorkshire moors."

"Wait, the moors where the Bronte sisters lived?"

"One and the same. I always wanted to travel in the northern country. Someday, I will take you there. It's a wild country. Something you really need to see to appreciate."

She caught herself thinking his offer was almost romantic, though she knew it would never come to pass. No, she wouldn't be in England for much longer.

"It was there when I finally realized that my father's life was actually one I envied more than I loathed. I may have grumbled about being dragged around old crumbling castles as a kid, but the truth is I loved every second of it. Being a scholar might seem like an unexciting occupation but, actually, it allows you more freedom than any old desk job ever could. Every day is an exploration, whether it's in a library filled with centuries-old manuscripts or traipsing around some ancient woods looking for a tiny artifact from a medieval battle. The world is never small. There is always that one Roman coin just waiting for the day you put your spade into the ground and find it. Being the one who brings that knowledge to other people is just about the most empowering thing I have ever done."

"I love your story, Daniel," she said, meaning every word of it. "You are such a remarkable person. There is so much more to you than meets the eye."

His eyes sparkled as he smiled. "I feel exactly the same about you. Whatever you do—whatever you want to do in this life—you will do it well. I know that you have this astounding gift that lets you see into the past, and that is truly something remarkable. Yet, even if you didn't, you are still capable of doing remarkable things on your own."

"Thank you," she said, almost in a whisper. "I am not sure this gift is as remarkable as you say. It seems to interfere with my life a little more than I wish. I am learning to be patient, but I also have to learn to control it myself, as it mostly controls me now. So much of what I have been fighting in myself for years was just a product of this ability I didn't know existed. And now, knowing it exists has helped me in so many ways."

She had discovered so much about herself since coming to Hampton Court, but it would be remiss of her not to give Daniel ample credit for his help. Without even trying, he had emboldened her to do more than she would ever have thought possible.

"What is it like to hear the voices of the past? You can't imagine how envious I am of what you can do. I have spent so many hours of my life digging for tiny fragments of information. I cannot begin to fathom what it would be like to watch these things unfold before me like a theatrical production. It is truly astounding."

She couldn't disagree, it was astounding. "Just as fear is a universal emotion, reading energy is something we all can do at some level, even if we don't realize our ability. Haven't you ever walked into a room where you felt unwelcome?"

"Probably more times than I care to admit," he said, shaking his head. "Believe it or not, I am not everyone's cup of tea."

She touched the back of his hand. "You can feel the way other people perceive you, even when they don't say a word, right?" He nodded. "You can feel the energy they project, positive or negative, down into the fibers of your being. Your entire mood can shift in an instant."

As he nodded again, she thought he might be recalling a time he'd experienced such a thing himself.

"Those who hear the whispering, as my grandma calls it, just read energy with a more fine-tuned sense. It's the energy of the souls whose lives were lived in that same space. We can hear them, but we can also feel their emotions. I haven't had the gift long enough to fully understand every aspect, but I can see how it has impacted my life over the years. As Grandma says, not all of the darkness we feel belongs to us."

"That has to be some consolation, knowing what you have been fighting for so many years."

"Honestly, it is, but it can be difficult to determine what is mine and what is just the energy I am sensing around me. How many times have I felt anxiety that wasn't my own? Fear that I couldn't make sense of because it was not originating with me? In truth, I was channeling it. Now that I know about the whispering, my life has a new clarity and a whole new level of complexity."

"So, the true question is: Now that you know what you can do, what do you want to do?"

"I am just ready to live," she answered, excited. "I want to be this adventurous person you see me as. I have dreamed of the day where I could be unchained and live freely. Move through life as I see others do so easily. I feel like my world just grew so much larger. I want to explore every square inch of it, even if it's crowded."

"I would like to explore it with you too," he said.

"I would like that very much, Daniel. If only it were possible."

"Anything that you want enough is possible, Adelia. There was a time, not so long ago, when I would have said that this gift you have is impossible. Had you not explained it to me, I might still feel that way. Somehow, by some shift of the wind, this remarkable girl came straight into my life. Now I find myself irreversibly changed, and I can say, in all truth, I don't want this change to end."

How simple words could set her soul ablaze was beyond her comprehension. Her apprehension evaporated into the summer air, leaving a reckless woman in its wake. Whatever she felt for Daniel was so unbound, every bit of caution was gone. She barely recognized the girl who leaned forward, eyes fixated on his lips. Excitement surged through her when he inched nearer, but just as she was close enough to feel the wisp of his breath mingle with hers, something shifted in her hand. She closed her eyes, not wanting to acknowledge what she knew had happened. Grimacing with humiliation, she cracked open her eyes and looked down to see the squished contents of her half-eaten sandwich splayed across the legs of his trousers. Either all of the stars are against me, or I am just a bumbling fool. She chose to blame the stars.

Chapter Fourteen

On the day of their departure, Adelia kissed her grandma goodbye, telling her she would be back by the end of the week. She had expected some hesitancy in allowing her to travel to Oxford with a male acquaintance, but her grandma had been excited, wanting nothing more than to see her gain all the experiences she could while in England. She insisted on Adelia taking the pearl necklace along on the trip, just in case. Adelia hadn't worn it since the day she'd received it, too afraid to lose something so precious. Reluctant, she complied, tucking it into a small wooden box in her suitcase before Daniel led the way to the train station.

She had worn her plain-gray traveling dress, while Daniel donned a brown, tweed suit. He looked every inch the distinguished Oxford professor he would soon return to being at the summer's end. Despite his professional attire, he still conducted himself like a carefree college boy. Over the past few days, she had heard him laugh more than she imagined possible. It was strange to see how he could bounce between his casual and professional demeanor without effort. Before meeting him, she had always pictured herself as steady and predictable, but now, somehow, he managed to bring out the lightheartedness in her. It felt like a high school romance. So fitting for two adults who never found the opportunity to have one before venturing into the adult world. As she'd noticed before, there was an inexperienced giddiness about them. It was still by far the sweetest thing she had ever felt.

They boarded the train and sat next to each other in a traveling compartment. Within a few minutes, another passenger joined them, an elderly woman with gray hair that resembled the tarnish on a silver platter. She wore a modest light-blue wool dress that sat snug against her plump frame. Her smile was warm and cheery, reminding Adelia of her grandma. They made polite introductions.

"Aren't you a picture-perfect young couple," the woman said as she pulled a ball of yarn and a well-worn crochet hook from her bag at her side.

Daniel squeezed Adelia's hand and, as always, a flush of heat invaded her cheeks. She lay her head back against the headrest and wiggled in her seat to find the most comfortable spot in preparation for the near three-hour ride to Oxford. As the train departed, her eyes were already heavy with the promise of sleep. She didn't want to think of anything just now. Being here with Daniel's hand grasping her own was enough.

When she awoke, they weren't but half an hour from the Oxford station. Daniel smiled as she stirred from her slumber. She looked down to see that he still held her hand. The sense of safety she felt with him was undeniable, like he would never let a minute's harm come to her. He was such a perplexing character at times, studious and educated, delving into his work with a ferocity that resembled her father and all the other academics in his circle. But he could be reckless and fearless, too, and unafraid of his vulnerability. Just the same, he could be guarded and awkward, and as insecure as you could get. Above all, he was loyal, and respectful of the people he let into his world. He embodied just about every quality a person could want in a friend. She couldn't begin to fathom how, in the millions upon millions of people in this world, she could have been this lucky to fine someone so perfect for her. The more she processed it, the more she didn't want this summer to end.

How could she just return to Boston and continue the life she had once lived? She missed her parents, without a doubt, yet she could foresee the hole in her heart when she left England that would be hard to mend. How on earth she had allowed herself to fall so head over heels for this man in such a short time was a great mystery. Here she was, though, brimming with affection for Daniel, unable to imagine that happiness could exist anywhere else without him.

Adelia sat on the bed in the quaint room at the inn, contemplating what she should do for the rest of the evening. After arriving in Oxford, they had stopped by one of Daniel's favorite cafés for a late lunch. Then he took her for an abbreviated version of a walking tour, pointing out some of his favorite sites in the city. He took her past the building where he worked at the university, promising to bring her in for an in-depth tour later in the week. Having worked at Hampton Court for quite a while, he wanted to run a few errands and do some catching up around his apartment. He'd accompanied her back to the inn so she might rest for the evening, assuring her that he would pick her up the next morning for the trip to Cumnor Place.

After a bit of sightseeing, she was more than willing to sneak in a little nap. Daniel had arranged for her to stay at the Golden Rams Inn, a fine example of Tudor architecture, with its timber frame and the steep pitch to its slate tile roof. The building had wonderful character throughout—the only negative being that centuries of settling had made it somewhat unlevel. Its old timbers had taken on a somewhat wavy shape in the upper floors, and walking around her tiny room made her feel like she was on the brink of intoxication at times. Even so, she was pleased that Daniel had chosen such charming accommodation for her visit.

Refreshed and rested, she picked up the local newspaper she'd grabbed from the front desk and thumbed through its pages. Too many thoughts running through her mind prevented her from even beginning to read. She put the paper down on the bed and chuckled to herself. Since the day she'd touched down in England, she had hardly read a newspaper at all. Having tried on several occasions, her mind was never quiet long enough to focus on anything. After a minute or so pacing around the room, she moved over to the lone window.

It was still warm, and the narrow streets of Oxford were alive with people walking along, making their way home from their workday. Though she had only been in the city for a few hours, she was surprised that she hadn't felt or heard any whisperings. No shortage of them at Hampton Court, and Oxford was as rich in history. Even this old inn had to have some secrets to reveal. It didn't make sense that her gift had stopped just because she'd left the palace. She chalked it up to a busy day of travel.

After another lap or two around the room, she decided she was far too restless to just stay inside. A little time outside might clear her mind. She took a cardigan out of her bag, but then dropped it onto the bed, thinking the temperature outside would be far too warm to need one.

Once out on the street, she took in the heavy air, ripe with the smells of the city: blooming flowers mixed with the tantalizing scents of food being served in the local cafés. Oxford was such an interesting locale. A unique blend of old and new sandwiched into one place. She passed by Tudor-era buildings that housed bakeries and shops, with newer façades sprinkled here and there, reminding her that despite all the rich history in the city, progress was still inevitable. She walked along without any real aim or particular place in mind—the time irrelevant. Twisting and turning down the streets, absorbing all the nuances of city life, reminded her of being back home in Boston.

Daniel came to mind. Oxford had been his home since childhood. She imagined that his days were rather predictable—waking up each morning and readying himself for his day ahead, then walking the short distance from his flat to the university. Afterwards, he probably grabbed something for dinner from the local market, went home, read to the wee hours of the morning, and repeated the same routine the next day. This pattern lent credibility to what he had said about being lonely. There was no doubt that, throughout his years in the city, he had managed to explore every nook and cranny. That afternoon, she could barely keep up with all the history he had shared. As a visitor, she was enamored with the timeless old buildings and stories of the city's past. Yet life had to be much different when you lived here day after day. One might start to take for granted what became part of your everyday existence, and there were only so many times you could visit a museum before you became less in awe of what it contained. Daniel was like anyone else, always looking for the next thing to spark his interest.

She looked at her reflection in a shop window. Am I just that—something novel to spark his interest for the moment? Will the affection he professes to have for me fade in time? She almost growled at her reflection. How is it that I'm able to sort out the thoughts and emotions of others who lived so long ago, but can't understand my own feelings in this here and now? Does Daniel really have true affection for me, or am I just a tool he can use to discover what his precious documents can't tell him?

Love was such a complex emotion for her to understand. So foreign, yet so familiar. And full of raging highs and bitter lows. Just as she became comfortable with basking in the euphoria of love, she sabotaged her own happiness with thought, imagining that her peace could not be real—that some hidden agenda lurked in the darkness, waiting to steal away her joy. While she believed herself to be intelligent, she also knew she was naive and inexperienced. That knowledge made her more insecure. Nothing could ever be this real or this good. At least not for her. Could she ever get out of her own way long enough to fully trust another person's intentions?

The café she and Daniel had visited earlier in the day was now closed but she stumbled upon another and stopped to enjoy some evening tea. She sipped at leisure, watching people pass by the windows. The after-work crowd had long dispersed by now, and the streets were filled with those enroute to whatever destination held their evening entertainment. Their mindless chatter filled her with the unpleasant sensation of envy. Just like Besse, there were people of her own age enjoying life as they should. Back in Boston, she'd become complacent in the life she had prescribed to herself, never daring to push for more. While she was filled with regret for the time lost, she had to give some shred of acknowledgement to the progress she had made. On setting out for England, she was determined that this trip would be her chance at reining her life back. Just as Daniel said of himself, she had been irreversibly changed, having achieved what she'd set out to do, and in that she could find peace.

She walked around the city center for the next while, with no real aim in mind but still enjoying herself. When she caught sight of a cabbie parked at the curb, a thought came to her: Daniel promised to pick me up after breakfast tomorrow to visit the old Cumnor site, to see if I can shed light on what happened there the day Amy died. Thing is, he has no idea how difficult that might be for me. I'm not in control of who comes through, or what they want to share.

Now she thought of it, she realized that not one feeling had come through the entire day. She looked around. Most unusual. Perhaps there is something here preventing me from being able to hear the whispering. Daniel would surely be disappointed. She was at the mercy of what energy existed, and its desire to make itself known. The last thing she wanted was for him to be disappointed. My goodness, if I can't get a reading at Cumnor, I hope he doesn't think I made the whole thing up. So much pressure. Hmm, maybe that might be the thing blocking the whispers.

It was then a crazy idea sprang into her head. She looked at the cab, then back up the street. It's a little reckless and even out of character, but why not go out there tonight, alone? The energies are always most powerful when I'm on my own. Maybe, this way, something will surface. Daniel had a way of clouding her mind with the giddy thoughts of a lovesick schoolgirl. Not the best conditions to achieve the desired result.

Somewhat reticent, she approached the driver's door. "Sir, are you on duty?" It came out almost at a whisper.

"Yes, Ma'am. Where do you need to go?"

"Can you get me to the old site of Cumnor Place? It's a few miles out of town."

He looked ahead, blinking a few times. "I'm not sure I know that spot."

"I believe it goes by Wytham Church, or even All Saints Church now."

"Oh, that one." He arched a brow. "It's about three miles out of town. But are you sure you want to go out there now? It's probably locked up for the night." It was clear he thought she was a tourist, and doubted she knew what she was asking.

"I am sure," she said, giving him a determined nod.

"Won't be able to find yourself a cabbie back this late. No buses run out that way after they close either."

"Thank you, but I will figure something out, I am sure."

"Suit yourself then." He motioned for her to hop in the back.

On the way, she used the daylight to her advantage, taking careful note of the route they traveled, knowing full well she would have to walk the three miles back to town later. The sun was easing its way into the west, the sky reminding her of a painter's color pallet. When she exited the cab, she took a moment to appreciate the quaint countryside around her.

Wytham Church was nestled at the entrance to the grounds leading to the large and imposing Wytham Abbey. The building, stretching up into the sky, dominated the surrounding fields and woods. Just as she'd suspected, the weathered iron gate had been locked up for the night. She stood there, peering in at the old building, and there was only one person she could think of. In Amy Robsart's time, the church had been the site of Cumnor Place. Amy had leased her apartments there from Sir Anthony Forester, a friend of her husband, so her presence couldn't be seen as anything out of the ordinary. All through her life, she and Dudley had never settled in an estate of their own, despite Amy's sizable inheritance from her father. That must have been difficult, to never have a place to call her own. Adelia could only surmise that it had made her feel unsettled. It was reported that she inhabited the finest chambers of Cumnor Place, which made sense given her elevated social status.

In the years following Amy's death, the estate had passed through its fair share of owners. A long-established legend existed, about her ghost haunting the halls of Cumnor each year at Christmas. It had been a favorite tale passed down through the years by the servants. Something used to frighten the young staff into submission.

In the 19th century, a group of villagers and clergy sought to rid her spirit from the halls of Cumnor Place. According to legend, they cast her ghostly essence into a nearby pond, which never again froze over, even through the harshest of winters.

While Cumnor had been cleared of Amy's presence—or so it was said—over time, the building fell into disrepair and was partially demolished, with portions of it incorporated into the Wytham Church. Standing at the gate, Adelia found it difficult to discern just what aspects were from the original structure. The most visible part of the church was the great stone tower, with its distinguished clock face staring down at her. If Daniel were here, he would have no problem pointing out those details. But he wasn't here—a choice she had made on her own.

Now that the sun was fading, she started to second-guess her decision to come out alone. It had been a foolish quest. Alone in a place that was both unfamiliar and inaccessible. And she wasn't suitably dressed for the three-mile trek back into Oxford in the dark. As she contemplated her situation, she tried hard not to scold herself for being so foolish, getting herself stuck out in the middle of nowhere, in a place she had only heard about from Daniel's stories.

With darkness approaching, she surveyed her surroundings again. Just beyond Wytham Church stood the enormous Wytham Abbey. Beyond that lay the infamous Wytham woods. Legend had it that the near-thousand-acre woods had once been the traveling path for monks on pilgrimage. Though it had been gifted to the university of Oxford in the 1940's as a place of research for naturalists, it was still steeped in local lore, which said that the woods were haunted with the souls of the monks. She knew that a place with such a reputed presence was not ideal for someone with her abilities. The last thing she wanted was to go traipsing through ancient woods in the dark with the energy of hundreds of long-dead monks as her companion.

She thought back to Daniel's childhood fear of dead monks following him home. This was a land steeped in terrifying legends. Ones that were not frightening to just children, it would seem. Feeling almost cornered by her fear, she moved back against the perimeter wall and slid into a seated position. seeking security of some kind.

Just what did I hope to gain by coming out here? Some part of her wanted more than anything to find the secrets of Amy Robsart, if only to impress Daniel, or at least to give her abilities some credibility in his eyes. She closed her eyes and leaned her head back against the cool stone, rough against her hair. At first, she felt nothing, just the light tickle of the breeze against her skin. Then a familiar sensation—a chill—moved over her like an invisible fog, enveloping her entire body. She shuddered. This place was so unfamiliar—unlike the corridors of Hampton Court. She almost feared what would come through here. If she felt overcome, there was nowhere to run for safety. Yet a curiosity burned within her—a desire to discover what or who desired to be known.

She released her breath, slow and steady, and focused, listening with her whole body, slipping into a state of relaxation she couldn't remember achieving before. Then the whispers came, and she almost flinched at the rapidity of the waves. They were loud, then quiet, then loud again, the cycle repeating over and over. Voices surrounded her, yet she knew she was alone. It was too much, but she had to continue. How? She thought back to her grandma's mentoring, and did something she had never tried before, not with real success anyway. It was a gamble, but one she had to take. She concentrated on a specific time—Amy's time—allowing the images of the few known portraits of her to enter her mind, focusing on the details of her face.

Then, as if she had been able to will it to life, a specific voice came to her. It came in hushed tones, as though sharing a secret with another person. She listened, a silent witness to a conversation between two women. However, much to her disappointment, it became apparent that it wasn't Amy Robsart. There were nuances to their accents she recognized as Tudor but, as the image of the two women materialized in her mind, she saw that they were gathered in a kitchen. Dried herbs and large iron pots hung from the walls, and a steady fire in the hearth illuminated the women in shadowy profile, giving her no clear image of either face.

"You must tell no one, you hear?" the older woman said.

"I dare not," the younger figure responded.

"If the authorities catch wind that you were in the house, Jane, it could spell disaster for you. Do you understand?"

"I do, Maggie. I do."

Adelia sensed the apprehension between them.

"The mistress was bound to get herself into trouble long before this happened." Maggie tutted to herself as she shook her head. "She never should have mixed herself up with Sir Anthony. They were both married. He is in service to her very husband. I knew all along that no good could come of this."

Jane pulled a pot off the wall. "She wanted us all to go to the Abbington fair. She was most insistent. I just did not think it was right for me to leave, so I stayed behind without her knowing. I should have just gone."

Regret radiated from the younger woman. It was clear she knew that she had gotten herself into a predicament by disobeying her mistress.

"You are right about that," Maggie said. "You would have saved yourself a whole heap of trouble. She had misdeeds in her mind. We both know that. I can't say as I blame her, though, with her husband floundering about with the queen right there for the world to see."

"Sir Anthony promised her they could run away together. I heard them speak of it just days ago." She proceeded to fill the pot with chopped vegetables. "She wanted us all out of the house so they could take their leave."

Adelia realized her mouth was hanging open. Is it really possible that Amy intended to run away? With Sir Anthony Forster, of all people. This was not a theory she had heard before.

"He was never going to leave with her, and you and I know that's the god's honest truth. Where would they go? They would have brought so much shame upon themselves, there could be no chance at a better life. No money. No shelter. A bad lot, no matter which way you spin it."

"Yes, Maggie, but she would have been free from the sorrow her husband brought her."

"On that point, I can agree. Still, she would have traded one sorrow for another. When they come poking around here, you tell them you were gone with the rest of us, you hear?"

"Yes, Maggie, I will never speak a word about what he did. I just wish I didn't know."

Adelia strained to hear more but the voices kept fading in and out, making it too difficult to distinguish what was being said. Never in her

wildest dreams did she expect such a revelation to come her way. She
was used to mundane conversations coming through but, for once,
here was something of true significance. While she had not been privy
to hearing from Amy Robsart herself, this was just as good.

She recalled that Thomas Blount, one of Robert Dudley's men sent
to Cumnor to investigate Amy's death, had referred to her as having
a "strange mind." At the time, that meant she had been melancholy
and possibly contemplating suicide. As she thought back to the conversation between Jane and Maggie, a different picture emerged. If
one could believe the scuttle of two servants, it seems that Amy had
considered running off with Sir Anthony Forster, not ending her own
life. Jane and Maggie had known of this plot but being mere servants in
the house, they would not have dared utter a word about it to anyone,
let alone anyone tied to the inquest.

Jane was in the house the day of Amy's death. If she had been bold
enough to disclose that information, she would have put herself at
considerable risk. It was clear that she knew who was responsible for
Amy's death, and it wasn't Amy. She had said, "I wish I did not know
what he did." So she knew the man who had hastened Amy to her
end. Had she spoken up to anyone, other than Maggie, she might
well have been his next target. She couldn't blame her for keeping it a
secret, nor could she blame Maggie for encouraging her to do so. The
life of a servant in those days was far from protected. Knowing the
superstitions of the time, poor Jane might have been accused of some
sinister plot to bring harm upon her mistress. The young woman had
far too much to lose, including her life.

When her skin prickled with warmth, she knew her window into
Jane and Maggie's predicament had closed. She was grateful for what
she'd seen and heard but it left many questions that had yet to be
answered. Darkness now shrouded her, and her tummy fluttered in

response. How long was I with Jane and Maggie? She rose to her feet, turning back to the gate to look at the church once more. The looming shape of the old building looked foreboding. How can a place made solely to praise God hold such dark secrets? The question intrigued her. Most houses of worship had survived dark and turbulent pasts, especially here in England, with persecution and death a common theme for many centuries.

Since the day she came to understand her ability, she had seldom felt alone, always aware of the presence of the unseen. Wytham was no exception. If anything, she felt almost crowded here, like there were more voices wanting to be heard than ever before. Even though her grandma had assured her that the whispering would never bend to her will, she now wondered if there was a possibility. She came here set on retrieving answers—decided to zero in on a specific time and person—and because of that, was able to find some of the answers she was seeking.

It hardly seemed like a coincidence. Tomorrow, she would return with Daniel. With luck, she might remove some more of the shroud that surrounded Amy's death. While she could just about contain her excitement at the prospect, her logic told her she should focus on getting herself back to the inn. She imagined the innkeeper would be irritated by her returning at so late an hour.

As she turned to make her way back up the pathway to the main road, a rustling not more than a few yards away had her nearly jumping out of her skin. Be it man or beast, it mattered little, because she had nothing to defend herself against it. All she possessed was her tiny handbag, and even its contents were minimal. To date, she was unaware of any woman who successfully fended off an attacker with a tube of lipstick. She stood stock still, her heart racing, not sure what she should do next.

"Why the hell are you out here alone?" a man called from the shadows.

She trembled when the dark figure emerged from behind a tree. Then she couldn't believe her eyes on seeing that it was Daniel, and breathed a hesitant sigh of relief, not sure whether to be pleased or irked at his presence.

"Why the hell are you out here?" she demanded. "You nearly scared me out of my wits."

"You first," he shot back, his tone stern, nothing like she'd heard from him before.

"I...wanted to think. I can't feel anything with a bunch of tourists about." She pursed her lips, not liking the feeling of being scolded like a child, or of being made to feel this way. Despite Daniel's protective nature, she was, after all, a grown woman, more than capable of making her own decisions, even if they were bad ones. To be fair, this was a bad one.

"That never stopped you at Hampton Court," he said.

"Well, this is different."

"How so?"

She almost stomped her foot. "I don't know, Daniel, I just wanted to come here tonight. By myself. Things come through clearer when I am alone." She didn't know why she even needed to explain her actions to him. He wasn't her guardian.

He remained silent for a long moment. "Okay. Do you want me to go?"

"No! Now that you have scared me half to death, I think you should stay." Her brows felt tight as she glared at him.

"Very good."

She couldn't be sure in the gloom but she thought he'd said that with a sardonic grin. "I rather think I loathe you sometimes." She

wanted to slap him but thought better of it. What an infuriating man
he can be at times. Okay, maybe he's right to be angry with me. It's
dark and isolated, and I shouldn't really be out here alone, but I will
never admit that to him.

"That is a shame, Adelia. I like you very much."

She ignored his all-too-satisfied grin. The breeze was cool, and she
clutched her bare arms, running her fingers along them for warmth.
Daniel, observant to the slightest detail, insisted it was time to leave.

"I guess we'd better start walking," she said.

"Suit yourself, but I brought my car."

"You own a car?" she asked, incredulous. "You never mentioned it
before."

"I didn't need it back at Hampton Court. I've kept it parked at
home over the summer. Truth is, I rarely use it anyway. I walk just
about everywhere I go, and the streets of the city are too crowded to
drive most days."

"I would much prefer the car ride back to the inn, if you would be
so kind, Doctor Brown?"

"My pleasure, Ms. Grey." He smiled as he led her along the path.

Once they pulled onto the open road, Daniel jumped into a stern
lecture about her irresponsible adventure. He was most displeased at
the thought of her wandering around an old churchyard at night.
While all the folklore about ghostly monks was nothing more than
fantasy, that didn't mean a lady should be out there on her own. More
harm could befall her from the living than the spirits of the dead.

As she took the brunt of his displeasure, she contemplated whether
or not to bother sharing her discovery. From his periodic pauses in
ticking her off, it was clear that he wanted to ask. Despite being
tempted, she decided it was best to keep quiet about it. Hearing the
whispers came easy to her at times but understanding the meaning

was a different matter. She wanted time to process everything a little further.

While intuitive, Daniel was easily distracted by questions, so she kept the conversation centered on his plan for tomorrow, and what time they should meet in the morning. When he pulled up outside the inn, he smiled, then leaned in to kiss her forehead. It was the first time she had ever felt his lips against her skin. Though it wasn't the kiss she'd thought of all too many times, nor the one that had been so irritatingly interrupted, she liked it just the same.

"We can do all the exploring your heart desires tomorrow, Adelia. You need some sleep, as do I. It has been a long day."

She slid her hand against his soft cheek, his warmth seeping into her fingers. "Tomorrow then, nine o'clock." Leaning forward, she placed her lips upon his cheek, the smooth scent of his cologne filling her nostrils.

Chapter Fifteen

In the morning, Adelia put on one of the nicer dresses she'd packed for the trip. It was the most flattering option, an emerald-green sheath dress, which she wore with a short-sleeved ivory jacket. She lifted the pearl necklace with teardrop pendant from the bureau where she'd left it last night and fixed it around her neck. Even though it was early, the summer heat radiated through the window of her tiny room.

As she descended the steep and narrow staircase to the breakfast area, she couldn't help but think about the one where Amy Robsart lost her life. Although made of stone, they would still be considered dangerous by today's standards. She took careful steps, trying not to lose her footing in her low-heeled shoes, understanding how difficult a task this would have been in a sixteenth-century gown like Amy would have worn daily. It wouldn't be unthinkable that she might have taken a fall in her haste to meet Sir Anthony. Still, that didn't explain what Jane said about "not believing what he did." A critical part of the story needed to be uncovered.

Once on the first floor, she entered a side room that had been set up with a few tables and chairs. None of the furniture matched, with the exception of the delicate white and yellow floral-patterned tablecloths. A long narrow table, set up along the west wall, had fresh-brewed tea and little pitchers of milk, honey, and sugar cubes laid out on it. She prepared herself a cup of tea and placed a biscuit on a small white porcelain plate, adding a dollop of Devonshire cream to the side. With Daniel due to arrive at 9 o'clock, she seated herself at one of the tables to wait, confident he would be punctual. She had come down a little early hoping to give herself time to prepare for the day.

"Did you rest well?" the innkeeper asked on entering the room.

She watched the small man walk over to the serving table, where he checked if anything needed refilled. His button-up dress shirt was in dire need of a good ironing, and that made her smile because, despite his somewhat disheveled appearance, he reminded her of someone's sweet uncle. The kind who always had a funny story to tell.

"I slept very well, thank you," she answered.

"Are you off to explore the city today then?" He brushed some invisible crumbs from a tablecloth and straightened a chair or two.

"Actually, I am headed back to Wytham Church."

"Wytham Church, you say?" He looked to his left, as if searching for a thought. "Oh, you mean All Saints Church, at the Abbey?"

"Yes, that's the one." She took another sip of her tea.

"Some call it the old Wytham Church, some call it All Saints Church. Just depends on who you ask, I guess. Things are always changing around here."

"I went out there yesterday evening but it was closed for the night. I hope to get a chance to look inside today."

"It is a peculiar place. You will find the inside quite a mash up. Over the years, they have added and tore down. Indeed, there is a little of just about every generation left in that building."

"I'm interested in the parts that were once the old Cumnor Place. It was a house where Amy Robsart resided in the fifteen hundreds."

"Oh, yes." He smiled, then pulled the chair opposite Adelia out from the table and sat on it. "My daughter once did a report on her when she was in grade school. My wife and I took her to the site to look at a few of the old surviving windows. There isn't much left, mind you. House was mostly demolished. Amy is buried not far from here, at Saint Mary's. I would recommend a stop there if you get the time."

Adelia sat up, intrigued. "What did your daughter discover about Amy? That seems like a pretty intense topic for a grade-school project."

"Well, most of what she found was just the same old stuff you find in history books. It was my wife, who has passed on now, who took the most interest in the story."

"Oh, I am sorry to hear about your wife. My condolences."

He inhaled a slow breath through a sad smile. "She has been gone nearly six years now. She always took an interest in the old tales of how Amy haunted the halls of Cumnor. She even wrote a poem about her." He nodded to himself. "Mary loved poetry. Even had some of her work published in the local Gazette."

Adelia drew back the urge to clap. "How remarkable. I would love to have read some of her work."

"You can, as a matter of fact. I have an old book just behind the desk. I read it now and then when there isn't much going on around here. I can fetch it, if you like?"

"Please do, if it isn't too much trouble? I have a little time before my friend arrives."

With a bright smile, the elderly man got up and nearly ran to the front desk of the tiny lobby to retrieve the treasured book. Adelia couldn't help but chuckle at his enthusiasm to share his wife's poetry. It brought her some inner joy to see the devotion he still harbored for her memory. In a matter of seconds, he returned with a weathered old leather-bound book that had loose yellowed pages tucked within. He unlatched a small leather strap and opened the book with tender care. As he thumbed through its pages, she got the impression he knew exactly where to find the page he sought. Its tattered corners showed wear, no doubt from the countless times he'd handled the old tome.

"Here it is," he said, handing the book over to her. "This is the one she wrote about Cumnor Hall."

She accepted it with a delicate touch, as if handling a priceless artifact in a museum, cognizant of the value it meant to the man across the table. Within their silence, she traced a fingertip across the beautifully crafted script. As they were still alone, she decided to read the words aloud:

"Peace to the ghost who walks these halls that are no more,

A vision of a living breathing soul

Who dwells in bliss and grief in tandem,

The Norfolk beauty, a June bride

Draped in black velvet in the palace of Richmond,

Behold, a sight fit for a king.

The carnal match of fire and sorrow

Reunited and departed time again,

Gifts meant to sooth the passage of days between

Love tarnished by ambition,

Devotion forsaken by selfish desire.

Death meets the June bride on a staircase most foul,

Her memories clouded by deceit and treachery,

Her story, left to the ages.

Yet, the June bride still walks in time,

She is not lost as once was planned,

She still walks the halls that once graced this land."

She took a long, slow breath, reflecting on Mary's intricate description of Amy's life. A June bride, married in the presence of King Edward VI himself. How many days and years she had held onto the love for her husband, only to be forsaken in the end by his ambitions. And while her murderer remained a mystery, she would never have met such an end had she not chosen Robert Dudley to be her husband. Regardless of his role in her demise, he had at least some level of responsibility for her plight.

Her story, left to the ages, was the line that most impacted her. The truth about that day mattered little—countless people had already written her story—yet, no matter how much they'd tried to cease her existence, Amy remained.

"Your wife captures Amy's story in such a way that I can't help but wish I'd known her. Mary. She shows so much respect for Amy's life, rather than just focusing on her death. This is really beautiful. Thank you so much for sharing it with me." She looked back down at the book, turning a page or two more.

"I am glad to share it, Miss. My Mary would spend many an hour out in the garden penning her poems. It was something she found soothing to her soul. She said it helped to calm the whispering." He shrugged. "Whatever that was."

"The whispering?" Her face went cold as she stared in disbelief at the man.

"Just something she would say when her mind was racing with thought. She was a quiet sort of person who kept to herself as much as running an old inn would allow. Always had an interest in old things and old places." He looked up to his left, as if some distant memory was replaying in his mind. "So, you are American?" He focused back on her. "What brings you here to Oxford?"

"Yes, I'm from Boston, actually. I came here to stay with my grandma at her apartment in Hampton Court. I just took a short holiday here to explore Oxford with a friend."

"Hampton Court? My, your grandmother must be a lady of great importance to have been granted an apartment there. Only Her Majesty the Queen can make such appointments."

"Actually, it was her father who granted the honor to my grandfather, Colonel Grey. My grandma was a Babington before they married."

"Babington?" he exclaimed with uncontained excitement. "Well, so was my Mary before we wed. What did you say your grandmother's name was?"

"M-Marjorie," she stuttered, unable to dampen her surprise.

He looked off again to his left. "Hmm... Doesn't ring a bell. Maybe they were cousins or something. Mary came from a large family, and in all the years we were married, I cannot say I ever met them all."

Adelia sat in stunned silence. Is it possible that Mary was a distant relation to my grandma? If she did possess the ability to hear the whispering, it would make perfect sense, as Grandma said it was a gift passed down through the female line of the family. The poem she'd just read now became so much more. What did Mary sense the day she took her daughter to the old Cumnor Place? Perhaps she felt and heard something just as I did?

She thumbed through a few more pages of the book, pausing to read certain sections to herself.

Beyond these designs, we are still clever. Always holding the key to the hidden reaches of our mind, just beyond our grasp. And so, the perpetual mystery remains, forever trapped as the ghost.

She glanced at the entrance to make sure Daniel hadn't yet arrived. Possibilities raced through her mind—nothing new considering her habit of overthinking. *Is it possible that I came to this particular inn in Oxford just by chance? That in all of the places in the city to stay, I ended up here by mere coincidence alone? The prospect of holding the writings of someone who may well have been my relation, possessing the same ability as me, could not be a simple happenstance.* She straightened in the chair and glanced from the book to Mary's husband. *Can the whispers call a person to a place? If my presence here is not simply by chance, then what more awaits me in Oxford?*

A vague sense of apprehension crept into her as she traced the lettering across the page. *Did Mary want me to know what she knew? Did Amy Robsart want her story told?* She closed her eyes as too many thoughts flooded her brain, then nearly jumped out of her skin on hearing the old wooden front door creaking open.

It was good to see the familiar figure of Daniel enter the foyer. The innkeeper got up to greet him, and she listened to their cheery exchange echo from the hall. Then Daniel walked into the morning room, greeting her with his chipper smile. He was dressed more casual than normal in basic slacks, and his button-up shirt wasn't nearly as starched as she'd grown accustomed to. Indeed, he looked like a man about to embark on an afternoon of leisure. She almost felt overdressed for the occasion.

"Good morning, Daniel."

"And good morning to you, too, Adelia."

She sipped the remains of her tea and stood, about to tidy up her plate and cup.

"No, Miss, allow me," the innkeeper said, his tone polite.

She acquiesced, picked up the leather-bound volume and placed it into his hands. "I do appreciate you sharing this with me."

"You remind me so much of her," he said. "My Mary, that is. It must be something in the Babington line. Perhaps you were family after all."

She smiled as she nodded, said goodbye, and followed Daniel out to the car.

As they drove through the narrow streets of Oxford, Daniel swerved in and out between parked cars, doing his best to miss the passing buses that transported tourists and locals alike.

"There aren't many cars in the city for this very reason," he said. "Most of us use the bus around here. Just too narrow to get around."

"Just why do you have a car then?" she asked, aware that her heart was thundering as she held the dashboard. Even in Boston, she never really had the need to use a car. Her entire world was within walking distance. She could have expanded that world, mind you, but it was her preference to keep it as small as possible.

"On the weekends, believe it or not, I do a bit of traveling. This country is rich with wonderful places to explore, you know."

"Yes, I do," she agreed. "I suppose, if I lived here, I would want to explore every square inch of this country too."

"You could, you know?"

"What?" She gave him an expectant look.

"Live here," he answered, without hesitation

"I could. I won't say the thought hasn't crossed my mind. I think I would love it here."

"Then it is a deal. You will stay in England, and I will show you every nook and cranny of this country. It will take us a great many years, but I think we have the time."

"It is not a deal, Daniel," she said, her laugh incredulous. "You know my parents would be most disagreeable about me going on a summer holiday and never returning home."

"What is in Boston that is not here, though? Well...besides your parents."

"I don't know, really," she answered, looking out her window for a moment.

"You could go to school here. I would highly recommend Oxford. They have outstanding professors, or so I hear. Of course, there are other schools in England, too, but none of their names come to mind at the minute."

She chuckled. "You make a compelling argument. Really, you do." She shifted her handbag in her lap, trying to think of a way to siderail the conversation. "Tell me, Daniel, just what do you hope I can do when we reach the church?"

"I honestly have no idea." He glanced at her and shrugged. "I guess I was just hoping you could shed some light on what might have happened to her. Anything that might help me understand her last days."

"That's a tall order," she said. "Things only come through to me at their will. What I feel, hear, or see is entirely by chance. They have to want me to know. I cannot pinpoint a certain person or a certain time. It all has to be on their terms."

"Have you ever tried it? Summon a certain person, I mean?"

"You make me sound like a gypsy fortune teller, channeling the dead in a seance or something."

"I didn't mean to. I just wondered if it is something you can control, or does it control you?"

"Up to this point, it controls me. My grandma assures me there are ways to control it, but I haven't figured that out yet. Perhaps in time."

He smiled, laying his free hand on hers. "If you hear nothing, then you hear nothing. It is a beautiful morning, and despite the promise of afternoon showers, the day should be just about perfect. Let's agree to go sightseeing today, and if something happens, we will take it as it comes."

"Agreed." She allowed a smile, glad to feel the pressure subsiding. Daniel wanted her to feel something, but it helped knowing that he wouldn't be disappointed if she didn't. As she watched the passing scenery, she marveled at how freeing it was to no longer be overwhelmed by anxiety. She understood what her fear was now, or what it wasn't—no longer some nameless force that inhabited her. Now it had a meaning. Her gift was invisible to the world but it made her content with being different. Daniel made her content too.

As they turned down the old lane, a mix of excitement and apprehension bubbled in her tummy at the sight of the old church just up the road. Daniel pulled the car over into a grassy berm and cut the engine.

"Shall we?"

She smiled and exited the car. He almost ran to her side, closed her door and linked her arm in his. There were already a few people walking around the grounds, as the gates had just been unlocked. The church and grounds were open to the public to explore, and visitors took photos and chatted as they milled about. Much to Adelia's surprise, there were no guided tours or staff on hand to answer questions, as was the case at Hampton Court. Visitors were permitted in any area that was accessible, with the only expectation that they deposit a donation in a little wooden box that sat outside the church's door.

Once inside, she found herself enamored with the mixture of architectural styles, evidence of the continued transformation the place had undergone over the centuries.

After making a small donation in the box at the door, Daniel led the way to a few gothic-styled arch windows at one end. His eyes lit up as he explained how they were some of the few remnants of the old

Cumnor place. Adelia focused on them, thinking something might come through, but she was met with pure silence. She walked around the church, sliding her hand along its old stonework and the ancient wood of its pews. Still nothing. Daniel never seemed to be disappointed, just walking along, sharing details and bits of information about the church and the nearby abbey.

Frustration bubbled deep down as she struggled to keep her mind at ease. She wanted to feel something, even if it was just to validate her ability a little more to Daniel. By now, they'd wandered around the grounds for a couple of hours, and she hadn't felt a single thing. She couldn't understand why things had come through so clear and fast last night, but not today. Nothing. She couldn't shake the possibility that her deep-felt desire of wanting something to occur was the problem.

As she glanced around at the other visitors, she considered that she had never experienced anything with so many people around. Maybe that time in the chapel, but that was her first time. For an obscure church in the country, there sure were a lot of tourists. Maybe her grandma was right when she'd suggested that her attention on Daniel had a way of changing things. He had a way of mixing her mind up, his presence making her feel guarded and vulnerable all at the same time. Though, on more than one occasion, she had experienced the whispers with him near, but that didn't negate the fact they'd been around each other several other times when nothing occurred. Did the whispers not come through on those days, or did her attention on Daniel block them without her even knowing?

After walking through every part of the church, several times, she was desperate to clear her mind with some fresh air. They departed the stuffy interior for the brightness of the afternoon outside. Out in the courtyard, she paced along with no particular destination in mind.

With any luck, some distance from the others might help her regain her focus. She had developed her abilities at a rapid pace but their lack of reliability was still problematic. Her trust was shaky, like a wizard picking up a wand for the first time.

As they exited the courtyard through an old gate at the perimeter wall, a light rain tickled her face, so they sought cover under a nearby tree. She slid down to sit at its enormous base, with Daniel following suit. They remained silent as they looked up at the church's old square clock tower.

"That is enough for today," he said, his voice slicing through the serenity of the afternoon shower, "let's have some fun." He sprung to his feet, stretching out a hand to help her up.

"Fun? I thought our trip to Oxford was for your research." She wasn't too disappointed that she might be off the hook for today.

He shrugged. "We work too hard. The great thing about history is it will always be there tomorrow. Nothing will change. On that we can rely."

"Good point," she said, slipping her arm into his. As they walked back to the car, a low rumble of thunder came from above.

"Oh no," Daniel shouted. He grabbed her hand and set off at a furious jog.

She couldn't stop laughing, struggling to keep up and catch her breath at the same time. He flung her door open and she fell into her seat, still giggling at his dramatic display.

He wasted no time in starting the car and pulling out onto the main road. As her laughter eased, a welcome sense of relief settled over her, and her breath fell into rhythm with the slow swish of the windshield wipers. The trip back into the city was short, three miles as she remembered, yet the lush green countryside was a welcome change of scenery and pace.

"So, what adventure shall we embark on now, Doctor Brown?" His newfound unpredictability made her all the more curious as to what he had in mind.

"Doctor Brown?" he said, his eyes wide. "Please, call me Danny."

"Danny? You like *Danny*?" She almost laughed at the sound of the name. For her, it didn't fit with the polished intellectual persona he normally sported.

"No, I actually hate it. My aunt Lois calls me that and I absolutely despise it."

"What's gotten into you today? Has Oxford brought out some long-suppressed side of the esteemed Doctor Brown?"

"I'm just happy to be here with you, that's all." He glanced behind then changed gears. "I don't want us to waste a moment. Don't you ever just want to throw caution to the wind and do something unexpected?"

That, for one thing, was unexpected. She touched her wet hair, now sticky from the mixture of rain and her setting spray. The umbrella she'd brought along wasn't doing her much good sitting in her suitcase back at the inn, and she was sure she looked a mess. Daniel had yet again managed to catch her off guard. He had this way of being romantic and chivalric at the same time. It was unanticipated on her part. She thought she knew his type so well, yet around every corner he managed to surprise her. He was subtle and exciting, could be cautious yet courageous, and there was nothing boring about him. If anything, she longed for more time to get to know his many sides.

"Well?" he asked, nudging her arm with his elbow.

"My life pretty much revolves around the unexpected these days, or have you forgotten?" She worked a big smile, trying to bury the bashfulness she felt at his compliment.

"Yes, I suppose you are right on that point." He followed this with a boyish grin. "I have just been cooped up in the office too long. Besides, I want to see your adventurous side."

Heat surged into her cheeks and she looked out her window. "I am pretty sure you are far more adventurous than I, Daniel. I don't want to disappoint you. After all, you are the one who goes wandering all over Scotland with nothing more than a map."

"You would love Scotland, but I have told you that before. Someday we will go."

She looked at him. "I imagine I would love Scotland, but I think Ireland is higher on my list. My mother's family was Irish, and Boston has such strong Irish roots too. I grew up surrounded by the culture. I always said I would like to go there someday."

"Irish, you say? That's perfect." He took a sharp left, and she shrieked as her handbag went tumbling to the floor. "Oops, my apologies." He chuckled as he maneuvered around oncoming traffic and parked cars. "Are you hungry?"

"A little, actually," she confessed, catching her breath. Neither of them had eaten since breakfast, so she was on the brink of ravenous. However, her stomach was now in her chest as a result of Daniel's questionable driving, and hunger was not at the forefront of her thoughts. She was grateful that he didn't own a motorcycle. If he did, she was sure she would have politely refused that adventure after today.

"I know the perfect place for us," he said as he turned onto a quiet street. The traffic was less congested and his driving became smoother and less erratic. "We can park at my flat and walk there. The rain looks like it will be ending soon. It will be the perfect evening for a stroll through the city. I promise not to get you home at a reasonable hour."

"Who are you?" she asked, smiling, though throwing him an astonished look. He responded with his brilliant grin and a coy wink.

She stared back in wonderment, trying to unravel how that glance had managed to render her as mindless as a love-struck schoolgirl.

After parking the car, he led the way through the narrow streets of Oxford on foot, telling her he had the most perfect Irish pub in mind called The Molloy. There were several Irish pubs in Oxford, but he assured her this one was the most authentic.

"It's as close as I can get you to the real Ireland tonight."

She just chuckled, shaking her head. In truth, she had never been to a pub. A nightlife for her back in Boston did not exist. She gripped her bottom lip between her teeth, a little nervous at the prospect of the pub being crowded. Come on, Adelia, shake that feeling off. It's the old you, who no longer exists in this new landscape. She pushed her natural instincts into the background, convincing herself that this experience would be worth a little discomfort. Daniel will be there. I have nothing to fear. No matter how overwhelmed I am by the people around me, I just have to focus on him.

As they walked along, Daniel shared factual information about every building they passed. She supposed some people might find his constant need to narrate somewhat irritating. Not her. She didn't find it the least bit bothersome. In fact, she liked having a built-in tour guide everywhere she went. She had grown up with her father doing the same thing, so it wasn't anything out of the ordinary. It was a sort of language of love for men in the academic world. Sharing something they loved with another had a deeper meaning than could be observed on the surface. She saw his sharing of knowledge as an unspoken display of affection, even if it was subconscious on his part. In just a few blocks, he'd showered her with more romantic sentiment than a delivery truck full of rose bouquets.

First, though, came an impromptu stop at The Martyrs' Memorial. Resembling the famed Eleanor Crosses that had once dotted England, the gothic-style memorial had been erected to commemorate the burning of three prominent protestant leaders during the reign of Mary I. According to Daniel, they had each suffered a cruel death, with two being burned at the stake just outside the walls of the city. The story was tragic and moving, reminding her of a gloomy spring day long ago when she had visited Salem Massachusetts with her parents. As her memory trailed back, a shiver slid down her spine. Learning about the ill-fated women and men of the notorious witch trials had left her with such a sickening feeling in her stomach that she had faked a toothache just to be able to return to the hotel early. Now that she knew of the whispers, she could surmise walking in a place where such atrocities had been committed was far more than a play on her emotions.

Not entirely unexpected, the brief detour took nearly two hours. Daniel resumed the trek to their intended destination, and not a moment too soon, for Adelia's empty stomach had started making audible groans. After a block or two, they stopped in front of a building with a mossy-green painted exterior. Old wooden casement windows, their leaded glass panes foggy with the recent rain, gave a glimpse into the happenings inside. The door was surrounded by a miniaturized version of a portico, painted a crisp alabaster, which reminded Adelia of something straight out of the Georgian architecture in Bath, rather than an Irish pub. If she had to guess, this building had been repurposed many times over its lifespan. Every painted surface told the story of the last few centuries of change.

The smell of familiar food reminded her of Boston, sending a shockwave of heat through her heart. Even from outside the door, the sweet sound of an Irish fiddle could be heard. Her anticipation swelled as Daniel led her inside. It was early evening—dinner time for most city dwellers—but the establishment was already busy.

She looked around the gloomy interior, its walls painted in the same mossy-green palette as the exterior. The decor conveyed an eclectic blend of Irish pride, with pictures of famous writers and poets on the walls, along with posters of famed actors or theatrical productions. Old instruments and other forms of nostalgia hung from any of the remaining spaces, giving the room a bit of a cluttered feel, though it was also homely. The music of the live performers, chatter of the crowd, and the tight configuration of tables played against her senses, threatening to overload her. She grasped Daniel's hand tighter, her own sweaty. He seemed in tune with her sudden rise in body temperature and led her through the crowd to a small wooden table in a corner.

When she slid into her chair, she couldn't hold back a breath of relief. The noise was all around her, but this dimly lit oasis felt removed from the chaos. Daniel brushed his fingers across the back of her hands, and that contact helped ground her. He asked a passing waitress for a glass of water for Adelia and a pint for himself, then leaned back in his chair, nodding to the beat of the bodhrán drum.

"I guess I should have asked you if you also wanted a pint." He arched a brow. "It looks like you could use one."

"Water is good." She glanced around. "This looks like it's a pretty popular spot."

"If it is too much for you, we can go," he said. "I guess this isn't exactly the most ideal spot to unwind after such a long day."

"It's fine." She tapped the back of his hand with her fingertips. "Really, it's wonderful, Daniel."

The waitress soon returned with their drinks. Daniel asked if they might have menus, and she departed to retrieve them. Adelia lifted her glass and drank with haste. She tried not to gulp down the whole lot in one swallow but the cool liquid felt exquisite. Never in her life had a simple glass of water tasted so magnificent. Her burning flesh started to cool and, little by little, she grew used to the swirl of activity around her. Keeping a sharp focus on Daniel helped the background noise fade to a tolerable level.

Once they had their menus in hand, the pangs of hunger she'd suffered earlier returned. She scrutinized the limited selection with a careful eye.

"What shall we have?" Daniel asked, studying the menu as he would a newly discovered treasure in a long-forgotten archive.

"I'm undecided," she said. "Colcannon is good, but it's hardly an Irish meal without boxty. Oh, and soda bread is a must."

"You had my heart the minute you said boxty. Add a side of smooth creamy Irish butter and that makes it perfect." He slapped his menu onto the table. "Let's get it all."

"Perfection," she said. "I really am hungrier than I thought."

After they placed their order, Daniel leaned against the back of his chair again, his pint in hand. He turned to face the band, now playing The Wild Rover. A few of the patrons were on the tiny space reserved as a makeshift dance floor, their glasses raised, and the entire pub came to life as they chanted in unison, "No, nay, never. No, nay, never, no more."

Adelia and Daniel laughed as they raised their glasses.

"Sláinte," he called out over the crowd, and then started singing along. Adelia followed suit.

Returning to herself, she watched as his blue eyes shimmered in the light. If anyone told her two months ago that she would be sitting in an Oxford pub with a handsome man, singing along with the crowd, she might have been hard pressed to believe such a thing. Now, in this smoke-filled corner, she couldn't imagine another place she would rather be. The prospect of her parents being appalled that their daughter was in such a place, almost delighted her, and she couldn't help feeling somewhat liberated in such a bold undertaking. In that moment, she understood the appeal of rebellion in people her own age. Perhaps she was a little late to this realization. Yet, in fairness, she hadn't anticipated having such a revelation so soon either. Just as she'd told Daniel earlier, the unexpected was now becoming her normal.

It was nearly half an hour before their food arrived, and she was almost embarrassed at the heaping plates that covered the table.

"This seems like an awful amount of food, for two people."

"What's the old saying? 'Boxty on the griddle, boxty in the pan. If you can't make boxty, you'll never get a man.' It's something like that." He shoveled an unhealthy amount of the golden potato cake into his mouth.

"I think you hit it right on the head!" She slathered a thick coat of butter on a slice of soda bread. With each bite, she felt herself transported back home, and found it intriguing that what made her think of home was not native to Boston at all. As she ate the rich flavorful food, she became more convinced that she needed to move Ireland up on her places to visit. She couldn't help feel a pang of guilt for not knowing more about her mother's heritage. As a youngster, she'd spent much more time listening to her father's stories of England, neglecting to learn about her mother's family history.

Daniel did his best to make small talk, but given the growing crowd, it was difficult. When she was sure she could eat no more, she pushed her plate to the center of the table. Daniel followed her lead, stacking his on top of hers.

"Do you dance, Adelia?" he asked.

She gave him a disapproving grin. "I think we established a while ago that the answer is no."

"Ah, I had forgotten."

She shook her head at his look of pure mischief. "For a man who can easily remember the circumference of Henry VIII's waistline, I doubt your memory failed you so quickly."

He lifted both hands, palms up. "Live a little. It's not every day you get to go out on the town with the most sought-after bachelor in Oxford."

"I had no idea I was being bestowed with such an honor," she said, laughing as she clutched her chest.

"Not really. I know, like, four people in this town, and none of those guys want to marry me." His eyes gleamed with delight at his little joke. "Hold on, I'll be back."

He got up and almost ran across the old wooden dance floor, stopping at the small stage. Adelia thanked the waitress for taking their dishes away, and watched as Daniel spoke to the band leader. Then he bent and dropped a few pounds into the open fiddle case at his feet. She could just about make out the tune they started playing but thought nothing of it until Daniel returned, grabbed her hand, and pulled her to her feet. As he drew her out to the dance floor, she blushed from head to toe, even more when he wrapped an arm around her waist, taking her other hand into his.

The melody was soft, almost making her forget that she had never really danced with anyone but Daniel. Even that was just a few moments in a rain-drenched hedge maze. Something of a disaster.

"What is this song?" she asked. "It's lovely."

"My Wild Irish Rose," he answered. "I am sure this song was written for a girl who looked just like you, Adelia Grey."

As they swayed to the music, she caught herself breathing in his cologne. It was different to last night's, or at least she'd never noticed it before, but now it filled her head with the most delightful dizziness. It was as if she could breathe him in, and still never get quite enough.

The way he held her—his warmth pressed against her—it would never be enough to sate her desire for more.

He hummed along with the song, and she leaned her head back, grinning at him in disbelief. She liked the Daniel she had known at Hampton Court, but the new Daniel was just as easy to adore. At the end of the song, he called the waitress over for the check. Adelia tried to pitch in part of the cost but he was adamant that his pride would be mortally wounded. Not wanting him to suffer some irreversible mental scarring, she agreed to allow him to pay the tab.

"Just this once," she said, giving him her sternest look.

"Okay, okay," he exclaimed over the noisy patrons. "I will let you make me boxty sometime as repayment. That's the only way to keep me, you know."

"I have never made boxty in my life," she said as they made their way out. "I guess that's the reason why I am single."

"But you're not single anymore," he said, squeezing her hand.

"I'm not?" She stared at him. The sudden quietness of the street felt as though a switch had been flipped off. Though they had been together all day, out here, it was like time had flown by. Now it was just the two of them, walking along the tree-lined path, their shadows playing off and on between the streetlights.

"I would like to think that you are not single anymore," he said, a hint of a tremble in his voice.

The serenity of the night had somehow diminished a little of his courage. Perhaps the pint was wearing off too. She took pity in his return to vulnerability and squeezed his hand in silent reply. He smiled at her, as though knowing what her gesture meant, and looked at her in silence for a long moment.

Her eyes made playful rounds along the curve of his lips, her curiosity refusing to subside. Why Daniel had not made the move to kiss her was like a melodious tune playing over and over in her head. Only once since traveling to England had she called Kate. It was far too expensive to have talked to her more often. When they'd spoken, she was all too eager to share about Daniel. Wanting every detail, Kate listened as though the story was a serial on an old-time radio show. It had only taken a minute before she asked why they hadn't managed something as simple as a kiss. With reluctance, Adelia shared the few failed attempts, only to be met with an exasperated sigh. Naturally, Kate wasted no words in insisting that Adelia get off her high horse and take the lead.

"I can walk you back to the inn," he said at last. "It's not too far from here."

She blinked, realizing that her runaway thoughts had caused her to forget where they were for a minute. Her anticipation was curbed but she tried not to show that in her reaction. "Will you have far to get back to your flat, though? That will more than double your distance home."

"I will be fine. I know you're tired and I don't want to keep you out any later. I don't mind the walk home. I like the fresh summer air."

"Whatever you think is best," she said, still feeling a little guilty. Daniel's day had been long as well, and he must be tired too. Despite her fatigue, she couldn't help being caught up in every moment of their evening together. She was sure she could search the world, end to end, corner to corner, and never find a man quite so wonderful as this one.

They were no more than a block away from the inn when he stopped without warning and pulled her into one of the shadows along the empty street. He looked right at her, his gorgeous eyes reminding her of some perfectly sculpted piece of sea glass she'd found on a beach vacation.

He smoothed his hands over her hair, never breaking eye contact. "I will always look back on these days with you and think they were the best ones of my life."

She could almost hear Kate scolding her from across the ocean to just hurry up and kiss him already. As much as she wanted to, in that moment, she couldn't find the courage.

"Me t-too," she stammered, her voice barely audible.

Then, without a word of warning, he did something else unexpected—he kissed her. It wasn't just her first kiss, it was *the* kiss—the one that sent a message straight from her lips to the infinite corners of her brain, raising her temperature so high that no glass of cool water could quench. Her heart swelled, almost lifting her onto her toes. There was no hesitation as she wrapped her arms around his neck, prolonging this glorious moment, unwilling to let it come to an end just yet. She had waited so long for this, dreaming of what it might feel like, and now she had no doubt that it was so much better than she could have imagined.

When, alas, his lips parted from hers, she could hardly contain the thoughts swirling in her head. Oh my goodness, I am in love with Daniel Brown. This is real. This is love.

One does not need to be educated to know the feeling of love, nor have experience in the ways of the heart either. Love in its truest form is simple. It's a sensation that fills the veins with air. Like the touch of the softest spring breeze on warm skin. Or like your body defying the laws of gravity. Thinking is no longer an option. There are no thoughts that you dare allow to sabotage the feeling. Reason and logic no longer matter, and whether things work out is inconsequential. There is no concept of time—even the present seems distant and fuzzy. Love is like lighting a match and savoring the slow burn.

Adelia Grey is in love, and there is no turning back now. I have got to learn how to make boxty!

Chapter Sixteen

I t was still dark out—not yet 4:30 a.m.—and Adelia lay awake in her comfortable bed at the inn, unable to sleep, no matter how hard she tried. The memory of last night played over and over in her head. Her thoughts skipped back and forth, like a vinyl record with an irreversible scratch on the surface. She pulled the covers up to her chin, smiling into the soft linen like a schoolgirl who had just returned from her first formal. This is love. What a wondrous feeling. What an undeniably, magnificent, wondrous feeling.

As she basked in her glee, she was also aware of the slow creep of reality. She tried hard to fight it, wanting to stay in love, to hold onto those feelings a little longer. But Adelia Grey had a logical side to her—one that never allowed her the joys of anything for too long. I can't keep him forever. I will have to return home soon. This will all be over, and I will be going home, broken heart in tow.

Does Daniel understand this too? He is older. So much more experienced. Maybe he knows this is just a summer fling, and he can return to his normal life, no strings attached. Why are you so good at bad decisions, Adelia?

She lay there for another hour, thinking about Daniel, then overthinking, wishing she could return to the lonely shadows of the street last night. Everything seemed to make sense then, because there was no sense to be made. Nothing mattered, just the moment—just the two of them.

With nothing to be accomplished from so much overthinking, she rolled herself out of bed, brushed her teeth, and had a wash before getting dressed. She lifted the pearl necklace with teardrop pendant from the bureau, fumbling with its clasp as she fastened it around her neck. Though she didn't know why, something inside told her to wear it today. Feeling like a lovesick schoolgirl made her think she might need it to keep grounded.

She didn't go down to breakfast like she had yesterday, a little embarrassed after returning so late last night, and because making small talk was just out of the question today. As she sat at her window, peering down at the narrow street below, her vision blurred. Tiny flashes of light invaded her line of sight, until they vanished, leaving her looking at a new scene: men in finely tailored suits and top hats, and women in flowing day gowns walked arm in arm along the sidewalks, past gas-lit streetlamps, with carriages rattling along the cobblestone street. The style told her the whispers had brought her to the Regency period of Oxford's past. She couldn't hear the voices or feel the thoughts—far too removed from them at her vantage point—but just the knowledge that the whispers had returned to her was more than enough. As the images faded away and the Oxford of the present came back into view, she smiled with relief.

Still, it irked her why the whispers had been so evasive since she'd come to Oxford. Why had she only been able to feel their presence at the church the other night? Someday, she might be able to hone her gift to her liking, but she was far from that day yet.

Daniel arrived on time, like clockwork, and she made her way down the narrow staircase. As she descended, she was caught off guard by the presence of a young woman coming up the steps toward her. She carried a wooden bowl filled with shabby rags. Her attire was Elizabethan, of servants' class. The woman never looked up, just continued on the way to her destination. Adelia moved to the side without thought, allowing the figure to pass by. She considered reaching out to touch her, feeling the light swish of her dress as she passed, but didn't. What would it be like? My hand would probably pass right through the specter. We are just sharing the same space, not the same time.

When she got to the foyer, she opened the front door just as Daniel was about to enter. He smiled at her in surprise, almost losing his footing on the front stoop.

I probably should have let him come in first. Do I look too eager to see him?

While he looked a little stilted, he greeted her with his normal warm demeanor. Ever the gentleman, he opened the car door for her. When he paused and leaned toward her, she just smiled and slid past him, plunking herself down into the passenger seat. It was only when she noticed him stumbling forward before righting himself that she realized he may have intended to kiss her on the cheek. Oh no, why didn't I catch that? The poor man must be mortified at my rejection. Best to say nothing—pretend I missed it completely.

He closed her door, looked left and right, then rounded the front of the car to take his place in the driver's seat. She said nothing but gave him a warm smile, hoping it would ease any lingering embarrassment.

When he pulled the car out onto the road, she prepared for a repeat of yesterday's perilous driving but, as he snaked his way through the morning traffic, it was slower and more reserved, which she was glad of. As he drove, he remained quiet—too quiet for her liking. Oh, goodness, something is wrong. It has to be more than my unintentional rejection. Is he regretting last night? Maybe that pint at the pub played against his judgment.

"Did you sleep well?" she asked, hoping to break the tension.

He chuckled. "I didn't, actually. How about you?"

"No, not particularly." That chuckle made all the difference.

"About l-last night," he stammered. "I hope I did not make you uncomfortable. If I did, I am sorry."

"I wasn't uncomfortable, Daniel. I would have told you if I felt that way." She turned to face him. He glanced at her, his eyes glinting like blue crystals behind the delicate gold frames of his glasses.

"I don't regret kissing you," he said, his tone somewhat definitive. "I would only regret it if you said never to do it again. Honestly, I would still want to kiss you again. I just wouldn't if you didn't want me to. Am I making any sense at all?" He smacked his left hand to his forehead in embarrassment.

"You are making sense." She couldn't help laughing. "You're rambling a little, but it's still coherent rambling, so I do understand what you are saying."

"Well then, can you at least put my mind at ease here, Adelia? Did I cross a line?"

"There is not one day with you that I regret, Daniel. I mean, I have done some things I regret. Stupid things I have said and done that I might change if I had to do it over again. There is nothing on your part, though. I would change nothing about you. Wait...am I making sense now?"

He laughed, took hold of her hand and gave it a little squeeze. "You are rambling a bit, darling. It's coherent rambling, though."

She laughed again, giving him a sideward scowl. "Okay, let's hope today is the day. The whispers have been strong this morning. I have struggled a little since we left Hampton Court, but I feel good about today."

"I won't deny that I am hopeful too." He let go of her hand to navigate a turn in the road. "I want to know so much about what happened to Amy, but if it isn't meant to be, then we will take it as it comes."

"I know this means a lot to you, Daniel. I know that it's a personal goal for you to finish your work." She grimaced inside, wondering if she was wrong not to tell him about her experience the first night at the site. By now she feared too much time had passed, and he might look at her needless withholding of such valuable information with distrust.

He bobbed his head a few times from side to side, as if fighting with something inside. "The truth is, my work is important to me but this particular project is a little more personal than most."

"Really? I hadn't realized. How is Amy's death personal for you? If you don't mind me asking?"

"This hasn't been something I talk about, ever, really. I trust you, though." He looked at her, then focused back on the road. "My mother didn't just pass away when I was younger, she was in a rather tragic accident."

"Oh, Daniel, that must have been terribly hard, being that you were just ten years old."

"Losing her was definitely tough. It was the circumstances around her death that made it worse, though." He kept his focus on the road ahead.

Adelia remained quiet, unsure how to respond. She searched his face, wanting to know more but too timid to ask. If this was something he wanted to share, she would have to let him do so on his own terms.

"I could never say that my parents were the happiest couple," he continued. "Mind you, I never saw them bicker or squabble. They were just always distant, in a way, my father doing his work, my mother pursuing her own interests. As I look back now, what I can remember is them just coexisting peacefully. I don't recall seeing much love and affection between them, though they always had it for me."

"I think a great many relationships end up on those terms at some point," she said.

"Whether or not they would have stayed together had my mother lived, I can't say. I just know that my dad took losing her very hard." He checked his mirrors, then ran his hand across the top of the steering wheel, maybe recalling some distant memory. The pained look on his face told her it wasn't a pleasant one.

"Dad and I had gone out to an antique fair that Saturday. My dad never missed one. He was always convinced that some lost artifact was just waiting for him to stumble upon it. The fair wasn't far from our house, so we took our bicycles to town. I remember thinking of how fun that was, cruising up and down the old country lanes with my old man. You probably have a lot of those memories too."

"My dad and I have been very close all my life. I used to love our weekend adventures." She smiled at the recollection but didn't bother to elaborate. This was Daniel's time to talk.

"We were coming over the last hill of the gravel lane on our way home when I saw them. I remember those two police cars parked in front of the house like it was yesterday. Dad motioned for me to wait on my bike as he approached the policemen." He took a deep breath, both hands clenched on the steering wheel. "Mum had been in an automobile accident. Somehow, she had gone off the road, overturning the car down a steep embankment. There was no evidence any other vehicle was involved. Just a fluke accident, they said."

"Oh, Daniel, I am so sorry. That must have been such hard news to take. Even harder for your father to tell you, I imagine." She put her hand to her chest.

"It was incredibly hard at first, but what came after made it worse. You see, my mother never drove a car. She had never learned. At the time of the accident, she had driven the car the opposite direction of town, from where Dad and I had gone. As more details emerged, rumors began to circulate. Some people thought she might have been running away. That she had taken the car and was heading out of town. She was attempting to abandon her husband and son. Other people thought she had driven the car off the embankment on purpose. That she had been in such a state of melancholy, she had taken her own life. Once, I even heard a rumor that my dad had murdered her, hiring someone to do the deed while we went into town. That he had intentionally left the car as part of the plot."

"Oh God, Daniel. That had to be horrible hearing those rumors. People are just so cruel sometimes. They owed far more compassion to you and your dad at such a time." Anger welled in her, and she wanted nothing more than to go back in time and box the ears of anyone who did that to a mere child.

"You can see now why I have taken such an interest in Amy Robsart's death?"

"Now that you mention it, yes. The rumors that were sparked by Amy's death are the same as you heard about your mother. Do you feel connected to her cause because of what you went through?"

"I do," he admitted with a half-smile. "If Amy's death was an accident, that is very unfortunate. If it was murder, then she deserves justice. If she took her own life, then I pass no judgment. This poor woman just deserves for her truth to be known and her soul to be put to rest."

"I watched Dad go through all the phases of guilt that happen when grieving. The last thing he needed was people who barely knew him adding their own fictional twist to my mother's death. That's the sadness in death, like I have said before—in the end, our lives are only what others believe."

Listening to his sorrowful voice filled Adelia with a newfound determination. More than ever, she wanted to help him find answers to Amy's death. Deep inside, she feared that he might one day call on her to provide him with answers to his own life. Answers she wasn't sure he would be ready to receive if they weren't what he hoped to find.

This got her thinking again on why she had been drawn to him, infused into his life with such ease. The whispers, it seemed, had some strange ability to bring not only the past into focus but the present as well. There was so much about Daniel she could understand now. Though self-determined, he was never pushy in his expectations for other people. Perhaps he was frightened. It wasn't unthinkable that if he had believed his mother capable of taking her own life, he might have felt some responsibility. Might have feared that he'd proven too much for her as a child. His reluctance to be too demanding could have made him scared that he might push yet another person away.

In her eyes, his unyielding desire to find out what happened to Amy was noble. He wanted her death to have some meaning. Not the meaning others prescribed, but one Amy could articulate with her own voice. He was the last of some dying breed of men. One who still subscribed to chivalry and justice. She found these qualities not only admirable but comforting.

He parked the car in the same place as the day before. It was only when she got out that she noticed a large picnic basket on the backseat. He smiled, telling her he'd made a packed lunch for them, and they could return for it after walking the grounds for a while.

As they pushed their way through the familiar wrought iron gateway, Adelia was surprised to see fewer visitors today. She reckoned the weather forecast was to blame, with showers expected. The morning sun was strong, though, and reflected off the face of the clock high on the tower. She mentioned how she loved the weathered patina of the old copper numbers on the clock face. It gave the church a romantic appeal.

Some of the stones from the original manor house had been repurposed into the gatehouse and garden walls but the exterior would have been unrecognizable to Amy. After her experience at seeing Maggie and Jane in what was once the old kitchen, Adelia knew how disorienting it could feel to have her surroundings thrust back into another place in time. Cumnor had experienced dramatic change over the years, yet the essence of the people who dwelled here was ever-present. The whispers would decide what was to be revealed.

After entering the main building, she headed straight for the far wall, the one that contained the only remaining fragments of the old manor house—two arched windows stretching just shy of the roof, still magnificent in their presence. She stood, trying to channel the sensations that had grown familiar to her but, just as before, nothing came. The interior of this old building seemed to act as a guardian to the secrets it held. After this morning, she had been so sure things would happen, and now she had to bite down on her rising frustration.

She knew the whispers could never be fully controlled but that made it no less agitating. There would always be a part of her wanting that control, no matter the reality. They did a couple of slow circuits, sometimes sitting, not just to await the whispers but to better appreciate beautiful aspects of the interior.

"Time for an early lunch," Daniel announced after they'd walked around outside for a while. "Wait right here while I fetch the basket from the car."

He returned a few minutes later carrying the wicker basket, along with a striped wool blanket slung over one arm. The man's devilish smile brought heat to her cheeks. His pride at having arranged yet another meal for them to share was clear, and she loved how he went the extra mile to make sure she was cared for in every possible way. That reminded her that she needed to make good on his request to make him boxty. Hopefully her grandma could help her with the recipe when she returned to Hampton Court at the end of the week.

Daniel set the wicker basket down, then gave the blanket a gentle flick so it fell like a soft cloud onto the grass. Just as they'd unpacked the basket and sat on the blanket, a light drizzle started to fall. Adelia pouted, releasing a heavy sigh of disapproval. Daniel leaped to his feet and began packing up before they were caught in a downpour. But then he stopped and pointed over at a lush old oak tree, and the two of them dragged the laden blanket to the dry patch of grass. Adelia held her hands out to gauge if the tree was thick enough to block the rain. She smiled in satisfaction, popping down to sit on the blanket.

After lunch, the rain was still falling in a slow steady rhythm.

"It should stop soon," Daniel said, looking at the sky. "Won't be long now."

"I am in no rush. Are you?"

"I have all the time in the world." He leaned over and planted a kiss on her head, sliding his warm hand through the silky strands of her hair. She closed her eyes for a moment, happy to stay in that position forever. When he reclined back against the massive tree trunk, hands folded behind his head and legs stretched out, she rolled onto her back and propped her head on his leg. As he stroked her chin, his touch tender, she fidgeted with the pearl pendant.

"What's this?" he asked, touching it.

"Oh, it's something my grandma gave to me. It has been in the family for years, she says."

He turned the pendant over. "The necklace itself is newer, but this looks much older."

Adelia closed her eyes. The light tapping of raindrops on the leaves above had a serene quality about it—so relaxing, she almost considered an afternoon nap. There in the quiet, all was right in her world. It wasn't long before her fingers tingled with a light buzzing sensation. Her fingernails hummed with electricity as a mix of heat and cold worked its way up her arms and into her neck. Her ears became warm, and she let out an audible sigh.

Daniel shifted, as though watching her, but her eyelids were so heavy they refused to open. Then the whispers filtered out the sound of the rain. They came as a low hum at first, steady and demanding, becoming many voices then, hushed but garbled. One by one they faded away, except for one, which came through with the same clarity as someone sitting inches from her face.

It was a woman. No, women. She smiled when she realized it was Jane and Maggie.

"I can hear them," she said, not sure if it was out loud or just in her thoughts. She shot up into a sitting position, as though it might help her hear clearer.

"Is it Amy?" Daniel asked, excited. "Amy Robsart Dudley?"

She looked at him. "No... I don't believe it is." She closed her eyes, focusing hard to block out the clamor of sound around her. "It's Jane. Well, Jane and Maggie."

Daniel's sigh of disappointment came as a low groan. "Who are they?" He got up and began pacing.

She closed her eyes again and listened. "She knows the Mistress Dudley."

"She knows her?" he asked, his voice closer.

"Or, *rather*, she knew her." She took in the flashes of visuals, trying to make sense of the vocal fragments. "She knew Amy quite well. You see, both Jane and Maggie were in service to Sir Anthony Forster here at Wytham."

Though Cumnor had long since been demolished, the old house in all its magnificence stood before her, clear as day. It was as if the Wytham church had disappeared, with the old estate reborn to its former glory. She marveled at the vivid imagery, which reminded her of liquid paint melting down the walls to reveal a masterpiece. It had all the markings of a grand Tudor estate: finely carved wood panels, embroidered fabrics, and beautiful stonework. She could even smell the aroma of freshly baked bread wafting through its halls. The visual was so real, she was convinced she could reach out and touch something—trace the embroidered upholstery with her fingertips.

"Amy trusted her. Jane. She gave her something in return for helping her."

"What did she help her with?" Daniel asked.

"She wants me to come this way." She motioned toward some unknown destination, then got up and left the shelter of the old tree, following the perimeter stone wall of the courtyard.

The grass was damp from the afternoon rain, and her heel slipped as she made her way. Daniel steadied her footing with a gentle but reassuring grip. His touch sent a spark of electricity through her arm. He had a way of making the simplest moment magnificent. She regained her composure. "It's over here."

"Here?" He sounded skeptical.

She nodded, opening her eyes to see that she'd stopped in a grass clearing at the foot of a small hill. "It's the staircase." She closed her eyes again and listened, shuddering, her excitement almost gruesome. "Jane said this is where the Mistress Dudley took the fall down the stairs. This is the spot where she met her end. Jane feels responsible somehow. She helped her pack her things. Amy was kind and gave her a necklace."

A shiver ran across her shoulders when she saw a small teardrop pearl pendant, identical to the one her grandma gave her. Somehow, she and Jane were connected, yet it was impossible to know how. She had no time to process it as the visions came at her with intensity.

"Jane just keeps mentioning the staircase. It's right here." Blinking, she met Daniel's puzzled gaze and could understand how ludicrous the whole idea must seem to him. Here she was, talking about a staircase, when all he could see was a blanket of grass. He couldn't see what was before her—the narrow stairwell of smooth gray stone, dimly lit by a small window at the top of the landing, the air musty with the smell of ancient wood that had soaked up the moisture of English rain. As she scanned each stair in its descent, she gasped on seeing a heap of fine fabric on the floor below. Her eyes widened in horror as she strained to make out the shape of the delicate hand, the long strands of chestnut-brown hair. She let out a soft cry on realizing that it was Amy's body.

"What is it, Adelia?" Daniel demanded.

She shook her head to shake the image from her mind, without success. In the midst of all the emotion flooding her, a deep-seeded morbid curiosity took over. Am I really seeing this woman who met her tragic end so long ago? In all the unexplained experiences that had plagued her throughout her life, she had never felt death.

As she waded through the panic and dread, a new emotion made its way through her: peace. She couldn't be sure but she no longer thought those emotions were coming from Jane. They were coming from Amy now. She stared in disbelief as she inched forward into the gloom. The fear was fading, replaced by a peacefulness that propelled her on. She wanted to see the face of this woman—this figure who had been shrouded in darkness for more than 400 years. So much of Amy's life had been a mystery. Who was she as a woman? What were her sorrows? What were her hopes and dreams? All that remained of her were vague details—documented dates of the aspects of her existence—but nothing that ever revealed who she really was in life.

Standing there, looking down at this woman, she had a strong urge to know everything—a desire that was beyond her understanding. Yet, as she made her way closer to peer upon the delicate features of this beautiful soul, the silent stillness became almost deafening. She stared for what felt like ages, but couldn't have been more than a minute or two. Jane's soft whisper reemerged, breaking the intensity of her gaze.

"The pond?" she said, turning to Daniel. As his face came back into crisp focus, she almost leapt into his arms. The sight of his somber eyes and tousled wavy hair was such a welcome sight to what she had just seen.

"The pond," he repeated, flicking a look left and right, then blinking several times, as if searching the archives of his mind. "Of course!" He snatched hold of her hand and pulled her along with gentle determination, and she followed without a word. "After Amy's death, the servants in Cumnor Place swore that the atmosphere of the estate had changed dramatically. There were reports of a foreboding presence that nearly frightened them away. So, a group of local men banded together to perform a ritual to cast her soul into the nearby pond. Legend has it the pond never froze over since that day. We have to find it."

They searched the property for what felt like a lifetime until, just over a rise sat a small, unremarkable body of water lying in the valley of a grassy field. Neither were sure if this was the spot but they still approached the water's edge with haste. Adelia tried again to summon the whispers. This time, it took almost no effort before the sensation of fire and ice ravaged her body like bitter flames. The feeling ebbed and flowed in waves, crashing into her with brutal force, then receding just as fast, each one closer than before, like the promise of the inevitable high tide.

"She loved him." Amy's thoughts were as clear as Daniel's voice. These were not words that Amy had spoken to anyone, they were mere echoes of the emotional firestorm that swelled within a woman who had found herself in the midst of deceit, with predators lurking in every direction. She had only ever wanted what any woman in her time would have desired: love and security. The tragedy of her life is that it mattered little to anyone, if there was power at stake.

"Dudley," Daniel said, matter of fact.

"No, not her husband. That love had vanished a long time ago." Another wave hit her, sending a surge of cold sparks through her. "She loved Anthony. He promised that they would run away together. Robert broke her heart, but Anthony came along and changed everything. She was desperate for affection."

Another wave came, and she clutched her chest with its ferocity. "She keeps saying he promised to take her away. They were to leave that very day."

"That explains why she was so adamant that the household staff go to the Abington Fair. She wanted them out of the house so they could make their escape."

She opened her eyes and let out a deep-felt laugh. Daniel frowned at her. "I'm sorry, it's just that Amy has a wicked sense of humor. She says that she ordered a new dress for the occasion, on Robert's account. She thought it fitting given all he'd put her through."

Daniel smiled as she regained her composure. "Remember her letter to the tailor?"

She nodded. "She has such mixed feelings about her husband, it's quite remarkable." She was elated with the reality that she was hearing from Amy herself. "At times, he could be dashing and romantic. She absolutely adored him once. Everything changed, though. He became so involved in his own rise to power that she quickly became forgotten. She went through a time of utter despair. A time when she had all but lost hope. Coming to Cumnor Place saved her, or she thought it did."

"What does she say about Forster?"

Adelia smiled at his persistence. She had never seen him quite so excited. Gone were his bookish refined manners. He was like a child anticipating the purchase of a new toy.

"You have to be patient, Daniel," she said. "This has to come through on Amy's terms. She wants to tell her story her own way."

"I understand," he said, disappointment etched in his jaw. His scolded-child look made her want to laugh all the more.

She let go of his hand and took a few paces along the pond's edge, feeling the tread of his feet close behind.

"She loved him. It was unconventional. No one would have approved but the way he made her feel alive again was almost blissful. He made her feel wanted, important. He listened to her. It was a feeling she'd always wanted from Robert. She keeps repeating, 'He promised.'"

Daniel chuckled. "If Forster betrayed Dudley by wooing his wife, how is that for karma?"

"It's far more complicated than that, though," she said, her breath quickening. "There is so much more."

"Adelia, you are killing me here."

She closed her eyes and listened. "Forster promised her that they would run away. She was to meet him at the staircase. When she got there, he was waiting." She held her breath. "I can feel her anticipation. It's like...pure exhilaration." She sucked in a lungful of air. "Jane helped her pack some things, and Amy gave her the necklace as a token, in gratitude. When the Sunday came that she and Forster planned to meet, she sent the servants away."

'So did she get to Forster?" Daniel asked, his impatience clear. "Did he change his mind? Was he the one who hurt her?"

Adelia strained to block out his questions so she could focus on Amy's voice, but it wasn't really her she could hear anymore. It was as if she and Amy had become one, her emotions raw and untamed.

"Amy made it to the staircase where they were supposed to meet." She took a step back. "Something feels wrong, though. Something isn't right. When she looks at him, there is something dark in his eyes." She covered her mouth with her hand. "She...is afraid he has changed his mind. He lets her go down the stairs first, and then—"

A flash of pain shot through her head and she grabbed the back of it, trying to find the origin. Her ears filled with a loud buzz, like white noise, and everything seemed to go black. Something warm trickled down her neck, then sheer panic and disorientation set in. She flailed about, grasping for Daniel to steady herself as she fell to the floor, feeling him reaching for her, his touch muted as she slipped deeper and deeper into the darkness. A looming shadow existed at the edge of her vision—possibly a man with dark eyes, but she couldn't be certain.

"Adelia," Daniel called, his voice pitched. "Adelia, are you okay? What's wrong?"

She faded in and out of consciousness at the sound of his words.

"It was always Cecil," she said.

"Adelia!" It came as a near scream. "Darling, tell me you are okay."

She blinked up at him, shocked with the clarity of what she had experienced. Not only had she seen Amy in her direst hour but, somehow, she had felt every single moment as though she were her. She now understood what her grandma meant by being overcome by someone else's story. With breath held, she remained still until the pain subsided. That fateful day, so much more tumbled down the staircase at Cumnor than a body. It was Amy's hopes and dreams too. The whole story stank of betrayal. Layers and layers of deceit.

Panic gripped her, and Daniel helped her to sit on the grass. She glanced around, trembling, trying to see if anyone had witnessed what just occurred. The area was silent, with not a soul to be seen. A living one, at least.

"Daniel." She looked up at him. "I know what happened to Amy."

"That's wonderful." He hunkered down, inhaling long and hard, as though he hadn't taken a breath in a century. "However, I am more concerned with you at the moment."

"I'm fine." She touched his forearm. "I mean, I wasn't fine but I am now. I know what happened to her."

"We don't have to discuss it now," he said. "Really, Adelia, you should rest. You are so pale." He brushed the backs of his fingers across her cheek.

She paid no mind to his insistence, not after having just bore witness to something so tragic she could barely keep it to herself a minute longer.

"Daniel, if I tell you what I saw... Well, you do understand that no one will ever believe us, right?"

He stared at her, then looked down at her trembling hands, which he grasped in his own. "You are about to share the answer to the greatest mystery of my career, and I can't reveal what I know, ever."

She squeezed his hands. "Even if you told someone, they would never believe either of us. You would discredit all the work you have done."

He eased himself onto the grass and sat there in quiet contemplation. "It doesn't matter. I can't believe I'm saying this but it does not matter to me at all. All I care about is that you and I know the answer and that you are okay. I would never be so selfish to put you at risk of ridicule for my own career." He held her hands to his chest. "You have to trust me."

"I do!"

"Well then, tell me the story I have waited to hear all my life."

"It was Cecil all along. He wasn't the man who pushed Amy down the stairs, though, but he was the mastermind behind her murder. Amy cleared the house that day, thinking Sir Anthony Forster was to meet her. The two had become romantically involved and he promised her they would run away together. Though the details aren't clear, I think that was a deceptive move on behalf of Forster, at the direction of Robert Dudley. But all along, William Cecil had been plotting and scheming on his own. He managed to convince Dudley's man Sir Richard Verney to double-cross him. On that day, Verney was visiting Cumnor and overheard the servants talking about the plan between Forster and Amy, and seized the moment. He surprised her on the landing and pushed her down the stairs. It wasn't Anthony Forster she saw on the staircase, it was Verney."

"Oh my God," Daniel exclaimed, his mouth agape. "That makes absolutely perfect sense. Even Cecil himself couldn't have hoped for such a lucky turn of events. He was so removed from the plot, no one would have ever suspected him. He used Dudley's man to do the deed, knowing full well that he would never be discovered. No matter which way things went, Dudley would be implicated, thus destroying all chances he had of ever marrying the queen."

"I feel such sadness for Amy," Adelia said. "She was never going to come out of that marriage alive."

Daniel nodded. "No. God, Cecil was such a clever man. Even if we brought this information out today, there is no more concrete evidence to implicate his part than there was back then."

"I suppose not," she said. She rubbed his upper arms, the action slow. "Are you sad to know the truth, Daniel? Does this closure make you feel like all your work has been for nothing?"

"I am sad for Amy. I am sad that she was nothing but collateral damage for power-hungry men who used her in their war against each other. I am not sad that I finally know what happened to her, though."

She smiled through her own sadness. "I'm glad to hear you say that."

"I have spent so much time researching this, and I cannot deny I will be sad to stop. It seems fruitless now to keep going. Yet, on the bright side, if I had not begun this journey, then I never would have met you. That is worth every hour of work I have ever put into this project." He shifted forward and hugged her, and she breathed in his scent and soaked up his support. Her body still felt weak, her limbs almost lifeless, as though she had just weathered a long crossing of the sea in the fiercest storm.

"What do we do now?" she asked after they parted. "I know it sounds preposterous but I don't think you can just stop your research so abruptly. People will wonder why."

"Yes, I suppose you have a valid point." He arched both eyebrows and angled his head to the side. "I guess I just hit a dead end. I was always going to, anyway. I will devote the rest of the summer to writing up my findings and just leave it at that, I suppose."

"What about the two of us, though? What do we do now?"

"Simple. I continue adoring you, as I have since the moment I met you. Nothing between us changes."

"Now that you have the answers, you still want to be with me?" She lowered her gaze, not sure she wanted the answer.

"Why on earth wouldn't I?" He held her chin, encouraging her to look at him again. "Did you think I only wanted to have you around to help me with my research?"

She shrugged one shoulder. "The thought has crossed my mind."

He chuckled, then went serious. "You have this remarkable gift, Adelia. One that could spread light on so many mysteries of the past. It's an ability that someone like me could only dream of possessing."

"Believe me when I say it is not always such a blessing." She rubbed the back of her head to ease the remnants of a burning sensation.

"I think I just witnessed one of its downsides, so I can honestly say I believe you there. Despite the remarkable gift you possess, I can assure you that it is the other remarkable traits making up Adelia Grey that I love." He leaned forward and fixed his focus on her eyes. "I am endlessly devoted to you. Just you."

Her heart swelled as she touched his cheek with her open hand. "Even if that means you must spend a lifetime keeping my secret with me?"

He held her hand to his face. "Are you offering me a lifetime?"

"Well, I guess that was a bit too forward. For a while, at least." She gave him a playful smile.

"You know, for a woman, you sure do have problems with commitment." He laughed.

She gave him a playful push, with just enough force to knock him to the ground. Before he could get up, she moved forward and came to rest beside him, with both of them staring up at the crystal-blue sky.

"I need some time to think," she said. "My life has taken on such a new direction, so quickly, that I can't quite settle on what I should do."

He took her hand in his. "Take all the time you need. The longer you spend thinking, the longer I have with you. Take years and years and years if you must."

Chapter Seventeen

A delia bit her lip as she waited for the connection to be made to her parents' number. She held the phone receiver to her ear, her palm sweaty as she replayed this conversation over and over in her mind, planning each response with careful consideration. Her breath caught at the sound of her father's deep melodic voice on the other end of the line. She started with simple pleasantries, until she took that step off the ledge and told him of her plans to stay on in England.

To her surprise, he didn't scream or shout. She wasn't sure why she thought he might have. When she considered it, she realized she'd never really known the man to get that angry. Quite honestly, she had never done much of anything to test his patience. This was probably the most brazen thing she had ever done.

"Give me a hundred good reasons why I should let you stay, and maybe I will agree," he said.

Holding the receiver tight, she looked at Daniel. "I only have one." She knew at that moment that she loved Daniel. Loved him enough to take the biggest risk of her life, by staying.

"Ah, I see. Well, Adelia, if this is what you want, I have no choice but to agree. It's not like I haven't been in a similar position. Just give me time to talk to Mom. She may take this a little harder than I. But have no fear, Doll, she will come around in time."

"Thank you, Dad," she said, unable to hold back a huge smile. "Chat soon." She finished the call and hung up the phone.

Daniel smiled back at her as he lounged on the sofa of his sparsely decorated flat. "Now, my dear, with the mystery of Amy Robsart Dudley solved, whatever shall we tackle next?"

She folded her arms and nodded to herself. There was no such thing as work ever being done with this man. "I have always had a fondness for the princes in the tower."

His eyes lit up. "I do believe I will marry you someday, Adelia Grey."

"That will be the fault in *your* stars, Doctor Brown." She took his hand in hers and planted a kiss square on his lips.

Dear Reader,

Dear Reader,

   As a writer, music has always played a vital role in providing inspiration for the stories I tell. Songs not only stir the soul but capture the spirit of the characters as they grow. Below you will find a list of songs that helped to spark my creativity and bring this book to life.

   "Begin Again" *Taylor Swift*

   "Fearless" *Taylor Swift*

   "Anxiety" *Jason Isbell*

About the Author

As a child, Tasha Sheipline wanted to be a ballerina, marry a doctor, and have a pony. Since none of these dreams came to fruition, she became a teacher instead. Teaching others has proved an empowering endeavor.

An avid reader, Tasha has a long held belief that you can never have too many books. Her favorite authors include Alison Weir, William Shakespeare, Edgar Allan Poe and Jane Austin. She is certainly not opposed to sprinkling in a good Tessa Dare romance novel when time allows.

She began writing as a creative outlet, and it soon blossomed into a real passion. A lover of history, Tasha has a specific fondness for the medieval through early modern eras. She loves to infuse characters and events from these areas into her writing.

Her favorite pastimes include traveling, watching historical documentaries, and adding to her growing collection of antique books. Tasha lives in a small town in Ohio with her husband, children and two corgi's.

Also By

Look for these soon to come titles by Tasha Sheipline:

Blood in the Chapel Royal: Book Two of The Whisper Series

Yorkshire Rose: Book Three of the Whisper Series